M. A. MORRIS

Take Me Home

Marivella House

First published by Marivella House Publishing, LLC 2026

This novel is entirely a work of fiction. The names, characters, and incidents portrayed in it are the work of the author's imagination. Any resemblance to actual persons, living or dead, events, or localities is entirely coincidental.

M. A. Morris asserts the moral right to be identified as the author of this work.

M. A. Morris has no responsibility for the persistence or accuracy of URLs for external or third-party Internet Websites referred to in this publication and does not guarantee that any content on such Websites is, or will remain, accurate or appropriate.

Designations used by companies to distinguish their products are often claimed as trademarks. All brand names and product names used in this book and on its cover are trade names, service marks, trademarks, and registered trademarks of their respective owners. The publishers and the book are not associated with any product or vendor mentioned in this book. None of the companies referenced within the book have endorsed the book.

First edition

ISBN: 979-8-9945986-0-3

This book was professionally typeset on Reedsy.
Find out more at reedsy.com

For my husband and our four children, who fill my life daily with love, laughter, and inspiration. You have all played a special role in this remarkable journey.

"An unexpected journey often leads us home... to love."

M. A. MORRIS

CHAPTER 1

June 2001

The plan was simple: tacos, margaritas, and forgetting for one painfully perfect hour that adulthood is an ongoing test I definitely didn't study for.

What I got instead?

A front-row ticket to my fiancé tonguing "Ho-bag Holly" in the middle of a godforsaken Mexican restaurant.

Soooooo, yeah. You can only guess that things escalated. And quickly.

"Let's go find his car and slash *all four* tires." An evil grin spreads across Jennifer's face, chilling, and it's genuinely terrifying. An eagerness in her voice materializes; devious, almost as if she's been waiting her whole life for this exact betrayal so she could unleash chaos upon the world. And the blind rage she has for anyone who hurts me doesn't go unnoticed.

"Ummmm, I do *not* want to sleep in jail tonight." Just the thought of wearing one of those hideous orange-and-white striped uniforms

1

makes my soul leave my body. "I just want to teach him a lesson." I caution her as I stir my fresh mango-margarita with a vengeance, its lime spilling out from the top and landing onto my untouched plate of fish tacos. I pick it up and brush off the few pieces of rice that cling to it, then drop it back into the glass. My mind goes through scenarios, plotting what to do next. Searching for the perfect plan.

"Come on, Charlotte! You never let me have *any* fun... that fucker deserves it," Jennifer snaps back a little too loudly, pointing her knife, meant for her steak fajita, toward the opposite corner of the room like she's selecting her next victim. "I always knew there was something I didn't like about him. I just never could put my finger on it." She snarls, baring her teeth like a warning. "What I'd like to do is stick this finger straight through his eyeball." She lifts her slender middle finger, the glossy black polish gleaming as she points it at him without a care in the world.

Worried looks come from the older couple sitting at the table next to ours, probably reconsidering ever dining out in public again. I truly admire Jennifer's loyalty to our friendship, but the wicked look on her face begins to scare even me a little. And I love her all the more for it.

"This can go one of two ways," I say, as I lean back into the vinyl-covered chair and feel it squeak beneath me. The sound echoes in the room like a warning. I start fidgeting with my straw, stirring it faster, glaring at the back of James's head from across the Mexican restaurant. *If only looks could kill. I could be spending the rest of the afternoon conspiring with Jennifer as to where to stash the body.* His hair is perfect like always, just like I thought *he* was, and now that I think about it, his good looks are his only likable attribute.

Our spontaneous little taco run has turned into so much more than I had bargained for. What started as a craving for chips and guac has now become front-row seats to James's blatant infidelity. I'm sitting here watching my fiancé lean over the table with such arrogance and kiss his skinny young secretary on her slutty, red-stained lips. Then dig right into his plate of beef chimichangas, without a care in the world, like he didn't just commit emotional homicide. Never giving a second thought that my heart is being shattered into tiny pieces.

"Ho-bag Holly," I mutter under my breath.

Her massive fake breasts practically fall out of her top as she leans in to greet him. I swear, if she moves even one inch farther, this Mexican restaurant could be turned into a strip club where you pay a cover just to walk through the front door.

I met her last week at the company picnic. She wore a skimpy white halter top and ripped-up denim shorts, cut a little too high for a respectable company work outing. Every guy from James's office could barely take their eyes off of her. I remember now just how sweet she had been towards me. At the time, I didn't pay much mind to it. *I'm such an idiot.*

I recall our conversation from this morning, in which I asked James to ditch work for a few hours this afternoon and meet me for lunch.

"Babe, I can't… I'm swamped at the office."

At the office… the new meaning for French-kissing Holly over Tex-Mex, I guess.

In hindsight, I should have seen through his pompous, bold-face lies.

"I'm probably gonna get something from the vending machine in the breakroom," the bastard said.

Is the vending machine named Holly?

"Maybe next time," he said, so nonchalant, without an apologetic bone in his pathetic little body. *Guess you're not so busy now, are you? Jerk!*

Not long after his denial, I called Jennifer, who was more than willing to escape work and spend the afternoon with me in Philly.

"What I should do is walk over to him, slap him, and pour the rest of this margarita onto his lap." I hold up my glass, clink it against hers, and smirk. "Then watch it soak straight through to his tiny dick underneath," the same one that he constantly insisted on me giving blowjobs to after indulging in one too many gins and tonics. "But that would be a waste of a very good margarita." I take a big sip, its fruity, refreshing mango lingers, and its tart flavor rests on the back of my tongue. "Or... I can go with a much less dramatic way, but equally just as effective." I reach into my purse, retrieve a one-hundred-dollar bill, and summon our waitress.

* * *

Outside on the sidewalk, Jennifer and I anxiously wait. It's warmer out than when we first arrived, and I'm beginning to rethink my decision as sweat drips down the middle of my back. For a moment, I have second thoughts. My nerves kick in at warp speed, but we continue to peer through the window, our eyes fixated on James's table. We watch as our waitress, Chloe, my hero, sets down a plate in front of him, leans in, and whispers into his ear. With much discretion, she looks our way and winks, a satisfied smile affixed to her face. The moment she does, I spy the crisp one-hundred-dollar bill peeking out from the back pocket of her skinny black jeans. *Money well spent.*

I concentrate on James, and the unfamiliar look on his face is one of utter bewilderment. Confused. He's never confused and is constantly in control of every situation. Which makes this all the more satisfying.

Between the movements of his tongue paired with the shape of his lips, I can distinctly make out what's being said. A pattern very consistent with the oh-so-familiar saying, "What the Fuck?" spouts from his stupid little mouth. And then he sees it.

Jennifer and I laugh as we watch him stare down at his plate in shock. The *masterpiece*. In front of him sits a single churro, flanked by two scoops of ice cream. He's looking at a food penis, and written beside it in chocolate syrup is one simple but powerful word, "Cheater."

4

Oh, and my engagement ring? It's slowly vanishing, disappearing into the whipped cream that melts alongside it. Out of habit, I rub my finger, which now feels strangely empty, where an abandoned, stained white circle is left in its place. James looks up with a frantic look, his eyes dart around the restaurant. Red Lips's jaw drops, wide open in shock.

The perfect dessert for the undeniable dick that he is. *Mission accomplished.*

James freezes as he spots the two of us through the window, his eyes land on mine, guilt smeared across his pathetic face like bad paint. We both flip him off, laughing, though I'm half-crying while doing it.

I continue to cry on Jennifer's shoulder the entire way home, cursing the day I ever met him.

CHAPTER 2

S *eptember 9, 2001*

I'm exhausted in every sense of the word. I'm sitting here staring out the window of a high-rise hotel room at the Las Vegas Hilton, the city's glittering chaos stretched out beneath me. My feet ache to the actual bone, and anyone who says that decorating cakes for a living is easy work clearly has never stood in one spot for twelve hours working an International Baking Convention. The decorating of hundreds of cakes, the demonstrating of countless amounts of piping tips, and the lifting of thirty-pound pails of buttercream icing all take a toll. Not to mention the disaster of a wedding cake from earlier. An entire tray of purple premade-frosted roses I intended on using fell from my decorating station and splattered on the floor, staining a client's brand-new pair of white tennis sneakers. I only know this because she screamed at me for what seemed like an eternity, telling me so. It was at that exact moment when I thought I was about to lose my shit.

"My sneakers! They're brand new! Look what you've done to them!"

"I'm so sorry... I don't know how that happened." I said, trying to convince her that it was only an accident. My boss, Jeff, quickly stood by my side, diffusing the embarrassing situation. In the end, she walked off with a wad of cash in hand to purchase herself a new pair.

I shake away the awful memory and dig my fingers deeper into my aching heels, desperately trying to relieve some of the pain, and all I can think of is the flashy king-size bed sitting next to me. It's all but calling my name.

"I just really need some sleep," I say to myself. "It's been a long couple of days... Hell, it's been a long couple of months."

I plant my feet onto the plush purple and pink carpet and head for the bed.

Rat-tat-tat, I hear coming from the door. All at once, it begins to open, and I can hear her heels before I even see her face. In comes Mary, my co-worker bestie, barreling through the door with a tiny pink dress and black high heels dangling from her hand. I instantly regret giving her the spare key to my room.

"We're going out. No arguments." Mary demands.

I blink. "I'm tired, and I just want to sleep. It's been a lon—"

"Nope," she cuts in. "You're one fondant rose away from a nervous breakdown, and you, my dear, are in Vegas. You didn't fly across the country to cry into a piping bag. Let alone sleep in the massive empty bed alone." Her hand moves swiftly in front of her, spread wide.

Before I can protest, I'm being stripped of my clothes, redressed in a dress that is entirely too small for me, and being pulled through the casino floor by my wrist. Past the clinking slot machines and the stale scent of cigarette smoke.

Mary has somehow gotten the two of us onto the guest list at a swanky, velvet-rope club that sits on the rooftop of the hotel across from ours.

One that features overpriced cocktails in glasses shaped like the Eiffel Tower. The base is thumping so hard I can feel it in my chest, and we've only just stepped out of the elevator.

The heels that Mary insisted I wear are digging a hole the size of the Grand Canyon into the back of my feet. But three tequila sunrises in, and those heels are thrown into a corner somewhere while Mary and I dance the night away. We're laughing so hard I can feel my mascara beginning to run.

"You need to make out with someone with a neck tattoo," Mary shouts over the music. "It's called healing."

"I'd rather lick buttercream off the bathroom floor," I say back to her.

"You say that now, but give it a few more drinks."

If Mary isn't decorating cakes, I swear on her off time, she could be a professional flirt, so sassy and fearless. She reminds me so much of my lifelong best friend, Jennifer.

I've just returned with two new drinks in hand, when I spot her dragging a pair of guys onto the dance floor like puppies on leashes. One is lean and grinning with a crooked smile and wild, tousled hair. The other is taller, darker, with just enough scruff and a sexy smile that, if I didn't know any better, makes my stomach flip.

"Look... I made friends," Mary says, like she's won the lottery.

I laugh, only because I don't know what else to do. *Typical* Mary.

"This is Conor," she says, pointing to the wild-haired one. "And that," she gestures to the other, "is... something you need tonight. No thinking. No James. Just music, tequila, and this hot stranger."

I laugh, roll my eyes, and my cheeks flush pinker than they already are from the tequila. "Mary—"

"Will you just dance?" she orders.

Conor spins Mary into the crowd, and the dark-haired guy offers me his hand. "I'm Evan."

I stare at his hand, and for a split second, I hear James's voice, the

8

voice that makes me question everything and not feel like enough. I push it aside as quickly as it appears. Tonight, I am thousands of miles away, in Vegas. Buzzed, broken, and maybe for the first time in months, ready to feel something else.

"I'm Charlotte," I say and take Evan's hand.

We dance for a while. At first, it's playful and fun. Until it isn't, turning more flirty. His hand finds my waist, while mine is around his neck. His lips find mine. The music blares, and our bodies move together in unison. Less like strangers and more like people who know what lines they are ready to cross.

His lips move from mine and brush my ear. "Wanna get out of here?"

"To where?" I ask.

"Anywhere a little quieter... no pressure."

My pulse skips a beat, and at first, I hesitate, then nod.

* * *

The tequila is catching up with me, snaking through my veins, slow and heavy. The hallway floor sways beneath me, like I've stepped into a carnival funhouse. Evan's hand is on my back, steadying me. He doesn't lead or rush me, just matches my steps.

My heart pounds in my chest like a bass drum as I unlock the door to my room. The second it clicks open, I feel Evan's hand on my waist, gently leading me in. I waste no time and turn to him, pull him in closer, and kiss him differently than I did on the dance floor. Deeper, with a need at the forefront of it. My fingers curl in his shirt and tug him closer until our bodies are touching. He seems to give off its own heat.

We stumble backwards, laughing in each other's mouths until we fall onto the bed. He hovers over me, kissing my neck, his lips trailing along my collarbone and across the strap of my dress. Mary's dress. My eyes close, and my breath catches. It feels good... too good. And suddenly... too much.

"Wait."

He freezes. "You, okay?"

I nod. "Yeah. I just... I can't... I mean... You don't even know my last name."

He looks at me, pulls away, without a hint of his ego being bruised, and understands.

"That's fair," he says, and pulls the strap back up that his teeth just pulled down. "Want me to go?"

"Actually, can you stay? Nothing else. Just this."

He smiles at me, soft and genuine. "Deal."

I haven't told him anything. Not about James or our ruined engagement. Certainly not how I've felt lost for the past few months, like I'm someone else. Someone I don't recognize. Someone who is consumed with frosting and fake smiles.

But somehow, he knows. He reaches over and wraps his arm around my waist and kisses my cheek. I close my eyes and swallow up the warmth of him. No promises or expectations. Just understanding.

CHAPTER 3

September 10, 2001

I wake up to an annoying light filtering through the curtains and the sounds of horns honking in the distant Vegas traffic. My bed is empty, the sheets are jumbled, and there is a faint smell of cologne lingering throughout my room.

Evan is gone.

Of course he is.

I stare at the ceiling, my throat is hoarse and dry, and my heart is torn between disappointment and relief. I'm still in my dress from last night, I notice a smeared lipstick stain on my pillow, and I still have my neon orange bracelet wrapped around my wrist from the club.

Slowly, I sit up, my head pounds, and my stomach is queasy. Not just from the tequila but from the weight of it all. The drinking. The night. The almost. It's all proof that I am *not* over Jack-ass James, no matter how far from home I am and no matter how many strangers I kiss.

"I should have just gone through with it," I say out loud to myself. "Just so I can stop feeling like the woman who'd been cheated on and left behind like the last slice of cake left in the box."

Once again, I catch a whiff of Evan's cologne and remember that he was different, the way he pulled back when I asked him to. He didn't make me feel stupid or accuse me of being a tease. He stayed, just holding me with no strings attached.

Suddenly, I realize I didn't say no because I didn't want him. I want more, something real, something layered and sweet and worth the mess it takes to make. I want the whole cake. Even if I'm still not ready, it proves I'm still capable of wanting.

It all feels like progress. A few months ago, I couldn't even say James's name without choking on it. Now? I can almost laugh. Almost.

I recall some of the dates after James and chuckle as I think back at the absurdity of some of them.

My family and friends all seem to think they're entitled to weigh in on the kind of man I should be dating.

"Girllll, I know you better than you know yourself," Jennifer had said while out for martinis one night over the summer. The gleam in her eyes was so intent, it looked almost painful as she searched through the smoky bar, trying to hand-pick the perfect guy for me.

I swear, they've ignored every other aspect of their own lives and made some sort of secret pact to find me a man. My soulmates, no less, they've said more than once, like it's some sort of destiny.

Even my mother thinks she knows what's best for me and my sorry excuse for a love life, "Charlotte, you need to stop being so picky when it comes to men... I know James was an ass, but not all men are like him. Look at your father," she proclaimed as she leaned over, plopping a spoonful of mashed potatoes on his plate as we sat at the dinner table just last week.

"Oh no! Don't go dragging me into this... I learned my lesson not to meddle in her love life," Dad had said with such finality, shaking his head so hard it looked like it might pop right off. But he never missed a beat, spearing his fork into the hefty slice of meatloaf on his plate.

"Oh, you're no help," my mother snapped, dumping another pile of broccoli onto his plate, fully aware it would never be touched. "Like the guy I introduced to you last week from the supermarket... *He* was perfect... You are never going to find your soulmate and give me grandbabies if you don't give someone a chance," my mother said from across the dinner table. Her eyes never left mine, all while passing me the bowl of mashed potatoes, as if the topic of my love life were no big deal.

Still, lying here, rubbing my throbbing head, thinking back on that ridiculous conversation, I laugh, because honestly, it's just so absurd. I'm pretty sure that if my family and friends are the ones playing matchmakers, then it doesn't exactly qualify as a soulmate. Of course, despite all the talks and every red flag waving from their handpicked suitors, I still gave in. Ignoring all my instincts, I went on the dates anyway. Each one ended the same way. I'd thank them for the dinner and tell them that I'd be in touch, knowing all too well that I indeed would never keep in touch. The 'soulmates,' as I call them now, always fell into one of two categories: either painfully boring and incapable of holding a conversation, or so obnoxious, self-absorbed, and loud that I couldn't squeeze in a single word.

"Hideous Harry," that guy my mother spoke so fondly of, you know, the one she thought was perfect for me to spawn her grandbabies with, showed up in those horrible "Jesus looking" style brown sandals on our first date. *And last, for that matter.* With socks no less. It was his toe that got me. Just taunting me, sticking out of a tiny hole in his faded black sock, the heel all frayed. And somehow, I couldn't look away. It was like watching a B-rated movie; you know you should stop and change the channel, but something inside you just won't let you. So, you sit there, watching, without investing even the slightest thought in it.

I can't blame it all on my mom, though. I do accept partial responsibility. How could I have thought that my fifty-six-year-old mother, whose soul passion in life is tending to her zucchini plants in her backyard garden, could ever know a thing or two about dating? I mean, she hasn't dated in over thirty years. *I should have known.* Needless to say, that poor guy never had a prayer: I wrote him off without a second thought, adding him to my ever-growing list of nevers.

"No more blind dates! I'm done," I said to my parents when I returned home that night. Then I marched my ass right upstairs and rummaged through my sock drawer, throwing out every pair that might have had the slightest hole. I laid down to sleep that night, wondering if my family and friends ever really knew me at all. After what I've gone through with some of my past relationships, I am in no hurry to date, let alone settle down. *Been there, done that.* I will not make those mistakes again. If Mr. Right, somehow magically, shows up on my doorstep, who knows? But I know one thing is for sure. Today is not that day.

What I need to do is focus, get my ass out of bed, and get ready for work. This awful headache isn't going to make it easy.

A groan escapes me as I drag myself from the bed. My hair is plastered to one side of my head, my mouth tastes like spoiled milk, I may still be a little drunk, and my stomach has gone from a feeling of queasy to slow rumbling in a matter of minutes. Seven-forty-seven flashes in neon on my bedside clock, a sharp reminder that I'm not in Vegas for fun.

"*Shit!* I need to get my ass in gear," I mutter to no one, rifling through my clothes like it matters. It doesn't. My work wardrobe never changes.

Gurglllleeee

My belly growls, loud enough that it startles me, and my hand drifts down to rub it, like I'm some sort of chubby Buddha statue.

It was three o'clock yesterday afternoon when I caught myself standing on the showroom floor, only then realizing I hadn't eaten a single thing. I was on what seemed to be my eighty-seventh cake presentation of the day when my stomach roared like an angry, ferocious lion. The sound was so obnoxious that a potential customer actually dug through her handbag and handed me a mangled granola bar.

"Here… take this." She said it just as a fiery heat rushed to my cheeks, turning them the exact shade of icing I'd been using. Probably stashed in there for emergencies, just like that one. I wanted nothing more than to rip it from her hands and shove it into my gaping pie hole, but of course, I politely declined.

"Aw, you're too kind… Thank you so much… I'm fine. I'll be taking a break in just a little while," I said appreciatively. Except she remained standing there, bar in hand, not taking no for an answer. The persistent look she gave me told me that she wasn't leaving until I ate the dang bar. She didn't budge.

"Please, I insist… You will thank me… These suckers are delicious, and anyway, I have plenty to go around." She magically held up four more to solidify the offer.

I did what I was told, I accepted the beat-up granola bar and bit into it, all without skipping a note, still piping swirls of buttercream onto the mum-flowered wedding cake I'd been decorating. Red, orange, and yellow flowers cascaded down the front. The chocolate fudge pinecones that poked out from them could pass for being real. I have only been training decorators on how to make them, on a daily basis, for the past month. I could probably do them with my eyes closed, and given the competitive side in me, of course, I would try if someone dared. The cake was stunning with its warm, autumnal hues, perfectly suited for this time of year, an ideal centerpiece for any fall-themed wedding.

I shake off yesterday's thoughts as I catch my reflection in the full-length mirror hanging by the door.

"Ughhh!" I let out a huff, already annoyed with my boring excuse for an outfit.

Beige, khaki capris, and a drab, white polo. Sexy, I know. A bold choice in everyday disappointment. My staple for any trade show I attend. It pairs well with how I pull my long blonde hair, now streaked with white from the summer sun, back into a low, ordinary ponytail. I give very little effort into the rest of my look, because why bother, really.

"Good Lord, this whole ensemble screams, I am twenty-eight years old, and I live with my parents." I laugh and shake my head, because, honestly, it's just too true.

CHAPTER 4

I take one final look in the gilded mirror, pressing down any rogue hairs back into place. I grab my tote bag, which holds the essentials: my purse, my last clean apron, and my trusty travel-sized cake supply caddy. Because who doesn't carry one of those around?

Panic sets in as the search for my room key unfolds, only to find it already in my back pocket. *Didn't I just put it there two minutes ago?* My head shakes from side to side, pretty much on autopilot these days; it's grown used to it by now. I don't even know why I'm still surprised. "You would forget your own head if it wasn't attached," my mother would always gripe. *She was probably right.*

"When will I ever learn?" I say to no one, and head for the door, and that is when I notice something poking out from under it. It's a piece of paper ripped from a hotel notepad. Mary's handwriting, pink-inked and slightly chaotic, scrawled across the page:

Char,

I'm heading out for my early flight back home. You were asleep and looking weirdly peaceful (gross, but also adorable) when I snuck in this morning to say good-bye, so I didn't want to wake you. I'm leaving your spare key as well… Oh, and I may have eaten your emergency Peanut Chews. Sorry, not sorry. Have a good rest of the convention.

Love you. You're a badass. I'm so proud of you for last night.

XOXO, Mary

I can't help but laugh and fold the note and shove it along with the spare key into my bag as I push open my hotel-room door and step out. I stand longer than any normal person should, double and triple-checking the lock, convincing myself that no one is lurking inside, waiting to attack me when I get back. Again, I reach around and feel my back pocket for the umpteenth time, to ensure my room key and cell phone are still there. *I'm starting to get on my own nerves now.*

Dinnnngggg

The elevator pings from down the hallway, and without even thinking, I run in hopes of catching it. My legs move faster than the rest of my body, causing me to stumble and almost fall into the elevator doors as I reach them. The potential that my arm could be severed is strong, but I risk it anyway and place it in between the automatic steel doors, propping them back open just enough for the rest of me to enter. My eyes focus on the floor, I step inside and reach for the quarter-sized "Lobby" button, and watch as it lights to life in a sultry red glow. In the muggy gray windowless death trap, Elvis's "Blue Suede Shoes" plays in the background.

"Good morning."

"Jesus, Mary, and Joseph!" I jump, and instinctively, my hands reach up to my chest, and the tote bag spills out onto the elevator floor, startling me. Piping tips and white plastic couplers are scattered everywhere.

With the amount of speed at which I darted in here, I hadn't noticed anyone else inside. I exhale a deep puff, unaware I'd been holding my breath.

"Is there some sort of fire that I don't know about?" the stranger asks, stepping closer as I fumble to gather the contents of my bag, just in time for him to kneel and start helping with the mess at his feet.

Just as he grabs for my apron, I look up, our faces now only inches from each other. I can feel the warmth of his breath on my skin as I take in a deep breath of my own at its intoxicating sensation. I'm caught off guard. He's the kind of guy who could land the *Sexiest Man Alive* cover just by showing up and breathing. I would know, because I may or may not have purchased a copy each year of my adult life. I mean, holy smokes, he is gorgeous, and the devilish smile he is giving me right now is to die for. *Damn.* Between his piercing, icy blue eyes, his tousled brown hair, and that smile that should be illegal, it's no surprise my face is heating up. *Oh, that smile.* Heat rises up the back of my neck, and I hope he doesn't notice. The restraint I have from leaning over and planting a kiss on those lips of his is real. *Do it, girl... You will never see this guy again. What happens in Vegas stays in Vegas, right?* I can't believe my reflection in the elevator doors. My face is flushed once again, deepening its hue to a shade of red that I didn't know existed. *Get a hold of yourself, Charlotte.*

"Slow down, speed racer... You're running like the world's gonna end in five minutes." The playfulness in his tone doesn't go unnoticed as we both begin to stand. "For a second there, I thought you were gonna get pinned between the doors."

The snug black t-shirt he wears clings to every inch of his chiseled torso, perfectly offsetting his golden tan and stretching just enough to show off his bulging biceps. A precisely sketched tattoo of a buffalo, in shades of black and gray, takes up most of his forearm. I've never seen anything like it, and it's beautiful. His tight blue jeans look as if they were stitched just for him, hugging him in all the right places. I want to reach over and touch him, just to make sure he's real. My hands push to their sides at warp speed, forcing myself from acting on the urge.

Upon his head, he wears a baseball cap, "CHEVY" stitched across the front of it, and, completing the look, a pair of very worn brown leather cowboy boots. *I mean, come on, what woman doesn't love a guy in cowboy boots?* I stare for a moment longer than I should have before my mouth registers what my brain is trying to convey. *Speak, you idiot.*

"Uhhh, yeah, I'm here for work, and I need to grab something to eat before the trade show starts, or else I will be starving all day because I might never get time for a break," I say, realizing that a novel just came spewing out in one ridiculous breath. *Why am I so nervous?* My head shakes, annoyed at myself as he takes a step forward and stretches out his hand toward mine.

"Well, we wouldn't want something like that to happen, now, would we? Hi, I'm Jaxson Lange, but everyone calls me Jax... And now, so can you." He winks. The moment his hand meets mine, it's like flipping a switch; electricity surges, fast and hot, straight to my core and settles with a pulse between my thighs. I want to pull him closer and have my way with him right here in the elevator. The fact that he is an obvious stranger is completely lost in the moment. *It's as easy as pushing the little red emergency button, halting the elevator, and letting me have at him.*

The rush of desire that hits me, intense and unexpected, for a stranger, no less, is like none I've ever known. In the three years I'd been with James, I can't think of a single encounter where he ever left me feeling this charged. The button is right there begging me to push it, taunting me. I can practically hear Jennifer's voice chanting, *DO IT, DO IT.*

Forcing myself back to my senses, I somehow muster up an embarrassing, flustered attempt at sounding normal, "Hi, I'm Charlotte!" in a much too excited voice. Still breathing a bit heavy from our encounter, as the last bit of my introduction spills from my mouth, the elevator doors open, and Jax steps out. But just before he walks away, he turns and pauses, looks over his shoulder, and says, "Enjoy that breakfast of yours, okay. If I'm lucky, maybe I'll run into you again... It is Vegas, right?" he teases as he continues to walk away, and out of my life forever.

Now, all I can think about is that I wish I were enjoying my breakfast with him back in my room, the two of us, completely naked, eating pancakes in my bed. *What is happening with you, Charlotte? Good Lord, get a hold of yourself, girl.* I think to myself and laugh.

Erasing the sinful thoughts invading my filthy mind, I look up, hoping to catch one last glimpse of his ass, but he's already gone, swallowed by the sea of early risers, probably headed for the casino floor, chasing dreams of hitting it big. Lady Luck has other plans; he is gone, just as any chances I may have had with him. Vanished. *Girl, you know you weren't ever going to do anything with that man anyway.*

CHAPTER 5

My fork spears a piece of waffle and moves it around the plate at a snail's pace, sopping up the puddle of syrup that has been left untouched. My mind is elsewhere, and I'm unable to enjoy them, and that fact alone irritates me. They sit uneaten in front of me, even though they're covered with two of my favorites: fresh strawberries and homemade whipped cream. On any other day, I would have savored every bite, but today, my mind is occupied, filled with a constant reminder of the "cowboy" in the elevator. No matter how good the waffles might be, they just can't compete with my thoughts of Jaxson and the way his backside looked when he walked away in those jeans. *The first guy I have been attracted to in what seems like forever, and I'm three thousand miles from home. Nice timing, Charlotte.*

"Thanks," I say out loud, glaring up at the heavens.

I pick up the untouched plate and toss it into the waste bin on my way out, and head toward the convention center doors.

* * *

The day is going as all the others have before. Long and uneventful. My voice is giving out from all the talking and shameless schmoozing, anything to convince potential customers to buy from "For Cakes Sake," the company I create cake designs for.

"How do you get your colors so beautiful and muted, yet vibrant for the fall?" one woman asks.

"If you add a smidge of brown food coloring or even some chocolate buttercream to your colored icing, it will blend together, creating the perfect shades of fall colors, I answer as I carefully place the orange-colored mum at the edge of the wedding cake I'm working on.

"Interesting... I never would have thought of that."

"Yep. And our specially formulated icing holds in the colors the best. Would you like to talk to the owner, Jeff Baker, and learn more about it?"

"Absolutely."

I signal Jeff over towards my decorating station, and I can tell by the look on his face, one of fulfillment, that he loves what he does, confident that a new customer is on the horizon.

"Jeff Baker's the name, and baking's my game," he says with a grin, reaching out to shake her hand. I laugh at the cheesy line, one I've heard more times than I can count.

I continue decorating as the two of them walk off together, trusting that he'll be pleased with my interactions with her. My role for this particular show has only been drilled into my head a million times in the past month.

"We need to bring in more sales!" he would bellow. "An international baking show like this one could bring 'For Cake Sake' to a whole other level. Charlotte, you are the face of the company, front and center for this one, so I want a lot of one-on-one interaction with potential customers. Do that thing with your eyes. It gets them every time." His eyes flutter open and shut. His smile widens. *Is that what I look like?*

"You mean, blink?"

He didn't find it funny.

Without ever coming out and saying it, I always knew what Jeff meant. Not only would I be demonstrating my impeccable cake skills, but I'd also be showing off my smile, batting my big blue eyes, and laughing at jokes that are seldom funny. I can play "the game" as well as the rest of them.

Just yesterday, before closing up the booth, an older gentleman, donning an awful dime-store toupee, decided he was a funny guy and insisted on telling me a "hilarious" joke, as he put it, about cakes, of course. While I kept myself busy decorating a wedding cake, fully on display to everyone crowding our booth, he stepped in front of me and started reciting it.

"A father is dying. All of his children are huddled around his bed. The aroma of chocolate cake comes from the kitchen. So, the father says to his daughter... Please go get me a piece of cake before I die... She came back a few minutes later and said, "Mom said no. It's for after the funeral." Laughter exploded from him, while others looked at me for pity.

On cue, I laughed so hard at his horrible, predictable "Dad" joke that it actually pained me as I forced a tear to escape. I waved my hand and indicated for Jeff to make his way over and hear it for himself. It only took fifteen minutes to pass, and a major deal was made. When I glanced over and caught a glimpse of the two of them shaking hands, I knew I'd be looking at a nice, fat bonus, come the end of the month. *Works every time.*

Little does anyone know, I enjoy "the game," and the men are always so predictable. If they are not driven by what is dangling between their legs, then most are driven by their egos. If I smile and laugh at one of those stupid jokes loud enough, their "heads" will grow, and so will my company's business. *Morons.*

* * *

It's nearing four-thirty, and only a few persistent stragglers remain. The convention hall now feels like a ghost town as the rest of the customers have long gone. The scene is much different from yesterday's, when the hustling of deals was still in full swing at this time of day. This particular show is on the shorter side, only three days, even though I've been here longer getting set up for it. Today is the last full day of the convention, and tomorrow will end by noon. With Vegas as the setting for this show, I can only assume the customers have already wrapped up their business affairs over the past two days and are now out on the Strip, gambling, catching a David Copperfield show, or sipping vodka with reckless abandon.

"Charlotte! Get cleaned up! I need to take my back pill, for Christ's sake!" Dick yells while slumped over in a chair that sits in the corner of the booth, meant for the customers. *Guess I know now where the company name came from.* I let out a huff as my eyes dart to Jeff, silently asking for backup when it comes to Dick. It's a secret game we have with each other when he's being extra cranky. Right now, I'm the one bearing the brunt of his rudeness.

His age is starting to show as these long, grueling days of work begin to take a toll on his frail body. He reaches around to rub the aching that's clearly formed in the back of his neck. Dick (I guess if I had that name, I would be crabby too) is the founder of the company and just so happens to be Jeff's father. Judging by the puzzled look that Jeff is giving him at this moment, I can assume he notices it too.

"I'm sure what Dad meant to say is that the two of us would like to take you out for a nice dinner tonight. You have been busting your ass off the past few days, especially today, now that Mary's gone, and deserve a good meal at the very least." The way he glares back at his dad tells me he's unhappy with his unpleasant choice of words. His eyes never leave Dick's as he straightens out a stack of company brochures that sit messily on the table next to mine.

Just the mention of dinner has me forgetting all about Dick and his god-awful demeanor. It's crazy what a decent meal can do for a girl on the edge. I clean up my demonstration area in record time and wipe the surface of my countertop with a vengeance.

"Ooooh, yummmmm. Can't wait, thanks... I'm almost finished," I say as I secure the lid on the last pail of buttercream, locking it into place. I use my foot to push it under the table and store it out of sight for safekeeping until tomorrow.

"Hurry up, too! I'm starving and want to go to bed early tonight!" Dick demands. *Ugh, why can't it just be Jeff that treats me to dinner?* Dick stands, taps his foot impatiently, drapes his annoyingly immaculate tailored suit-jacket over the crease of his arm, and scowls at Jeff and me.

"Hey Dad... Didn't you also mean to say, take your time, you must be exhausted from decorating hundreds of beautiful cakes for our thriving company? How about, go get ready, then meet down in the hotel lobby at six-thirty?" He gives a wordless shake of his head, and for a moment, he looks exactly like one of those bobblehead dolls people stick on their dashboards. Jeff looks at me, and we both laugh, then the three of us begin walking toward the exit doors. *Lord, I hope to never get so grumpy when I get to be his age.*

When we reach the entrance to the hotel casino, we all head our separate ways toward the direction of our rooms. It's like a maze in here with elevators in every hallway. Just yesterday, I took the wrong one and walked around the halls for half an hour before I even realized I was on the other side of the hotel.

A thousand things run rampant through my mind. *What to wear? What am I going to eat? When was the last time I talked to my parents?* I make a mental note to set aside time and call home and check in with them, letting them know how things are going here.

I'll make a quick call to Jennifer, too, and give her the lowdown on the cowboy that got away this morning. My breathing quickens, and I gasp for breath at the mere thought of him.

Opting out of the direct and obvious route through the hotel lobby, I decide to take the fun "people watching" path, straight through the casino floor toward the west end elevators. Flashing neon lights engulf the room, the *clinking* sounds of quarters drop from the machines and spill into their pans below, all accompanied by a thick fog of cigarette smoke that nearly chokes me, making it difficult to see at times.

"Ahemmmmm." I clear my throat. *Maybe going this way wasn't such a good idea after all.*

I navigate through the usual Vegas crowd: gamblers of all ages, businessmen in overpriced suits, tourists in matching shirts, and a few brides dressed in tacky white wedding gowns, champagne sloshing in their half-empty glasses. I envision them on their way to one of the dozens of cheesy wedding chapels that Vegas has to offer, inviting couples to get married by the famous king of rock and roll, "Elvis" himself. On any other day, this would be my favorite pastime, a prime location for people watching. If I were here with Jennifer, we'd be sitting for hours observing and giggling, giving each and every person their own personal backstory. Yet instead, I find myself searching only for a "CHEVY" hat amongst this melting pot of risk takers, gambling their hard-earned money away. Even though I know the odds of seeing him again, in a city of millions, are slim to none. But it is beyond question worth trying. I'm more than willing to risk a little smoke damage to these otherwise pristine lungs for another run-in with Jax. Sadly, though, the elevator doesn't reward my bravery. No Jax in sight.

Just a whoosh of stale air and utter disappointment.

Before hopping in the shower, I call my parents to check in, the phone balanced between my shoulder and ear as I rummage through my dresser drawers, hunting for the perfect dinner outfit while I wait for someone to pick up.

"Hello?"

"Hey, Pop. How are you and Mom doing? Anything new?" I ask. The immediate sound of his voice makes me smile.

"All good...Just getting ready to head up to bed," he says. "Oh... Guess who I ran into today at Wawa this morning?"

"Well... judging by the harsh tone in your voice, I'm afraid to ask."

"That pathetic excuse for an old boyfriend of yours from high school... Derek... He turned the corner of the coffee station and almost bumped right into me. The scared shitless look on his face was priceless." There is a sinister tone in his statement. "He turned three shades of white, then threw his things on the counter and darted out the door empty-handed." The wicked way he laughs tells me that he is enjoying the thought more than he should be.

"Oh Lord, I'm surprised you didn't hit him even after all these years." I laugh, a hint of truth hidden beneath its surface.

"Believe me, the thought crossed my mind." There is an undeniable pride in his voice at the protection of his little girl.

"He's a coward and not worth your time. I've long but forgotten about that little jerk," I assure him, "and anyway..." I shake my head, still irritated whenever I speak of him. "I gotta go." I yank off my shoes and throw them at my shiny new suitcase on the floor, making a louder thump than I anticipated. I guess I'm more annoyed than I originally thought. "I need to shower and get ready for dinner."

"Charlotte, don't think about that loser. I shouldn't have brought him up." His voice is now soft and kind. His ability to know when something has bothered me is remarkable.

"It's fine." I stand up and square my shoulders. I refuse to think of him. "Tell Mom

I love her."

"We love you, too," Mom yells from the background, and I can't help but laugh. That woman hears everything, even other people's phone calls.

With a few minutes to kill before I shower, I decide to call Jennifer.

"Yo... Bitch!"

"What's up, Dummy? How's Vegas?"

"Dude... I met the hottest guy this morning in the elevator." My entire body feels toasty at the very mention of him.

"Did you have sex with him?" Her laughter echoes throughout the phone. I rub my ear to wipe away the ringing still left behind.

"Yup. The best sex I've ever had. Right in the friggin elevator too."

"Shut up! Seriously?" I don't think I've ever heard her so proud of me as she is right this second, and I can't help but enjoy every bit of it.

"Oh my God... No! We talked for five seconds... But on another note, I did come close to doing it with a stranger I danced with at a nightclub last night." I admit. "But that's a story for another time... We're talking about the love of my life right now." I laugh, knowing just how ridiculous that sounds.

"*Ughhh*," she sighs, and I swear I can hear her excitement deflate like a bicycle tire with a nail in it. "Oh, well, that's a bummer... Next time you call me about a hot guy that you meet, it better have a more exciting ending."

"Oh... I almost forgot the best part. The sexy one from the elevator... He's a cowboy... Well, he wears cowboy boots so...."

"Cowboy? Never had one of them. We'll have to see if I approve." She chuckles.

"Approve???? You don't get a say... You remember that last guy, Sam, that you picked out and 'approved' for me?" I wince at the very mention of him.

"Sniffy Sam." Good Lord, I'm not sure how to even explain that guy. Let's just say, during the course of our forty-five-minute coffee date that we had, he sniffed his fingers a total of twenty-three times. (Yes. Twenty-three.... I counted.) My stomach churns just thinking about it.

"Would you like some creamer for your coffee?" he had asked as he grabbed a handful of the tiny white containers filled with cream, then set them down in front of me.

"No. I'm good. I like mine black." I cut him off with a bold-faced lie. *Give me all the cream and sugar.* I can still feel the sting of bile when it rose in my throat at the thought of his disgusting, gross fingers touching them, and it made me sick. I remember my nose scrunching up in such disgust that he asked me if I was okay. I excused myself to the bathroom because I'd become so nauseated, I thought I was going to hurl my pumpkin scone right there all over the table. On the way to the bathroom, I took a right turn and sneaked out the back door, and never looked back, my hand cupping my mouth the entire way. Leaving him to his stinky fingers and my untouched coffee. Good Lord, he was creepy.

"Yeah, I still need to get you back for that guy," I promised her with retaliation. "What the hell were you thinking, Dummy?"

Thud, thud, thud! A sharp and steady pounding echoes from my hotel room door, jolting me upright.

"What's with all the banging?" Jennifer asks, concerned.

"Dunno... must be housekeeping... I'd better go. I'll talk to you when I get home in a few days and fill you in about the Cowboy, then," I say.

"Talk to you later, Bitch."

"Love you too, Hussy." I set the phone down and walk toward the door. I press my right eye to the peephole, squinting to see if it's actually hotel staff or a serial killer dressed as one and here to murder me. *Phewww, it's safe.* The tag that is pinned to her shirt has just enough room to fit her name, "Anastasia," and I open the door.

"Miss Evans, Ma'am? These are for you," she says with her hands extended out toward me, her broken English soft, a stark difference from her harsh pounding on the door.

I grab the most gorgeous flower bouquet that I've ever seen. *Who could these be from?*

Brrrring Brrrring. My phone rings from across the room.

"What the hell? It's like a Grand Central station here!"

"Ma'am?" asks Anastasia, her face contorted with a look of confusion.

"Ohhh, sorry, I was just saying... Oh nevermind... Thank you so much." I hand her a few dollars I had stashed in my back pocket from earlier, then close the door behind me. I run for my cell phone that's buzzing on the end table. *Geez, it's only been two minutes, Jennifer. It must be something good if you couldn't wait.* I laugh.

"Whaja forget, Dummy?" I can feel my chest rise and fall as I attempt to catch my breath.

"Did you receive the flowers? I miss you, Babe." My body goes limp, and my excitement disappears at the immediate sound of his irritating voice. *Jerkoff James*

"How the hell did you know I was here?" Anger builds inside of me. My jaw tightens as my teeth clench together, and I shake my head in disgust.

"You wrote it on the kitchen calendar... Remember, Babe?" The words roll off his tongue with such ease, as if he had forgotten the fact that we haven't spoken a word to each other in months.

"How's Holly... James?" I ask. Like a scalded cat, I remind him of his heartless infidelity.

"What? Holly... She meant nothing. I'm sorry, Babe... I want you." *Gee, thanks, glad you clarified that, Douche.* The cockiness in his voice, thinking he can call me Babe and offer up apologies, brings me to my limit. An immediate heat radiates up my spine, and I feel like a volcano about to erupt. My words are like lava, ready to flow, and James will not be spared in their path.

"Fuck off, James... We are done... And don't ever call me again... BAAAABE!!!!!!" I slam my phone shut, flowers still in hand. *Damn. That felt good.* I drop them both onto the bed, then head to the shower.

Under the gold-plated shower head in the gaudy marble bathroom, I embrace the scalding hot water and invite it to wash away any unwanted lies that James has left stained on my body.

* * *

I rummage through the dresser drawers once more and decide on a short spaghetti strap black dress, ruched at the waistline, accentuating my every curve. I bought it for the third anniversary of our first date. James and I were just one week shy of it when I caught him that dreadful afternoon in Philly. Needless to say, the celebration never happened, and it has been hanging in my closet, untouched ever since.

The curve of my bare back is on full display, perfectly framed by the loose blonde curls that cascade down, tickling my skin with every movement. A world of difference from the pulled-up mess that I've had all week. I decide on a bold choice of footwear, my favorite shiny red high heels that I rarely get a chance to wear back home. *Thank God, I didn't waste these on any of those ridiculous 'soulmate' dates back home.* My subconscious was in full Dorothy mode when I packed. I threw them in at the last minute, thinking Vegas might just be the kind of place where ruby slippers wouldn't raise eyebrows.

"Damn... These are smokin'." I'm pleased with my ensemble choice as I admire my reflection in the mirror. "You really screwed up, James." I pretend to kiss into the air and wink at the face that stares back at me.

I grab my purse along with the tainted flowers, gifted by my ex, and take one last look in the mirror, give myself a quick once over, then head out the door, towards the elevators. But not before handing the bouquet to a young woman in white, skipping down the hall, singing *"Going to the chapel, and I'm gonna get married." Ummmm. Yeah, good luck with that.*

CHAPTER 6

Turns out, we don't have far to go; Jeff chose a restaurant right here in the hotel. *How have I not noticed it before?* The world-renowned Japanese steak house, SAMURAI, is anything but ordinary and sits hidden and tucked quietly into the corner of the first floor. Not only is it known for its delicious culinary cuisine, but for its impeccable decor it displays from floor to ceiling. From the moment we walk in, I can't help but stop and stare. I'm in complete awe of just how stunning it is.

Fountains of pristine blue waters stream down the walls, spilling into a huge koi pond set in the dead center of the room. My eyes are immediately drawn to it, and it sets the tone for the entire theme. Lily pads lie atop the water as if suspended and floating above the sky. Gardens full of beautiful exotic flowers, shades in every color imaginable, all placed with such precision that they can be seen from every inch of the room. The aroma that exudes from them reminds me of the sweet plumeria candle my mom lights when she sits in her favorite chair reading one of her trashy romance novels. An impeccable shine beams off the glass elevator that sets off to the left of the entryway and carries you up to the second story, housing private hibachi-style dinner settings. I can only imagine that if I were ever to vacation in Japan, this is what it would look like. So beautiful, peaceful, and serene, and it's absolutely breathtaking.

"I hope they seat us soon. The stench coming from the damn flowers in here is giving me a headache," Dick complains, and interrupts my tranquility.

The imaginary angel sitting gracefully on my shoulder forces my hands to my sides and supersedes the sudden urge to push Dick into the pond. The sinful plan invading my thoughts is definitely the handiwork of her evil twin. I mean, how can you be in such a beautiful setting and still be so damn miserable? It boggles my mind in more ways than one.

The hostess approaches with caution, relieving Jeff and me from Dick's constant negativity. *She must have heard him complaining.*

"Jeff, party of three?" She asks no one in particular but directs her attention towards the three of us. The hopeful look on her face tells me the table is ours no matter what, but no one else seems to notice. *Even she is annoyed at Dick.* Jeff raises his hand like a good little schoolboy, excited to answer the teacher's question. "Your table is all set, and we are ready to seat you." We turn and head toward the glass elevator. "Enjoy your dinner, and don't shy away from the sake." She looks at me and winks just before entering. *Girl, you have no idea.*

The "show" is in full swing by the time our butt cheeks hit our seats. Our chef is already tossing knives into the air, captivating our attention as he catches them blindly when reaching behind his back. Eggs dance off the silver spatula, like a child on a trampoline, bouncing up and down until the last one is sent soaring up high. Eventually, landing in his tall paper chef's hat, never to be seen again. A volcano is constructed from a stack of sliced onions, carefully placed on top of one another with such precision, just like a stack of building blocks. They slide with ease across the scalding hot flattop, while steam erupts from its top, as our chef yells, "Choo Choo!"

Our eyes are fixated on the hibachi show, fascinated by our culinary surroundings. We talk about the day's profits, share a few stories from the past few days, and consume way too much alcohol.

"*Sake!!!*" the chef yells, and we all oblige as he squeezes excessive amounts of the sweet wine like alcohol straight into our mouths. I mean, it would be rude to say no when he offered, right?

Next up, the shrimp toss, always my favorite part of any hibachi experience, and yes, I'm undefeated. Everyone, except Jeff, catches the flying piece of prawn in their mouths. Jeff's shrimp goes rogue and flies through the air, bouncing right off his forehead and landing smack dab onto Dick's plate, causing laughter to erupt from everyone. So much so, Dick lets out a snort, causing more laughter, even now from our chef.

"*Sake!!!*" he yells once more, but only this time to celebrate our victories. I laugh out loud, even though I'll be sure to feel the repercussions in the morning, but at this moment, I'm sort of okay with it.

It's not often that I get to experience this other side of Dick and Jeff, the two of them always so proper and "ready for business." It's nice hearing them laugh this way. (You know, like normal human beings.) But I'm sure it might be the sake talking.

* * *

Jeff turns to me as we ride the elevator back to the first floor. He reaches out and hands me a crisp one-hundred-dollar bill.

"Here. Take this and go win big. Have fun," he says and gestures down the hall towards the casino floor. His cheeks are rosy, and his words are slurred.

"Well, only if you insist." I smile, take the money, and place it in the back zipper of my purse that dangles from my shoulder.

He doesn't have to tell me twice. I will do just that, I intend to have a lot of fun, and I know just where I'm going to use it. The slots have been taunting me since the second I arrived.

The two of them extend their hugs my way, and we say our goodbyes.

"How about the three of us meet down at the buffet for breakfast in the morning?" Jeff hiccups, and I laugh to myself. "Let's say eight o'clock. Then we can all walk to the convention together for our last day."

"Sounds like a plan. Have a good night's sleep and maybe take a few ibuprofens before bed. We've all had a lot to drink... I'll see you in the morning," I say, then turn toward the casino.

A slew of tables swallows up the center of the casino floor. Blackjack, Roulette, Texas Holdem, and Craps, you name it, and they have it. Cheers erupt from a crowd of onlookers at one of the Craps tables, and I wish at this moment that I knew how to play. Tables aren't my thing; I barely know how to play Gin Rummy, let alone Craps. The slots are much more my speed.

I'm not sure if it's the amount of alcohol I've consumed or if it's the long hours that I've put in this past week that've finally caught up to me. Either way, I, too, feel the sudden urge to head up to bed. But the crisp one-hundred-dollar bill that Jeff has given to me is suddenly burning a gaping hole in my purse.

"Jackpot Party" slots are my go-to choice when my girlfriends and I go to Atlantic City for a night. They're so obnoxiously fun, with those pounding horn sounds blaring from the machine. And no matter how much money I waste on them, I still love playing.

I can feel eyes coming at me from every direction. My outfit of choice is working its secret magic, causing everyone to turn heads at my red-hot heels and little black dress. Only I didn't wear it for them. *Damn it, Jax, where are you?*

The stench of stale cigarette smoke burns at my nose as I peruse the aisles of bright diamond-shaped carpet, surveying each machine in search of the one that will at last "call to me." As I do, my eyes are also on the lookout for Jax and his gorgeous blue eyes, in hopes of seeing him once more. I stroll past the Blackjack and Roulette tables, scrutinizing each gambler's profile, in anticipation of spotting the sexy cowboy. *Oh, stop, Charlotte, you have better odds of winning the jackpot than you do of finding him with all these people.*

"Oh my God! I don't believe it... There you are!" I yell.

In a flash, I find what I've been searching for. *No, silly. Did you think it would be that easy?* By good fortune, my "lucky" machine is vacant, and without hesitation, I sit and slide Jeff's one-hundred-dollar bill into it.

I pull down the lever attached to its side and bring the machine back to life, allowing it to work its magic. It isn't long before I hear the most glorious sound, "Jackpot Party!" screams so loud that passers-by stop in their tracks and lurk behind me, gawking at the flashing bright lights. One woman is so close that I can smell the exact flavor of coffee on her hot breath. French vanilla with a hint of cinnamon.

The multicolored party horns line up on the screen in a perfect row as quarters begin to fall in a steady fashion, for what seems like an eternity.

"*Holy shit!* I think I just won five hundred dollars."

"You sure did, young lady... I hope to be so lucky." Coffee breath lady says, then pats me on the shoulder, using it for leverage as she lowers herself down to sit at the machine beside mine.

Clink! Clink! Clink! The sharp ringing sounds of coins echo through my ears when they land in the pan below. *My lucky day.*

Five hundred dollars and some change is my total winnings. The temptation to keep going is real, but my gut's waving a red flag. History reminds me that those girls' weekends never ended with me on top, unless you count a hangover and an empty wallet as lucky. I'm taking my money and making a clean getaway.

Lugging my buckets of quarters, I make my way to the cashier's counter at the far end of the wall to cash out before heading up to my room for the night. Unfortunately, though, so many others have the same idea, delaying my bedtime. My arms begin to falter as the quarters grow heavier with each passing minute. The wait is longer than anticipated, and I continue to shift them from one arm to the other, an attempt to relieve some of the numbness that's developed. An excruciating pain has materialized in both of my feet, and I contemplate slipping out of my heels, but realize I haven't a free hand to hold them. The sexiness I felt in them only an hour ago is long forgotten. *Could this line be any slower?*

I patiently wait in this unhurried line, thinking about tomorrow and what it may have to offer. It is sure to be an exhausting one with lots of extra work, given it will be the last day of the convention, so I need to get a solid night's sleep. I'm banking on the fact that the amount of sake still flowing through my veins should help speed that process along.

"Those buckets of quarters can buy an awful lot of pancakes, Ma'am." I hear someone say from a few feet back.

I ignore the declaration, confident that the words aren't meant for me, until something inside me clicks. The sound of the familiar sexy voice has brought life back to my tired soul as my head swiftly turns in the direction of it.

"They look a little heavy. Can I help you with that?" he repeats, the hint of a slur in his voice catching my attention. I don't know why that little detail gets to me, but it does, and now my pulse is racing.

"Well, if it isn't thee Mr. Jaxson Lange." My eyes trail from his broad shoulders straight down to his belt buckle. Lingering there for a moment longer than they should. The direct result of too much sake, and I pray he doesn't notice.

"And if it isn't thee Charlotte, who is always so hungry." He winks at me. *He remembers.*

The seductive way in which his body leans against the chair of the vacant slot machine makes me wish I could be it. His thumb is tucked underneath and grabbing hold of his belt buckle with a can of Coors Light in the other hand. The rosy hue in his cheeks glows brighter than I remember from this morning, flushed from what I can only assume is one too many beers. I smile as he makes his way over, joining me in line. He stands so close that I feel the heat radiating from him. *Or maybe it's me.*

"Well… I was gonna offer to buy you a drink, but judging by the amount of quarters that you're juggling, maybe you should be the one buying instead."

I laugh, looking down at the absurd amount of money I'm clinging to, and agree with him.

"I think that sounds like a great idea." *Sleep is overrated.* "Let me cash these in, and then I'll buy *you* a drink at the bar. But only one, I gotta work tomorrow. Deal?"

"That's the best deal I have made all night." With a tug of his cap and a smile that could melt buttercream, he looks at me, and suddenly, my legs forget how to hold me upright.

I collect my winnings, and together we walk to the bar in the far corner of the casino. With each stride, I catch a whiff of the woodsy scent of his cologne. It's sexy and masculine, just like him. Both of which are making it very hard for me to focus on anything other than him walking so close to me. The red high heels I'm wearing fail me, and I stumble, falling directly into him.

"Geez, are you okay?" he asks and reaches for me.

I catch my balance first. "I'm good," I blurt, even though something in me feels a little too awake now, like my body's bracing for something I can't name.

"Are you sure?" he asks, and this time he gently places his hand on my shoulder, steadying me as I regain what's left of my balance. An unexpected fiery heat creeps up my neck and settles in my cheeks.

"Yes. I'm fine… As you can tell, I don't wear heels much." I laugh as we continue our way over to the bar.

"Well, you should." My body grows hotter than the surface of the sun at his bold choice of words.

We find two vacant stools at the bar and settle in next to each other just as the bartender walks up.

"My name is Dakota… I'll be your bartender tonight. What can I get ya?"

Without bothering to ask, I order a Coors Light and a coconut mojito, along with two glasses of water. Then I laid down a crisp fifty-dollar bill on the counter, enough to cover our drinks.

"Listen, I know we made a deal, but what kind of gentleman would I be if I let a beautiful lady pay for my drink?" He reaches over and pushes the money back toward me.

"The kind that made a solid deal, and given that we are in *Vegas*, of all places, Cowboy, you need to abide by the rules." I wink at him. The sake still flowing through my veins is clearly making its way into my words. "Speaking of, what are you doing here in Vegas?"

"I'm here with a few of my buddies celebrating our friend Patrick's bachelor party," he says, and against my better judgment, I can't help but laugh.

"Why is that funny?" he asks. *Good goin', Charlotte. Five minutes in, and you've already offended him.*

"It isn't, I'm sorry," I say in haste, trying to rectify the awkward situation I just put myself in. "It's just when you mentioned your friend's name, it made me think of an awful blind date that my Aunt Eliza set me up on."

"Well, now I need to hear the rest… You can't leave me hanging," he says, intrigued.

"Oh Lord... Okay...Wellllll... Political Patrick, my name for him now, wouldn't talk about anything other than his one-sided political views." *I mean, who does that?* "I'm with the Democratic Party... Was his actual first words to me," I snicker. "From the moment he opened his mouth, I knew it was going to be a long night, so I quickly ordered a drink and made it a double." My head shakes while Jax laughs and takes another sip of his beer. "I sat there having to listen to him talk crap about our President, all while popping an entire buttered roll into his big, obnoxious mouth. Spitting out pieces of crumbs and sending them flying onto the table as he continued with his offensive personal views. So *gross*. Going on and on about gun control and minimum wages, both of which I couldn't care less about," I continue.

"So, what did you do?"

"I shit you not, I said to him.... If we can get through this drink without me knowing who you voted for last year, that would be great."

"No, you did not?" His laughter catches hold of me, making it impossible not to join in.

"The hell I didn't! Then I ordered another mojito during one of his next rants, attempting to dull the pain I had been enduring... It didn't work, though; no amount of alcohol could drown out his ignorance... What I wouldn't have given to shove the entire basket of rolls into his pie hole, shutting him up for even two seconds." I laugh.

"Well, now I know not to talk politics with you." He winks, clinging his bottle to my glass once more.

"Enough about that idiot... If you are here with a bunch of your buddies, then why are you sitting here with me and not out partying with them, wherever that may be?" I find myself wanting to know more about him and ignoring the fact that I should be in my bed sleeping.

"Let's just say, I'm in a different place in life than the rest of them right now, and my mind is a bit elsewhere. And anyway, you're much better on the eyes." He smiles as he holds up his bottle, pointing in my direction. "Cheers."

"Cheers." I smile back, and sure enough, my face lights up red again.

"I didn't want to bring the vibe down, so I told them I'd had too much to drink and was gonna head back to my room and sleep it off... That's when I saw you." The tone of his voice changes at the latter end. *Did I just imagine him smiling at the sight of me?*

"Besides, they're pulling an all-nighter, drinking until the very last minute, then heading to the airport, catching the last flight out of here tonight." He takes a slow sip of his beer, and all I can think about is how much I wish it were my lips he was tasting instead. "I didn't book the same return flight... Mine leaves tomorrow, and given the state they all were in when I left them, I hope they don't miss their flights." His tooth clinks against his beer bottle as he tries to take in another sip while laughing. He doesn't seem to notice.

"Ahhh, gotcha. So your buddy is getting married? Exciting..." *Not really.* "I'll probably never get married... I'm not sure if I buy into the whole forever type marriage thing these days, ya know? Recent dates that I have been on keep solidifying that notion." We both laugh, but I don't know why.

"Oh... I believe in marriage... Just as long as it's with the one special person you're meant to be with." He says with more conviction than I anticipated. "People marry for so many different reasons," his eyes move from mine as if carefully choosing his next words, and he pauses for a moment. "Marriage has to be for love." He says at last, stumbling on his words as he takes in one long sip and finishes his bottle.

Without thinking, I lean over and playfully whisper in his ear, "Aw, a true gentleman you are." And before I knew it, I plant a kiss on his cheek, leaving a light red stain where my lips just were. The alcohol is reaching its full potency because doing something as fearless as kissing a stranger, no matter how handsome, is completely out of character for me. Jennifer must be rubbing off on me.

I pull away just as quickly and smile at my spontaneous, bold decision. Only Jax isn't as enthused; he looks apprehensive and uneasy. But why? *Good Lord, it was just an innocent peck.*

"And with that, I am going to head back to my room for the night… Thank you for the drink, it was nice." *Then why are you leaving?* "Have a great rest of your show." He says and walks away, out of my life for good this time. The clicking sound of his cowboy boots against the tile floor fades, leaving me alone at the bar, questioning what the hell just happened and why he left in such a hurry. *Maybe if I click my heels together three times, they can magically "take me home," away from here, because, needless to say, that didn't end well, and for the life of me, I have no idea why.*

Back in my room, still baffled, I focus on the mundane task of ironing my clothes for tomorrow morning, being more careful than normal as my senses are dulled from the amount of alcohol I drank. Relieved I hadn't burned a single hole this time. I arranged them at the foot of the bed like some kind of domestic triumph, then grabbed my phone to call Jennifer.

"Helloooo???" Her voice is groggy, and I almost hang up.

"Shit!! I forgot about the time change. I will call you back tomorrow." I feel awful for waking her.

"No… I'm awake now, Dummy. What's up?"

"Alright… Guess who I had a drink with tonight?" I say, half expecting her to somehow know. "The cute Cowboy!" I blurt out before giving her the chance to guess.

"Are you fucking with me again?" She questions my story, knowing it's completely out of character for me to have drinks with a stranger of my own accord. Usually, that kind of thing only happens when someone like her twists my arm.

"Nope, I'm dead serious." I push the window curtain to the side and peer out into the bright city lights as I continue. "But it doesn't matter anyway... In mid-conversion, he decided to get up and leave me sitting alone at the bar." My head shakes, still trying to make sense of it all.

"Ahhhhh... Screw him then!" she yells into the phone, her voice echoes in my ear. "You're three thousand miles from home... It's not like you're ever gonna see him again anyway." My eyes squint together and focus on an accident that has just occurred on the street below as she finishes her rant. "Forget about him and get some sleep."

"Yeah... I guess," I agree. "Thanks for listening and sorry for waking you... Love you, Stupid," I say, then hang up the phone.

The moment I lie down, my eyes grow heavy. With little resistance, my eyes fall shut, and sleep comes easily. I'm out, lulled to sleep by thoughts of Jax and that heart-melting grin.

CHAPTER 7

S eptember 11, 2001
Brrring... Brrring...
The ear-piercing noise of the telephone rings throughout my hotel room. It wouldn't be surprising if the rooms next to mine could hear it as well. By the time I realize it wasn't a dream, it stops, and silence once again swallows the room. *It must have been the wrong room because why on earth would someone be calling me this early in the morning?*

My head pounds as I lay it back down on the lumpy pillow, cursing myself for having that last bit of mojito the night before. My eyes still burn from the haze of casino smoke hours earlier, making it hard to see. The room's alarm clock that sits on the tiny dresser alongside me is still a little fuzzy. After some time, the fluorescent red numbers come into focus and read six fifty-five.

"Ugh!"

Without more sleep, today's bound to be miserable. I remind myself to grab ibuprofen from the front desk later. Once again, I lay my head down and close my eyes.

Brrring... Brrring... Brrring... The phone screams once more, and I have the sudden urge to hurl it across the room, silencing it once and for all.

"Oh, good Lord! Not again!" I yell a little too loudly for my aching head and reach up to massage my throbbing temples, a futile attempt to relieve the pain.

Two times in a row could only mean one thing: pranksters, and I am in no mood. They are about to get an earful as I roll over and grab the receiver.

"WHAT? YOU LITTLE PUNKS, YOU BETTER KNOCK IT OFF, OR I'M GON—"

"Charlotte? Is that you?" A nervous tone comes from the voice on the other end. It's Jeff, and he sounds different than normal.

"Oh my God... I'm so sorry..." The swift motion in the way I sit up is unlike me. On any normal given day, it takes the alarm clock five times to go off before I even attempt to get up. "I thought you were a kid, prank calling random rooms... Again, I'm sorry." My fingers squeeze at the base of my nose, trying to make sense of why Jeff would be calling so early in the morning. "What's up? Everything okay?" Worry suddenly crept in.

"No, Charlotte, it's not." Something doesn't sit well with his words, and all of a sudden, my stomach feels nauseous. "I need you to turn on the television to the first news station you can find." His voice sounds off, a bit shakier, scared even, and it causes every follicle of hair on my arms to stand at attention.

At record speed, I frantically rummage through the bunched-up rubble of blankets that cover my bed, searching for the tiny black remote that's been trapped underneath from the night before. I find the power button marked in red and push it with a vengeance, awakening the television and bringing light into the dark, ominous room.

"What sta-" I begin to ask, but quickly realize it isn't necessary. I am stunned.

Every channel is flooded with the same horrifying news. Harrowing scenes of a smoke-filled New York City; fires, rubble, and rescue personnel flicker throughout the screen. Gruesome videos of a plane crashing straight into the World Trade Center, one of the twin towers. Complete and utter devastation. *Are we under attack? How could something like this happen by accident?* Scared and panic-stricken faces have been captured by the soot-covered cameramen and their dedicated crews. Hundreds of people are screaming and running anywhere they can for safety. *Are they also thinking the same?* While other brave men, women, firemen, police, and volunteers run in a direct line towards the devastation to help in any way they can.

My eyes fixate on the events that unfold on the television, my mouth wide open in shock and frozen like a mummified statue. I can feel myself shrinking, curling myself into a ball on the edge of my bed, shocked at what I'm seeing on the screen before me. My breath feels trapped somewhere deep inside me, and I have to remind myself of the simplest thing: just breathe.

From the anchorwoman openly crying on live television to the haunting footage playing on the screen, it's clear that something terrible is happening. Our country, under attack? I can't even process it.

"Oh my God!" instinctively, my hand covers my mouth in disbelief, for there is nothing else I can do but sit and stare. *How is this real?*

It's like something straight out of a Hollywood movie, only there are no actors, no second and third takes, and the camera doesn't stop rolling to wait for a stunt double. It's horrifying, and it is, without a doubt, undeniably real. I can't just change the channel and flip to a different story; it's real life, real time, and it is more than terrifying. No horror movie ever made could come close to the terror unfolding before me, and the entire world, right now.

A steady stream of tears masks the worry that covers my face as I reach for my cell phone in a panic to call my parents. Oblivious to the fact that I'm still on the hotel phone with Jeff on the other end, my mind is now mush, in a fog, and unable to focus on what he's saying. I hear him mention something about a "rental car," driving home, packing my bags, etc. Sad to say, and no offense to him, my mind is a blur. Everything is drowned out by the sound of my parents' voices in my head. *I need to hear that they are okay.*

I'm twenty-eight, and I feel as though I'm aging backwards, shedding years by the second, but not in the way that feels youthful. Reverting to a time when I was young, and making me feel more like a scared five-year-old. When I heard loud, scary noises coming from outside my bedroom, I was always so sure it was monsters trying to get inside. Always finding out later that it was the dog next door nosing through our trash. I remember my mom lying with me, brushing her fingers through my hair, singing the same song every time, "You are my sunshine," on repeat until I fell back asleep.

Somehow, I know that hearing my parents' voices, without question, will make things feel a little bit better. The knack the two of them have for always knowing what to do and say is a remarkable gift they have. Or at least that's what I tell myself, because truth be told, I've never been more scared than I am right now. The room appears to be shrinking, closing me in, and I feel my breath being sucked from me. I take a deep breath and attempt to calm myself.

"Charlotte? Are you still there? Are you okay?" Jeff asks in an anxious tone.

"Yes. I'm sorry. I need to call my parents, then I will call you back. Okay?" My tone is much softer than it was just a moment ago, but it begins to crack through my muffled cries.

"I'm not letting you off this phone until I know that you are alright. Got it?"

"I promise you, I am. I just need to make sure my parents are good. Thank you." I articulate in a more confident manner, trying my hardest to convince him that I am fine. *I am not.* I'm not sure that I will ever be "okay" again, if anyone will be, for that matter.

The television volume is set to silent as I phone my parents, keeping the picture on the screen so I can follow the up-to-date footage of the carnage. My anxiety level is higher than usual, at maximum capacity. In fact, I should look away from the black box that sits on top of the dresser, but I can't. The world is quite literally crumbling right in front of me.

My hands tremble as I dial my childhood phone number without ever looking down, just as I have so many times before. So many phone calls home, letting my parents know that I'd be home late, in need of a ride home from a friend's house or field hockey practice. But this time will be different, because I will call home to make sure they are the safe ones.

"Helllooo? Cccharlotte, is that you?" Pop's voice sounds tired and shaky, and his character is unlike him.

Up until this very moment, Pop has always been the strongest man I have ever known. Nothing ever rattles him. If something bad happens, he is our constant rock, always finding a way to make things bearable. When something broke, his greasy hands would always find a way to mend it. Only this time, the unfortunate truth is that we both know he won't be able to fix anything. So, when I hear the sound of his uneasy voice trembling through the phone, it frightens me, and I wish I could reach through it and give him a big ol' bear hug. He sounds so helpless and lost inside, so vulnerable, something I have never experienced before with him.

"Pop... Oh, my God, have you seen what's been happening? Are you and Mommy alright?" A desperate need to be home with them builds inside me.

At rapid speed, I burst into tears.

Without a moment to spare, his entire demeanor changes, and the tone of his voice becomes more upbeat than when our phone call began. He's always been the strongest person I know, and quick as lightning, he becomes the rock that I've always needed him to be in situations like this. Even if I know that deep down inside, he is feeling the same way that I am. *Probably like the whole fucking world, for that matter.*

"Honey, your mom and I are fine... We are safe." I let out a sigh of relief. "Our only concern at the moment is you... How are you?" My body begins to relax as I lie down on the side of my bed, allowing my head to sink into the pillow. "But the most important question is what we are going to do to get you back home, safe and sound, here, together as a family?" The confidence with which he speaks makes me feel at ease, and the calming effect he has over me is immeasurable.

Thanks, Pop. You have no idea just how much I needed that.

He assures me that, given the obvious circumstances, they are fine and promised me they would stay put for the time being until I can get home to them. Before I hang up, the three of us pray together, my mother reciting Psalms from her favorite book, the Bible.

"The Lord will keep you from all harm – He will watch over your life; the Lord will watch over your coming and going both now and forevermore," we collectively say together.

I can't remember a time when I didn't see my mother with her Bible. It has always been her safety net, her "blankie" if you will, keeping her comforted, just as I had when I was young, only mine was an actual blankie, made of chenille with tiny little pink elephants on it. Having it close has always calmed me. *I should have packed mine.* In this moment, talking with the two of them and praying, I am beyond grateful for hers.

Out of nowhere, a commotion erupts in the hallway. Shouts echo off the walls, joined by the heavy clunk of shoes pounding against the floor. Luggage wheels clatter behind them, dragging noisily against the tile. Banging fists pound on doors, sounding so loud it rattles through my room and makes me jump from my bed.

"Charlotte! What is that noise? Is everything okay over there?" The worry in Pop's voice becomes more frantic with each question.

"Yes… It's coming from the hallway." I look toward the door. "I'm guessing it's others, just like me, trying to figure out a way to get out of here," I say to reassure and not worry him any further. "Which reminds me, I need to call Jeff and find out what's going on with the plans for getting us home."

"Mommy and Daddy love you, Charlotte… Everything will be fine… I promise…" His confidence in this unthinkable situation is welcome. "I know that we are not together at the moment, but come hell or high water, I will never let anything happen to my little girl." He declares with such confidence, and like always, I believe him.

"I love you guys. Talk to you soon." I set the phone down and sit for a moment longer.

The weariness that's consuming so much space in my head needs a moment to clear. I fall back into the covers once more and allow my mind to calm itself. The recent phone call has me thinking about my parents, and I admire just how long they have been together.

All at once, I marvel at the many storms they've weathered and the multitude of obstacles they've overcome together. They've been a couple since their early teens. Such a crazy concept nowadays. Thoughts of my friends and family, along with their significant others, all flash through my mind. A pang of jealousy hits me, smacking me in the face as I envision them, sitting on their couches, hand in hand, weathering this crazy, unnerving storm together.

Aside from myself and Jennifer, it appears that everyone I know has someone to share their lives with. After my break-up with James, I convinced myself that being alone was okay. But as I sit here thinking of so many that are close to me having a companion to rely on through this horrific tragedy, I begin to doubt myself. *This sucks.* Tears spill out from the corners of my eyes, once again. They continue to flow in a steady stream, like the "sweat" that drips from the bottle of an ice-cold beer on a hot New Jersey summer's day. It doesn't end. Not only do I weep for the current state of my country, the victims, and all their families affected, but I also shed tears for myself. As so many sit hand in hand, comforting each other as they huddle together on their couches, I lie on this uncomfortable bed, alone in this lurid hotel room. I have no one, and I am alone in every sense of the word.

Brrring... Brrring... Brrring... My self-induced pity party screeches to a halt as the outdated telephone beside me blares to life.

Ironically, right next to it is a small purse-sized Bible. *How have I not noticed it there before?* Reminding me once again of my mom back home, so far away. I place a hand on it, leaving it there as I pick up the receiver with my other, already knowing Jeff would be on the other end of it.

"I secured the last available car in the rental lot... Pack all of your belongings and meet Dad and me downstairs in the hotel lobby in forty-five minutes." Jeff spews out this imperative information in one long, drawn-out breath.

"Okay," I whisper. That's all I can manage.

Without hesitation, my head drops, my shoulders slump forward, and for one selfish moment, I think to myself, *oh good Lord, how the hell am I going to survive being trapped in a car for three days with my boss and his seventy-five-year-old opinionated father that always smells like mothballs?*

The gratitude I have towards the two of them is immense, but it doesn't stop the fact that this trip home is going to be nothing less than pure torture. Tension builds in the back of my shoulders, sending a sharp, piercing pain straight through and up to my neck. I reach back, digging the tips of my fingers deep down into the crease of where the two meet, in hopes of relieving some of its pain. I can almost hear it already; Dick will complain of Jeff's driving, Jeff will yell at Dick for switching the car's thermostat from boiling to scorching, and the list goes on and on. A memory from the ninth-grade pops into my mind. My English teacher, Miss Bill, was writing a question on the chalkboard when her hand slipped, producing an unbearable screeching sound that sent chills down my spine. *Uhhhhhhh, that sound.* I look down and see goosebumps forming at the very thought. I contemplate at this moment, which would be worse. Either way, it doesn't matter because in mere minutes, I'll be meeting the two of them downstairs to begin our grand adventure back home. *God help me.* I take a long-awaited deep breath in, then slowly let it back out, and begin to pack up my things.

* * *

I grab my belongings and exit the hotel room door, again checking its handle and lock a few too many times, never minding the fact that I will never be back in this Vegas hotel room again.

"Do you think we are safe here in Las Vegas?" asks an elderly woman to the man who stands beside her in the crammed elevator I just stepped into. Her hand clings to him like static, and her head is affixed to his shoulder as they lean against the back of the elevator that appears to be holding the two of them upright.

"We will be fine, dear," he whispers, attempting to calm her worried fears.

"I'm scared... What if whoever it is that attacked the towers comes here next? I mean, there are a lot of people here in Vegas." She seems to be growing more worried with every breath she takes.

"Over my dead body will I let anyone hurt you. I love you." He pulls her in a little closer, a look of fear in both of their eyes, and it reminds me once more of what is happening in the world that is quite literally crumbling around us. I look at them both and give a half-hearted smile with pity at the very forefront of it. *God, I hope he is right.*

For the past few months, I have assured myself that I haven't needed anyone to help take care of me, but as I am a first-hand witness to this couple's undeniable love they have for one another, I realize just how wrong I've been. *I am alone.* The world can be a cruel place sometimes, and I am tired of having to go through it alone.

The stifling, muggy air hits me like a ton of bricks just as the elevator doors open into the crowded, hectic hotel lobby. I force myself not to push the button once again and send it straight back up, taking me away from it all. It is pure chaos down here, insane even.

"Get out of my way!" a woman yells, as she barrels right past me.

"Move!!!" screams another.

"Hurry up, will ya?" a man shouts and elbows the stranger beside me, knocking his cup of coffee to the ground, splattering onto the floor, leaving some of its remnants stained on my shoes.

Wall to wall, people can be seen yelling, shoving each other, fighting, and scrambling, all with the same common goal: to find a way to get the hell out of this godforsaken city. Each face is the same, blank, tense, afraid of what's next, while unanswered questions eat away at all of us. *Could Vegas be the next targeted location for yet another attack?* I'm reminded of the conversation between the couple in the elevator that has now disappeared into all this pandemonium.

Since the initial tower had been struck, a second plane had crashed into its twin. It only took seventeen minutes for that second plane to crash to solidify to the world that these incidents were no accidents. Our country is, indeed, under attack. Reports have shown there have been other targets as well, all ending in the same unthinkable way.

Amongst the mayhem, it takes me a few minutes to spot Dick and Jeff in the sea of crowded people. The first to come into view is Dick, leaning against the far wall with his bags beside him on the floor, donning his oh-so-very proper work suit. Always the same boring gray one with his trusty old blue and white striped tie that hangs from him. Thoughts run through my head that being trapped in a car with a man who thinks wearing a suit on a three-day road trip is a good idea is soon to be my unfortunate reality. *"Uggghhhhh."*

Finally, I spot Jeff. His very distinct salt and pepper curly hair with a bald spot beginning to form isn't very hard to miss. I have seen it enough times that I could probably pick it out of a lineup if I had to. He wears the same light blue polo shirt to every show. If I didn't know any better, I would swear that he bought multiples of it and has a special drawer in his bedroom dedicated to them. It never fails that he will always pair it with his khaki dress slacks along with his hideous brown, very worn loafers, the same outfit that he wore yesterday. For a moment, I smile to no one but myself. The sight of Jeff makes me feel at home, and for one split second, I forget all my worries and feel a little safer with him in my sight.

Even with Jeff's back to me, I can see that he is talking to someone other than Dick. The man is taller than Jeff (which isn't hard, he is on the shorter side, standing only an inch or two taller than me) and donning a baseball cap. I can tell that Jeff is laughing, which makes him shift slightly to the side, bringing the unknown man more clearly into view. Whoever it is has just reached into his pocket, pulling out his phone, flips it open, and places it to his ear. His head falls back in a way of relief. He faces the opposite way, focused on whoever is on the other end of the line. His impeccable physical shape catches my attention, but given the angle from which I stand, it's difficult for me to tell if I know him or not. *I'm thousands of miles from home. Who am I going to know here? Maybe a customer?*

"Charlotte!" Jeff yells over the deafening crowd, waving his arms back and forth like he's swatting at invisible bees, an attempt at catching my attention as he moves a little to his left.

My body tenses as I catch a glimpse of the buffalo tattoo. Instantly, my stomach, and let's be honest here, *every* inch of me, lights up with a sensation that feels like a hundred volts of electricity crashing through me in the most oh-so-fucking-good-way.

It is Jax, the hot cowboy from last night, the exact one that I have been thinking about for the past twenty-four hours. The very same one that I had been dreaming of when I received the dreaded phone call, waking me into this nightmare, we are all so desperate to escape. *But how? Why? Like seriously, what are the fucking odds?*

CHAPTER 8

L ittle progress is made as I attempt to move through this madhouse. The casino lobby that once was so alive with lights and laughter has transformed into a chaotic, uncontrolled mosh pit. People are everywhere the eye can see. Wall to wall, the room is filled with anxious, scared patrons who are desperate to try and find a way out. Over all of the noise, I impress myself that I can still make out the words to Elvis' "Jailhouse Rock" that plays in the background. *Well, isn't that ironic?* Most of us feel trapped and are trying to escape this obnoxious, potential deathtrap we call 'Sin City.' Each face I see wears the same unspoken expression: to just get home, to hold their loved ones, to breathe a little easier, and feel safer.

The attempt I make to break through this three-ring circus is proving more difficult by the minute. My suitcase, which I'm trying to maneuver, makes it harder than it should. I pull it behind me as it continues to hobble and twist with every shoe that bangs against it. My other bag that once hung from my shoulder now dangles at the crease of my elbow. The violent way its canvas material rubs against my skin makes me wonder if there will be a purple bruise left in its place.

Throughout the crowd of insane chaos, someone barrels straight through me, and I am reminded of my dog, Sage. The way she runs haywire, the very second we set down her bowl full of food, running through anyone and anything that might be in her path. *I miss her.* A pang of sadness washes through me as I can still recall her head peeking out from the windowsill when I left for the airport only a few short days ago. *I wonder if she knows what's going on.*

I'm about to hit the ground when out of nowhere, someone grabs my arm and helps me up just as fast as I was knocked down. A muscular arm with the same tattoo I had just admired only seconds before reaches down, saving me from being trampled. *How did he get here so fast?*

"Are you okay? Have you been hurt?" Jax's tone is calm, but I note the concern in his voice.

I am momentarily paralyzed while I stare back at his piercing blue eyes as he waits for an answer.

Forcing myself to break from his gaze, I manage a shaky "I'm okay. Thank you for rescuing me," I say, grinning from ear to ear.

"Let's get out of this craziness and out to the car, and I will explain everything," Jeff breaks in, now standing to my other side. "All hell has broken loose in here."

I have never been more thankful for Jeff, easing the awkward tension between Jax and me without even realizing it. I notice that not only is Jeff talking to me, but directing it to all three of us, which includes Jax. My eyes dart to the three of them in one swift moment, and I can feel my eyebrows lift, squinting together in confusion. But instead of questioning him, I remain close and do as I am instructed. Before I take notice, I feel the gentle touch of Jax's hand resting on my back, guiding me throughout the congested lobby.

"I've got you," In every literal sense, Jax assures me that he indeed has my back and won't let me get hurt.

We are about ten feet from the exit doors, and I can already feel the unbearable Vegas heat assaulting my body. It's sure to be a scorcher outside, the kind that will leave the ground itself burning, sometimes melting the soles of your shoes.

"Good Lord, I hope the car has decent air-conditioning," I say to no one and everyone.

With each step closer to the exit doors, it grows even hotter. Beads of sweat drip from my brow. It's the type of heat where you have to change your shirt and bra like twenty-seven times in the matter of an hour. *Yeah, yeah, I know that's a bit of an exaggeration, but you get what I mean.* It's friggin hot!

Once outside, our car is only a few yards away, parked in the closest spot to our right. In its space sits a shiny four-door silver Toyota Camry. In an instant, I'm taken back to my seventeenth birthday when I was taking my driver's license road test. I used my grandmother's car, which was the same style and make, only in navy blue. I can still smell the stale scent of cigarette smoke, even though she denies smoking to this day, along with the stains on the driver's side seat from her spilled coffee, remnants from her morning trips to the post office. Thank God I passed the test that day because later that afternoon, she surprised me with the Camry as a present for my birthday. The thought of Mom-Mom Carol and all our Camry adventures warms me like a hug, and for once, the sweltering heat outside isn't to blame.

"Everybody can put their bags back here, then get in the car," Jeff says as he fumbles with the keys. His thumb frantically presses every button, trying to figure out which one will open the trunk, all while we patiently wait and melt. Well, some of us, that is.

"Unlock my door first so I can sit!" Dick yells at Jeff. The tips of his fingers are already resting on the handle of the passenger side door. His suitcase sits by the rear tire with a garment bag draped over it, waiting for one of us to stash it in the trunk for him, as if we are his personal assistants who cater to his every whim.

"And so it begins," Jeff mumbles to himself, just loud enough for me to make out what he said.

"You're a good son, Jeff. A saint," I whisper over his shoulder, then kiss him on the cheek. The two of us laugh, not because anything's funny, but this is the hand that life's dealt us.

The rest of us begin strategically storing our bags, filling every available space with luggage as if we are trying to win a game of Tetris. The fact that my bag is larger than the rest doesn't go unnoticed, taking up more room than the others. It's no secret that I tend to overpack, but I am grateful as I recall the way Jax checked me out in my little black dress and red high heels last night. *Not that it mattered with the way he left so quickly.*

"Can you hold this for a sec?" Jax reaches over and hands me Dick's garment bag, then reaches for the suitcase that it was covering. It is an older style with no wheels attached, probably a hundred years old, just like its owner.

After all the luggage has been stowed, we make our way to a vacant door of the four-wheeled silver bullet we will call our "home" for the next several days.

Jeff will act as captain, taking the front seat and driving the first leg of our journey home. Dick sits to his right and is already settled in as copilot, leaving Jax and me to occupy the last two remaining seats, alone together in the back seat. Before my fingers touch the handle, Jax appears at my side in one swift motion, making me jump as he opens my door.

"After you." He gestures with his hand to enter the car.

You're being awfully nice for someone who left me without a warning last night.

I thank him for the gallant gesture, shaking away the unwanted memories of last night, as I slide into the car. Aside from my father, I can't remember a time when someone opened a door for me. *Maybe this trip won't be so bad after all,* I think, feeling a devilish grin creep across my face.

An air freshener in the shape of a Christmas tree dangles from the rearview mirror, sending wafts of crisp pine scents throughout the Camry and reminding me of fresh-cut pine trees in December. The engine roars to life, the air conditioner kicks on full blast, spreading around fresh new scents that hit me square in the face, and oddly enough, I don't mind.

The car is silent as we wait in bumper-to-bumper traffic, along with every other person trying to escape this busy lot. Anxiously, I wait for Jeff to reveal how this whole 'Jax coming with us' thing even happened. On cue, he cranes his neck from his driver's side seat, addressing the two of us.

"Jax, this is Charlotte." Jeff cocks his head and gestures towards me. His neck looks like it could break in half at any given moment; if he tries to move it even one inch farther, it might snap. Visions of my favorite cousin, Amelia, and me, breaking the wishbone in half at our annual family Thanksgiving dinners, pop into my head. The thought of its sound makes me wince.

What Jeff doesn't know, just hours ago, I was dreaming about this stranger, naked in my bed, feeding me strawberries with those strong, capable hands.

Jeff then turns towards me and says, "Charlotte, this is Jax," freeing his neck and relieving it from snapping like a stretched-out rubber band. "Jax was standing behind me in line as I waited my turn for the car. We got to talking, and he mentioned he was from New Jersey, just like you." *So, the cowboy lives in Jersey, huh? This story just keeps getting better.*

He continues to explain that after he was awarded the coveted last car in the lot, he then turned to Jax to offer his apologies. I don't even need to hear what happened next; I already know. Being the generous guy that Jeff is, I knew it wouldn't be long in that conversation that he would offer to bring Jax home, along with us.

"There is no reason that you need to be stuck here and figure out another way home. That's just ridiculous, you can come along with us, we are going in the same direction." I could almost hear him say. They struck a deal; Jeff would pay for the rental fee on the car, and Jax agreed to pay for the gas that it would take to get the four of us home. Leaving me with the best part of that deal: sitting in the backseat of the car, only inches from the sexy cowboy. *There is no escaping me now.*

Finding out that both of us reside together in the tiny garden state of New Jersey excites me. I turn towards my window as the heat rises in the back of my neck, making its way across my face, causing me to blush a few shades of crimson.

"Are you okay?" asks Jax.

"What? Who? Why do you ask?" My words stumble, fearful that he somehow can hear my thoughts.

"I was just wondering if you have enough room. Because I don't." He laughs, gesturing to his legs. I look down at his scrunched-up limbs and then over to Dick sitting comfortably in the front seat, with enough legroom for a seven-foot-tall Sixers point guard.

"Dick… Maybe you could move your seat up a few inches for Jax to sit more at ease? His colossal body looks like it's crammed into a matchbox," I plead.

Without a word, I notice the seat moving forward, allowing Jax to stretch out his legs to a more comfortable position.

"Thank you," he softly whispers, keeping his words between us.

"You're welcome." I lean in closer to him. "And by the way, I didn't mean to insinuate that you are huge."

"Well… You're not wrong." Heat rushes to my cheeks and leaves me wondering if there's some truth behind that statement.

CHAPTER 9

A fter some time, I settle into the back seat and reach into my
bag at my feet, pulling out the most recent book I had been
reading. It was a spur-of-the-moment purchase just before
boarding in Philly, something to keep me company on the flight. (THE
WEDDING, by Danielle Steel) It hasn't been opened since that day. The
second I landed in Vegas, work had consumed my every moment. *I can't
wait to find out what happens to Allegra!* Not for nothing, but given the
catastrophic events that have transpired in the past few hours, I could
use a little something to transform me into another world and not think
about anything other than a steamy love story. I lay the book on my lap
and search for the little folded corner from the page I had left off, and
begin reading.

"You like to read?" asks Jax.

I guess it can wait.

"I do… The funny thing is, though, as a child I hated it, but now, it's one of my favorite things." My eyes close as I pull the book to my chest, squeezing it tight. "I love the idea that a book can take you on journeys without ever leaving the comfort of your own home... Or in this case, a car." My eyes flutter open, only to find his forever-ending eyes staring back at me as I set the book back on my lap.

"I guess... I was never into books." Judging by the look on his face, the concept of reading one just for fun looks foreign to him. "I would much rather wait for the movie to come out," he admits.

"What??? Really??? I am forever on the hunt for a new book to read, taking suggestions from anyone who wants to share them. This one in particular was suggested by a woman waiting in line behind me at the grocery store." I tap on the face of the book. "So, when I saw it in the airport duty-free store, I felt compelled to buy it." I think back to that day and laugh. "There's a funny story behind it too... a cute guy who had wayyyy too much to drink in the airport bumped into me and knocked it out of my hands... He apologized and told me I was hot and that I would be perfect for his best friend Jay." My head shakes at the memory, and I can't help but laugh. "I mean, who says that? It was just all so random." He leans over, his shoulder almost touching mine, to catch a glimpse of its title, and without thinking, I hold my breath at the thought of him being so close.

"THE WEDDING, huh... I thought you didn't believe in marriages?" His elbow nudges into mine, and he laughs. *At least I know he was listening.* "Well, if it ever becomes a movie, we should go see it together." His smile is contagious, and I can't help but return it. "Unless you would rather go with that guy Jay," he jokes, and I can't help but laugh with him.

* * *

Gurgggglllleeeee! The obnoxious growl of my empty stomach echoes through the car. I press a hand to it, hoping to calm the noise. Embarrassed, I glance up from my book, my eyes scanning the others before finally landing on Jax.

It's only been thirty minutes into the ride when the oh-so-familiar pain in my stomach makes its appearance. It's rumbling louder than a late-night summer thunderstorm, and I'm certain everyone in my so-called 'home,' a glorified cardboard box on wheels, can hear it too. If there is anything I'm sure of, it's my body, especially when food is involved.

"Hungry?" Jax snickers.

"If a snack run isn't made soon, the inside of this car is going to become even more uncomfortable than it already is, for everyone. My "hangry" self isn't pretty, and no one wants that," I joke to ease the embarrassment my uncontrollable stomach has caused.

"Maybe we should stop and grab some food and essentials at the first place we can find. Top off the gas tank and then head on our way." Dick suggests, coming to my rescue.

I don't think that until this very moment, I have ever been more grateful for Dick – and yes, I laughed at myself as I thought it.

Through the window, the cars pass by, and the green mile markers on the side of the highway decline with each passing moment. There's nothing but blue skies, and it feels eerie without a single airplane soaring through it. The usual hum of life above, the contrails, the occasional gleam of a metal wing catching sunlight is gone, leaving behind a silence that presses against the glass. I lean my forehead against the cool window, watching the world blur past. It should be comforting, the open road and clear blue skies, but instead it feels like the world is holding its breath. Every few miles, flags hang at half-staff. Gas station attendants move slowly, in a fog. The whole country is in motion, but no one knows exactly where they are going.

"All aircraft have been grounded across the entire country for safety precautions. Many planes en route to the U.S. have been grounded in Canada," comes from a woman's voice blasting through the car radio. I shake my head in disbelief, still processing what has transpired in the world around us. Only a day ago, I was decorating wedding cakes, and my biggest concern in the world was deciding on how many tiers there should be. *How can this be happening? It doesn't seem real.*

"I found one!" Jeff screams out in excitement. *Jesus, Mary, and Joseph!*

The passion in his tone scares the living daylights out of me. I leap from my seat, sending my book flying onto the floor and landing at Jax's feet. *My God, Jeff, I'm already scared enough. Was that really necessary?*

I lean down to retrieve it, just as Jax reaches down, grabbing it just moments before I can.

I take the book from his hand, but his fingers graze mine, and our eyes meet. The hold lingers just a second too long. For a moment, I am caught off guard by the warmth growing between my thighs. It's ridiculous to feel this way about something so trivial, but I start to fumble and the book slips through my fingers again.

"Everything okay?" his breathing quickens when he hands it over to me. *Did he feel that, too? Good Lord, now I'm imagining things.*

Although Jeff's sudden excitement nearly gave me a heart attack, I welcome it; it turns out he's spotted a convenience store. Either way, the rumbling noises that are coming from my empty belly will soon be at peace.

For me, stepping into a convenience store and perusing the junk food aisles is the equivalent of a four-year-old running the aisles of a Toys "R" Us searching for the perfect gift. For the next few minutes, the Circle K that we are about to set foot in is my own little slice of heaven.

My left arm is nearly collapsing under a basket filled with Funyuns, Chex Mix (the kind with that ridiculously addictive orange powdered cheese), a package of off-brand chocolate-covered mini donuts, Skittles

– taste the rainbow, yes please – and a large Gatorade. All of these are staples for any decent road trip. Without a doubt, Peanut Chews would have made the top of the list, but they are made in Philadelphia and are only sold in a few of the surrounding East Coast states, and Lord knows, we are far from any of those. I doubt anyone from Nevada has ever even heard of them, and for that, I feel a tinge of pity for them; they are *that* good. *Sucks for them.*

I continue to stand in the potato chip aisle contemplating another impulse purchase when I spot Jax in the next aisle over, having words with a man, and for some odd reason, I get a funny feeling in the pit of my stomach.

They are both tall enough, making it easier to spot them over the shelving units. I make my way around to ask Jax which flavor he would prefer. Salt and Vinegar or Sour Cream and Onion chips cling together in my free hand, in case I decide to share. When I turn into the aisle, I see Jax with a firm hand squeezed around the stranger's arm, who appears unable to move. *What the hell?* I freeze, and that's when I notice the little boy standing next to them, a look of sheer terror on his poor little face.

"Why don't you mind your own fucking business!" The man snarls at Jax as he tries to pull his arm free. Jax tightens his grip and moves in closer; their noses are only inches from each other. With extreme caution, I take a step forward.

"Jax! Stop!" I yell and take a step closer to the little boy, trying to ease him from being so frightened. I still have no idea what the hell is happening.

"Yeah… Listen to the little lady." His smug words only fuel Jax's anger even further. He looks like he wants to kill this man, and he is beginning to scare me in the process. Reminding me that we really don't know a thing about Jax at all. *Does anyone ever really know someone?*

"Does that make you feel like a man?" His teeth are clenched so tightly together that they look like they'll crack. "I don't know exactly what was going on, but I know what I saw... Only a fucking coward would hit a little boy over taking too long to decide what kind of cookie to buy!" he shouts. "Especially after what happened yesterday... A lot of families lost their loved ones... Lost a child... You should be grateful you still have one... Not lose your temper over something as stupid as this." Jax swipes a pack of chocolate cream-filled cookies and knocks it to the floor. The grip that Jax has on him eases while his eyes never leave the man's. That's when I noticed the red mark on the little boy's cheek, the exact shape of a handprint left in its place. *Asshole.* The man looks at Jax, fear in his eyes, then backs away, grabbing the package of cookies as he and the little boy walk away.

Jax turns around, his face still boiling, blood red from his encounter, and notices me still standing there.

"What a piece of shit," I say, and give my approval of the way he handled the awful situation.

"Yeah... I guess they let just any old asshole be a father when there are so many good guys out there that never get a chance to." His reaction leads me to believe that this is a personal topic for him. I nod my head in agreement and place my hand on his arm just as Jeff and Dick make their way into the aisle.

"Everybody find what they were looking for?" asks Jeff. The plastic bag hanging from his hand is turning the tips of his fingers white from the lack of circulation. *I think I have.* My eyes focus on Jax. "Dad and I already paid for ours; we'll meet you in the car." The two of them turn and walk through the automatic doors, leaving Jax and me alone together once again.

I look at Jax and place my hand on his bicep and give a gentle squeeze, my attempt at diffusing the awful situation that has just occurred. I am certain that he can see straight through my pitiful smile as we both turn toward the checkout counter. I set the bags of chips down in the cookie aisle, leaving them behind.

Purchases in hand, the two of us make our way back to the car, and I lag a few steps behind, lost in my own thoughts. My eyes focused on Jax's backside. *Not a bad view, I could watch this all day.* He stands tall, walking with such confidence. What I just witnessed back there, the way he stood up to that douche, only adds to the many layers I'm just getting to know in him. It's intoxicating. There's a certain air about him that exudes arrogance, but not in a bad way. Honesty, it's incredibly sexy, and I can't take my eyes off him. The way he stuck up for that little boy was nothing short of amazing. I've been the victim of a few dickheads in my life, so seeing a man do what he just did is kind of hot.

Before hitting the road, we take a few minutes to get ourselves situated for the long journey ahead. Drinks are placed into their cup-holders, "first choice snacks" are chosen with precision and lay on each of our laps, and clicking sounds of seat belt buckles being fastened fill the air. Jax is the last to achieve that task. He leans in to snap his buckle into place, and his fingers graze over my thigh. Subtle enough that to most it would have gone unnoticed. A wave of heat pulses through me, and it takes every ounce of willpower not to react. My body betrays me, and my face goes fifty shades of red. For some odd reason, I'm reminded of a woman I once trained at work. She complained of hot flashes due to menopause. One second, she was smoothing out her cake, and the next she was red as a beet and fanning herself with her spatula. *This ain't got nothing to do with menopause.* At breakneck speed, I turn my head towards my window and away from him in hopes he can't see my cherry red, stained face, along with the huge smile that accompanies it.

Having him this close to me for the next several days should be classified as pure torture... the good kind, though. Well, all except for the nasty Funyun breath situation. Poor guy. *He might as well get used to it.*

With that, the stench of stale onions swallows up the air in the Camry as I pop two of the yummy dried tasty rings into my mouth, enjoying every bite.

"Interesting choice of snacks you got there." Jax jokes, pointing to the strange array of goodies sitting on my lap. "What are you, twelve?"

"What? Doesn't every girl you know eat freeze-dried onion rings and chocolate-covered donuts at 10:30 in the morning?" My tone is playful. "If not, then you must be hanging around the wrong ones." The sound of the wrapper is ridiculously loud as I rip into the donut package, like the donut is announcing itself to the entire car.

"Maybe you're right. I may have to change that, I guess." Jax winks at me, and I smile back in agreement.

Rush Limbaugh's radio podcast blares throughout the Camry. Naturally, Dick's choice, of course. He seems to be hanging on to Rush's every word. Dick's age shows as he leans in closer to the dashboard to hear it more clearly, even though I have no problem hearing it from the back seat.

It must be a generational thing, because my dad's always talking about this guy Limbaugh, and his views, agreeing with everything the guy says. I close my eyes and can almost picture my own father, three thousand miles away, sitting on our old, weathered couch, next to my mom, glued to the television or radio station, listening to this very same speech that echoes throughout our car. Suddenly, I am sad, thinking of them home alone, and I could use a distraction.

"So, Charlotte, do you have any brothers or sisters?" asks Jax as if he is somehow blessed with the gift of reading my inner thoughts. He nudges my leg with his hand. *Thank you.*

"Nope," I say, shaking my head from one side to the other. "I'm an only child… And a spoiled one if you asked my parents." The truthfulness in my words makes me laugh. "I wish I did, though. It would have been fun to have a sister… But I have a Jennifer, and that's the next best thing."

"What in the world is a Jennifer?" He laughs, and I can almost feel him questioning my sanity.

"She's been my best friend since the second grade and is the closest thing I have to a sister." I smile at the mention of her. "She knows everything about me... Even you." *And you thought you would get off easily, didn't you?*

"Me?" His face twists into a scowl, puzzled by my admission.

"Well, yeah. I mean, you practically left in mid-sentence last night when we were having a good time. Or so I thought." I say, putting him on the spot. "When I got back to my room, I called her and told her all about it...Well, not everything." My cheeks flush with embarrassment. "Why did you leave anyway?" I finally ask. *Straight for the jugular.*

"WAIT...You two knew each other before this morning?" Jeff asks, his eyes glued to the two of us through the rearview mirror. *Good Lord, I forgot you were up there.*

"Yes." I laugh, but I'm not quite sure why. "We met in the elevator yesterday morning, then again in the casino after dinner last night." I look out the window and remember the way he looked as he stood leaning against the slot machine. "Long story short, Jax and I were having a drink at the bar when all of a sudden, he got up and left." My eyes wince at the thought. "He looked like he had seen a ghost." I look right at Jax, my eyes never leave his. "Then the next thing I knew, I was left sitting alone at the bar." My voice grows louder by the time I finish, bringing back all my frustrations at the thought of it once again. *Seriously WTF? Just another reason to add why I swore off men in the first place?*

"It wasn't like that." He is quick to explain.

"Sounds like someone's got commitment issues. *You* can do better, Charlotte," Jeff jokes, lightening the mood in the car, and together we all laugh.

"I swear I didn't mean—"

"Now you listen here... Charlotte is like a daughter to me, and she has been through enough over the past few months…" Jeff interrupts him; his tone is stern. "You mess with her, and I will pull this car over right now and leave you stranded on the side of the road and never think twice about it." Jeff stares back at Jax through the rear-view mirror, toying with him but with a hint of truthfulness in his tone. Jax swallows the lump that has developed in his throat and doesn't say a word in return.

An unsettling quiet weighs heavily throughout the car, the mood all but changed, and I begin to feel bad for Jax, putting him on the spot like that. It wasn't fair of me to pass judgment on him for my trust issues with men. *Fucking James.*

"Anyway… You seem fascinated that I'm an only child. I'm gonna go out on a limb and assume you are not." I say changing the subject and breaking through the bitter cold that now fills the car, freeing Jax of the hook he was dangling from.

The stiffness in his shoulders begins to soften. "Far from it…" He laughs. "I'm the youngest of three very protective older sisters. Growing up, I never had a hot shower… I was always the last to use the bathroom in the mornings," he admits playfully.

"In all seriousness, though, I love them… We're very close and would do anything for each other. Growing up, my house was always full of people, so loud and chaotic." His words swell with pride when he speaks of his family.

"Sounds like it would have been a lot of fun in your house."

"It was… But there were also times when I couldn't wait to get to my best friend's house. Sean was an only child like you, and sometimes I just needed the quiet."

The way he speaks of his sisters is endearing. It can't be easy being the only boy in a house full of females, and for a moment, I pity him as I recall my hormonal teenage days and the way I was at that time, a ticking time bomb of emotions. *My poor dad.* I make a mental note to tell him just how sorry I am for all the years he had to endure me as a teenager. I now realize it couldn't have been easy.

"You poor thing." My condolences have never been more real. "I can only imagine having all those girls on their periods at the same time in that household." He wrinkles his nose as if he just smelled a skunk, and yet I notice he doesn't disagree. "I can almost see you and your dad taking cover for a week every month." *Really Charlotte? PERIODS? You're so awkward and weird. No wonder you don't have a boyfriend.* I'm annoyed with myself.

"What's your favorite soda?" is the first thing that comes to mind, changing the subject once again. "Mine is root beer, or any version for that matter. Root Beer, birch beer, sarsaparilla. All will work, except for the diet versions, ain't nobody got time for that." I claim.

He laughs harder than I expect, "You're not going to believe this, but birch beer is also my favorite. And a McDonald's fountain Coke would be a close second."

For a man that I just met only a day before, holding a conversation with him comes very easily; he has a calming effect over me, and the words just come with such ease. We keep talking as the miles continue to roll by, flowing from the meaning of life to its darker shadow, death. We talk about politics, then somehow end up swapping stories of every sport we ever played, all the way through high school. Nothing seems off-limits.

"I played three sports during high school. Football, wrestling, and baseball, but wrestling will always be my favorite... It teaches you so much more than just the sport itself, like mental toughness, discipline, and even leadership skills. One day, I can only hope to have another...." His body stiffens and pauses for a brief second before correcting his words. "Have a son, so I can teach him all of my moves," he says, relaxing. *I'll volunteer. Work your moves on me, right here, now, if you want.* Without thinking, my hand begins to rise, and just as quickly, I pull it back down and laugh at myself.

"I went to all the wrestling matches at my high school. Well, I kinda had to, I was the manager for the team and worked the table during every match. Wrestling was kind of a big deal there…What weight were ya?"

"165… I placed in States my junior and senior years." He claims. "You may not believe it, but I was recruited to wrestle for a few D1 schools." He boasts. "One was from the very prestigious West Point Academy." His face beams with pride.

"Wow! That's awesome!" My eyes open wide, knowing just how unbelievable an offer like that is. "You must have been really good."

"Wait!" Dick shouts, interrupting our conversation. "Did you say *West Point?*" He reaches over to turn down the volume on the radio, silencing it, then positions his body a little to its side to gain some view of Jax. "That is a once-in-a-lifetime opportunity, yet you chose not to go?" He just shakes his head slowly, like he can't quite fathom what he is hearing. "You must have had one hell of a good reason to turn them down."

"Dad!?" Jeff cries out, annoyed by his father's abruptness.

"Let's just say, a lot of key factors at the time went into my decision not to accept their offer. Not that I regret my decision, but it's definitely something that I have thought about every single day since, believe me. The what ifs…"

Dick finally shuts up. Just sits there wide-eyed, shocked into silence.

The fact that Dick chooses to stay quiet and not say anything else on the subject leaves me dumbfounded, like I'm sitting in the back of a car in another universe or something. *Progress.*

He turns up the volume on the radio once again, and Limbaugh's voice now lingers in the background.

"Placing in the New Jersey state tournament isn't easy. I've attended enough of them to know. But getting recruited by one of only four academies in the country is just plain impressive." I speak more quietly, directing it only to Jax. I get the feeling the topic of West Point isn't something Jax wants to relive, and I decide not to press on. "Believe me, I get it." His face softens as I sympathize with his decision. "I didn't go to college either; I had no interest in leaving. I wanted to stay home and be close to my parents." I admit. "I worked at a local bakery and taught myself everything I know about cake decorating. Until Jeff stumbled upon me one day."

"Yup... I snatched her right up, before anyone else could." He butts in, sounding way too proud of himself.

I smile back at Jeff through the reflection of the rearview mirror, then turn my focus back to Jax.

"Funny, you mention that about having a boy, though, and teaching him wrestling. I always say that I hope to one day have a little girl just so I can teach her how to play field hockey. I'm gonna make her a little beast." I laugh. *But I am one hundred percent serious.* "And the stick can always be used as a weapon if needed," I say in a serious tone, as a memory flashes through my mind. "Just sayin."

"Whoa, remind me never to get on your bad side," Jax says as the sound of laughter erupts from everyone in the car.

No matter how deep the topic gets, talking to Jax comes naturally. It's not as daunting as the way first dates can sometimes be. I know it's not a date, but it feels just as personal. Honestly, it's as comfortable as talking to Jennifer, the way we used to stay up late in high school, whispering in the dark about the boys we had crushes on. In all the years that I've gone out on dates, I can't remember a single one that I could talk so openly with. I mean, I did mention his sisters and their menstrual cycles, and he didn't feel the need to unbuckle his seatbelt and jump out the window. Sitting here, so close to him, sharing my life details, everything about it feels right; he feels right, to me, he feels like home.

The more we share, the more my feelings grow. I could stay in this moment forever. *Well, with unlimited snacks, of course.*

CHAPTER 10

Hours have passed as we make our descent from climbing through the mountains, and the scent of pine fades to asphalt. I reach for my phone, and for the first time in what seems like forever, bars flicker across the screen and then come the notifications. Missed calls. Voicemails. Too many to count.

"Finally," I whisper to myself.

Jax glances over, and his brow lifts in confusion. "Huh?"

I shake my head. "Sorry... Not you... I've finally got a signal." I hold up my phone. "I swear it's been since right after the attacks that I haven't had any service. I need to call my parents. They've gotta be worried."

My chest tightens as I hit play on the first one. It's Mom, and her voice is trembling with what sounds like panic. "Honey, we've been trying to call you, but nothing seems to go through. Please call us when you can, okay?" Her voice cracks on that last word, and I have to stare out the window and bite the inside of my cheek to stop myself from breaking.

The next voicemail is from James. For a second, I almost don't listen. I tell myself that he isn't worth it, but curiosity wins. His voice is low, steady, and careful, like he's afraid of what to say. "Charlotte... I heard about the attacks. I don't know exactly where you are right now, but please call me. I really just need to know you're okay."

I swallow hard, and suddenly my mouth is as dry as the desert we've just driven through. For a tiny moment, I almost forgot why I hate him. I almost forgot why I shouldn't care. I almost press replay. Almost. Then the next message auto-plays.

This time, his voice isn't gentle, it's not caring, it's short and impatient. Self-centered. "You could at least let me know you're alive. I deserve that much. I'm not the bad guy you think I am, Char." *Deserve? You deserve nothing.*

That does it. My bitch-switch has just been flipped, spinning around like a roller coaster. My thumb slams down on the delete button before he finishes. The ache that had crept in a minute ago, that familiarity that we shared, hardens into intense anger, sharp and clean. In an instant, I am reminded of what an ass James is.

Jax looks over but doesn't ask questions. His hand rests freely on the seat in the space between us, close enough that I feel calm radiating off him. It steadies me more than I'll admit.

I take a deep breath in and scroll back to my mom's message and press call. She answers on the first ring.

"Charlotte?" Her voice breaks when she says my name.

"Hey, Mom," I say, my throat still dry that it barely makes it out. "Yeah... I'm okay. I've had no signal until now. I'm safe."

She exhales like she's been holding her breath for days. Then come the questions, rapidly, like an auctioneer at an estate sale, but laced with love. I let her talk as I stare out the window. Hearing her voice is soothing; it's the only piece of home I've felt since everything changed, and I can feel a tear slipping down my cheek.

When she finally takes a breath, I steal the moment to tell her we're en route home. Somewhere past the mountains. Her breathing is steadier, more normal, and I can almost picture her trying to calculate just how long it will be until I get home.

"We've been so worried. I love you, sweetheart," she says. "Please... Just be careful. And check in when you can."

"I will, I promise... I love you... Tell Dad I love 'em too."

When I hang up, the silence in the car creeps back, quiet, but not empty and alone. Jax's eyes are on me, not wavering.

"She sounded relieved," he says quietly, and only meant for me.

"She was," I answer. "Guess I needed that call just as much as she did."

He nods and gives me a faint smile, like he understands more than I've said, and the hum of the engine fills the quiet that's left in the Camry. I lean my head against the window and stare out at the stretching road ahead of us.

CHAPTER 11

T he sky outside blazes with deep reds and oranges, saying farewell to the day as the sun settles in. Hours have passed since our last stop, and right on cue, our stomachs start composing a full-blown symphony. They are empty. Even the gas meter joins the chorus; it too is empty.

Just as I wonder if Jeff has noticed, a flashing neon-green sign screams from the roadside: **EAT HERE.** It looks like one of those construction warning signs, which doesn't exactly scream "fine dining." *I hope this isn't some sort of foreshadowing.* But at this point, I'd risk food poisoning for fries.

"Judging by the growling in this car, I'd say it's time to stop," Jeff says. "And the tank needs filling—two birds, one gas station." He laughs at his corny joke.

He pulls in and snatches the last spot beside a weathered mom-and-pop station. Out front, a rusted telephone booth leans like it's given up on life, guarded by a drooling hound dog. Charming.

"Would you get a load of these gas prices?" Dick bellows. "Un-American! Taking advantage of people in a time of need." For once, none of us disagrees.

"Well," Jeff sighs, "as much as I hate it, the tank's running on fumes. Lucky Jax volunteered to pay." He laughs.

When I step out, my legs wobble like strawberry Jell-O. It takes a moment to steady myself before pins and needles invade my toes. We all stretch, crack joints, and moan like we haven't walked in weeks.

"Ow, my neck," I groan, rubbing the side that's sore from talking to Jax for hours. Maybe he'd give a good massage. Maybe he could start with—

"What are you smiling about?" Jeff cuts in.

"Nothing... you wouldn't get it." I smile because I just can't help it.

Three pairs of eyes land on me like I've grown extra heads, but I've got more pressing issues—namely, my bladder. "Meet you at the table!" I shout, sprinting toward the diner in a half-panicked dance.

In the bathroom mirror, my hair is a disaster. I scold my reflection for not packing a brush, it's tucked safely in the trunk, then realize why I suddenly care—Jax. I free my hair from its bun, finger-comb it, splash some water, and manage to look halfway human.

Feeling somewhat normal again, I step out into a wave of greasy fries and fresh coffee. The diner looks like it hasn't changed since 1972—gingham tablecloths, faded booths, and tired patrons staring blankly out the window. Fear hangs in the air. I smile at them anyway, trying to reassure both them and me that life will go on.

"Charlotte! Over here!" Jax waves both arms like a flag in a storm. I pretend not to see him—until he shouts louder and the entire diner turns my way.

"Good lord," I say to myself, and my face flushes from embarrassment. I try not to notice the eyes and walk over to the guys and scooch into the booth.

Jax slides a root beer toward me just as I do. "I remembered it was your favorite."

Is there anything hotter than a man who listens? "Perfect," I say, taking a long sip as the fizz tickles my nose.

"You look beautiful with your hair down," he says, brushing a loose strand behind my ear. His fingers graze my cheek, and suddenly the diner feels twenty degrees hotter.

Jeff clears his throat. "I agree—but in a father/daughter kind of way." Laughter breaks the tension, and I silently thank him for saving me from spontaneously combusting.

The waitress rattles off the specials in a tone that suggests she's dead inside, like she's repeated them for the hundredth time today. Dick predictably orders the senior pot pie special and proudly announces his discount eligibility. Jeff goes with an open-faced turkey platter.

When it's my turn, I freeze. "Uhhh… grilled cheese with the soup of the day. And, um, gravy fries?" The waitress looks puzzled, apparently not a local delicacy here; she's never heard of them. *Where are we exactly?* I give her the full Jersey rundown, and her mood lifts instantly. "That sounds amazing," she says. "I might make a double for myself."

Then Jax orders—confident, specific, sexy. "Bacon cheeseburger, barbecue on the side, fries well done, and honey mustard for dipping." The waitress blushes, and so do I. *I feel ya, girl.*

"Charlotte," Jeff teases, "that's twice I've caught you smiling for no reason. What's going on in that mind of yours?

"Just a memory," I lie, giggling. "You wouldn't understand."

Dinner arrives, and I devour everything like I haven't eaten in weeks. The waitress returns beaming, apparently the chef loved my gravy fries so much that they're adding them to the menu. I grin, smugly proud of my minor culinary influence. *Told ya.*

The guys step away, Jeff to pay, Dick to the bathroom, Jax outside for a call. Through the window, I see Jax's face tighten with worry as he rubs his temples. When he catches me watching, I look away, pretending to admire the sunset.

He soon joins me, sliding closer until our legs touch. "The sky's unreal, isn't it?" he says softly.

"I was just thinking that. Most people love sunrises, but sunsets feel more… magical. My mom and I used to sit on the deck after dinner, watching them fade while eating whatever dessert she whipped up from the garden."

He nods but stays quiet, still guarded.

"Everything okay? You looked upset on your call."

He hesitates. "Yeah… just stuff. So… What's your favorite dessert of hers?"

"Huh? Who?" I say, confused. *What is happening right now?*

"Your mom, and her desserts."

I laugh, caught off guard. "Chocolate-chip zucchini bread. She'd make it in winter from the frozen leftovers. It's ridiculous how good it is."

He brushes my hair to one side, resting his chin near my shoulder as we stare at the sunset. His breath is warm, clinging to my skin, and his closeness is leaving me unsteady. For a moment, the chaos unraveling in the world disappears.

Then— "Ready to get back on the road?" Jeff's voice startles me. I jump, hand landing on Jax's leg.

"Jesus, Jeff. Warn a girl." I snap back. "You scared the crap out of me."

Reality returns—terrorist attacks, fear, uncertainty—but somehow, sitting here next to Jax, everything feels… right.

"Jeff, I can drive if you're tired," Jax offers as we walk back to the car.

"Nah, I've got a few more hours left in me."

"When you switch, I'll move up front with Jax to help him stay awake," I chime in. "Usually, all-nighters mean tequila and dancing, but I'll adapt."

"Fine by me," Jeff says, yawning.

"Sounds good," Jax adds with a grin. A faint scar near his brow catches the light that I hadn't noticed before, making me wonder what stories he's hiding.

They'll think I'm being helpful, but really, it's selfish. I just want time alone with him.

CHAPTER 12

The road has been quiet for some time now. Too quiet actually, as I stare out the window at the long stretch of Oklahoma highway. It's the kind of quiet that makes you want to scream, just to feel something. Anything. After countless hours of Dick's obsession with the radio reports and his endless rants about the government "not telling us the whole story," silence is both a relief and oddly nerve-wracking. It's almost like it's warning us that something bad is about to happen.

Dick is snoring away in the passenger seat, his head propped up against the window, and a dribble of drool escapes from the corner of his mouth. Jeff is still driving, but not for much longer. I can tell by the way he squints at the lights of the cars passing that it's getting more difficult for him to see. He is driving with both hands on the wheel, his fingers gripping it like a vice, as if that will help him see any better. And Jax sits beside me, unwrapping a stick of gum, trying desperately to be quiet about it. My head rests against the window, and the cool glass feels nice against the side of my warm face.

As I peek out the window, I notice a blur of brown and white on the road up ahead.

I blink for a second, trying to focus. "Um… is that a friggin cow?"

Jeff lets off the gas. "You've got to be kidding me."

Jax chimes in as he leans in between the seats to see more clearly. "That's not a cow… that's an entire herd of cows."

The cows have no intention of moving and are completely unfazed by our car heading directly toward them. Jeff slams on the brakes. Dick jolts awake with a full-on attitude. "What the hell is going on?"

"Bovine parade," Jax jokes.

"Is that fancy talk for cow traffic?" I ask.

"So, you speak cow too?" he laughs. "Where I grew up, if you didn't time it just right in the morning, you would be late to school because of the daily cow-crossings."

I look at him side eyed. "Are you messing with me?"

"I am dead serious… Once in the morning and the other in the evening, our neighbors' cows would cross the street from one side of the pasture to the other… If by unfortunate chance you arrived a minute too late, you were screwed. It's the equivalent of having to wait for a train to cross."

One of the smaller heifers is staring at me through the window, like she doesn't have a care in the world. It's evident that they have no worries about the national emergency that our country is currently in or about our road trip schedule. A dozen or so more are scattered across the asphalt and along either side of the road.

"Are they hitch-hiking?" I ask, jokingly.

"Well… they certainly aren't gonna fit in here," Jax says, playfully. "I can get them out of the way. It's nothing I haven't done before." He says, like it's no big deal.

I look at him with a questioning eye, "What exactly are you going to do?"

"We move 'em," Jax says, like it's an everyday occurrence to him.

"Well… You are the one wearing the cowboy boots." I sigh and open my door.

I barely have time to close my door when a woman's voice calls from across the field, loud and urgent. "Hey! Don't let 'em get too far!"

An itty-bitty woman in overalls and boots runs frantically toward us, waving a coiled rope in one hand and a flashlight in the other.

"Y'all mind lending a hand?" She shouts out to us. "Gate busted from the storm last night, and the cows are getting frisky."

"Guess we're wrastlin' some cows," Jeff says in a pretend western voice that seems completely out of character for his normal khakis and polo stature. "My 4-H days are finally gonna pay off."

I creep up to one particularly stubborn cow that has taken a liking to the center of the road. "Okay, now Bessie, let's keep it mooooving," I say, and laugh at my goofy joke.

Bessie blinks at me, unimpressed and unmoving.

"Really, Bess? I thought mules were the ones who have the reputation of being stubborn." I plead with her. I even try waving a road map in the air, flapping it like a fan. Anything to get 'ole Bessie to move. She sneezes.

"Gross," I say, wiping my arm on the back of my shirt. "Cakes are so much easier than cows."

Half an hour later, the cows were safely wrangled. Dick is telling us a story of how he would take Jeff to 4-H fairs every summer back in Lancaster County. Jax has a grass stain across one leg of his jeans from leading two steers, and I have managed to corner the last rogue calf with the help of Carla, the owner of the farm.

"I owe you all a gallon of sweet tea," she says. "Come up to the house… It's the least I can do."

Dick says, "We really need to be –"

"Nope," Carla interrupts. "You wrangled my cows; you're gettin' some cornbread."

Ten minutes later, the four of us are sitting on white rockers underneath Carla's screened front porch, sipping on sweet tea from mason jars and eating warm cornbread with homemade strawberry preserves on top.

"You folks clearly are not from around here... Where y'all headed?" Carla asks.

"Back to the East Coast," Jeff says. "Work convention gone sideways."

Carla shakes her head and sets the pitcher of sweet tea down on the tiny side table next to Dick's rocker. "There is a whole lot of sideways these days, it seems."

On the same table as the tea is a vintage-style radio giving its latest update. Words like recovery, efforts, and first responders drift softly throughout the air of the porch. None of us look at it, but we all hear it.

I've suddenly lost my appetite, and the cornbread I just inhaled doesn't seem as appetizing.

Carla leans against the porch railing and offers a gentle smile. "I know it doesn't seem like much, but ever since the attacks, I've been wondering what I can do... Maybe feeding good folks like yourselves, just being a decent person, and lettin' others know they ain't alone is enough."

No one says a word. Everything is silent except for the distant sounds of the cicadas in the background.

Jax raises his glass. "To cows and cornbread."

Everyone laughs. It feels like the first genuine laugh I've heard since the horrific acts of terrorism happened.

Jeff lifts his glass next, "and to good people."

We all clink our jars and drink.

The world may be broken right now, but out here, on a porch in the middle of nowhere, a little kindness and a shit ton of cows are starting to glue it all back together.

I guess 'ole Bessie knows best.

CHAPTER 13

The moon outside is putting on quite a show, as if Jax and I are its own private audience. The dark night sky is filled with endless amounts of tiny twinkling lights, stars for eternity, it seems. The beauty of the perfect night sky always has a certain romantic feeling about it, immediately sending my thoughts to the cowboy sitting next to me.

"You were great back there. You know that?" I say softly, just above a whisper, and not enough to wake Dick and Jeff in the back seat. "Just like you were with that little boy and his douchebag dad back at the convenience store… You seem to be good at a lot of stuff."

He glances over at me and smiles, "You should see me when I'm trying."

And for just a heartbeat, there is something different in the air between us, unspoken and electrifying. Not love. Not yet, at least. But something that could be if I allow myself to let it.

I am the first to look away and redirect my focus back to the stars.

"The stars are unreal tonight, don't you think?" asks Jax. In one swift motion, I turned back his way in shock. *Can he hear my thoughts? What man notices a gorgeous star-filled night sky? He must be part of some sort of alien experiment sent down to fuck with us mere mortals, because this guy cannot be real!*

I stare at him a second longer than I should, to reassure myself I didn't actually say those thoughts out loud, that they were safely tucked away in my head. And for extra insurance, I pinch myself.

"They really are beautiful. I feel like we could be in one of those snow globes at Christmas. The ones that you shake, causing snow to float down over a tiny north pole village scene... Only instead of snow, it's replaced with millions of twinkling little stars." I'm marveled by the luminous sky. "You just don't see a sky this magnificent in Jersey, do you?" He shakes his head in agreement.

The stars spark a chain of conversations that carry us through the night. I want to learn every detail that he's willing to share. I monopolized most of our conversations during the day's drive, and one could argue that he knows my entire life's story by now. I mean, I'm pretty much an open book, rarely hiding anything. He knows I'm an only child, my favorite soda, and my profession, but I know next to nothing about him. The tables are about to turn. Hours ago, he only offered glimpses into his life, but I want more. No... I need more.

"Okay, enough about the stars, I want to know more about you," I joke. "I mean, there must be some good stories you're able to share. You've got to have some skeletons rattling around in that perfect little closet of yours, dying to escape."

"What do you want to know?"

"For starters, why don't you have a girlfriend? What's wrong with you?"

He laughs at my bluntness, but the pause that he takes before answering doesn't go unnoticed. "The timing just isn't right, I guess."

"Okay, fair enough... But just so you know, this is gonna be a long night, and if you think that I can keep you awake on my looks alone, then you're dead wrong." I laugh. "You will soon learn that I am relentless and won't stop until I'm privy to every detail of your life."

"Well, at least you warned me."

"I remember you saying that you lived in a small town, like how small are we talking here?" I ask, hoping to break through the ice that holds Jax's secrets about his life. "How many kids were in your class? I mean, I'm sure I have driven through your town at some point in my life, but honestly, I really have no idea."

"Well, in the sixth grade, there were only seventeen kids in my entire class. Then, after more surrounding towns all joined in, I graduated high school with one hundred and seventy-six total kids... I knew everyone in the entire school." He says.

"Wow... Really?" I am stunned. "I might have had more in my graduating class than you had in your entire school. That's crazy." The thought alone is unfathomable to me. I thought every school was just like mine.

"I know that coming from a small town might sound like all we did was milk cows and husk corn, but small or not, we were teens just like the rest of you 'normal' people, and nothing stopped us from knowing how to party," he boasts, flashing that irresistible smile. "Every Friday night, following the football games, everyone would head to one of the local fields, drink whatever could be stolen from our parents' liquor cabinet, then party by a bonfire." His hands released from the steering wheel, opening up wide to show just how big the fire was. "And... If you must know... I got my first kiss from my best friend, Joanna, in the tenth grade at one of those bonfires." His eyebrows rise, and the beginning of a smile emerges.

"Get out? She must have been some friend."

"Yup... Her girlfriends dared her, and she was never known to ever back down from a challenge, soooo." The way he speaks of his high school years is sweet.

Learning about a younger Jax blows me away. He's got layers, more than I ever expected. And I'd love nothing more than to peel back every last one… Until there's nothing left but that sexy, gloriously naked shell.

I imagine him as nothing but the heartthrob of the school, the boy that every girl had a secret crush on. His eyes alone can make any woman melt. *I mean, I do feel a little warm right now.* He seems almost too perfect, and I wouldn't be surprised if he ended up telling me he was the Valedictorian of his class.

"I bet you were crowned the King of your senior prom, weren't you?" I tease him, nudging him with my elbow.

He pauses, for just a moment, before answering, as if he is thinking of the perfect way to answer, "not possible, I didn't go." He sheepishly admits. A hint of sadness in his tone lingers on his tongue.

"No… Way… No freaking way!" I'm completely floored.

"Way… Really." He laughs.

"I don't believe you. There is no way someone didn't snatch your ass up as their date." My head shakes, slowly and disbelieving. I can't wrap my mind around it.

"Welllllll, what about you? I can't imagine anyone else in your class was even half as pretty as you are, no matter how many girls there were. You had to have been voted your Prom Queen." He turns towards me, certain that his assumptions are correct. "Am I right?"

"Hardly!" I can't contain myself. "I was a tomboy, and my life pretty much revolved around sports, especially field hockey… So no, I was not crowned the Prom Queen." The sheer obscurity of it makes me laugh. "But I did go, just with a group of my friends though… I wore red, in case you were wondering." Giving him a playful wink, his eyebrows raised at the thought.

"I bet you looked beautiful in red." The confidence in his voice makes me blush, and I can feel the temperature in my cheeks rising. "Which reminds me of the red high heels you were wearing last night. I liked them."

"You liked my heels, huh?" I tease. "I guess they were money well spent then."

"Most definitely... They were hot!" he looks away and is lost in his thoughts for a moment. My face flushes at what could be going through his mind.

"Enough about me, back to you." I laugh. "Well? Did you ever end up dating? Joanna, was her name, right?"

"Uhhh... Let's just say, we were together for a very long time, years even...But in the end, we both knew that we were much better as friends than we ever were as a couple." He looks away and doesn't say another word.

I want to press on and know just how long ago that had been, but in the end, I refrain and let him off the hook, stopping the inquisition.

I sit back and lean my head against the headrest, allowing my eyes to grow heavy. For only a moment couldn't hurt, even though I made a promise to Jax. His eyes are focused on the road, and I'm positive he won't notice.

CHAPTER 14

"Wake up, sleepyhead." Jax says playfully and low. "You're supposed to be my wingman and keep me awake, remember?" His hand nudges my thigh, and I can't help the small smile that tugs at my lips.

"Okay, wingman is back on duty," I murmur, stretch, and let out a yawn, "but first..." My stomach twists. "Bathroom break. Urgent."

Jax raises an eyebrow, and his blue eyes flicker in the dashboard glow. "Bathroom? Already? I thought you were holding out to stay up for me?"

"Don't judge," I snap back, laughing. "You'll thank me later, when you don't have to pay a cleaning bill for the 'accident' I'm about to have all over this rental."

He shakes his head, grinning. "Fine... I can't argue with that."

The rest stop appears like the universe has been secretly spying on our conversation. We pull in slowly. Jeff and Dick remain curled up in the back, lost in dreamland, completely oblivious.

I hop out and stretch once more, taking in the crisp night air, cool, tinged with scents of gasoline. Jax leans against the car, arms crossed, alert, his eyes scanning the empty lot.

I walk toward the restroom and can feel his eyes on me the entire way. When I reach the door, I peek inside, then turn back to him and give him a thumbs up. He nods, silently giving his approval for me to enter. When I return, to no surprise of mine, Jax has my door open and ready for me to climb back in. Just as I do, flashing red and blue lights light up the darkness, and I straighten upright. My stomach twists once again, and not from needing the bathroom this time.

"Uh… that can't be good," I say.

Jax stiffens. "Stay here." He says and places his hand gently on the small of my back. Easing my nerves just a little.

A patrol car rolls to a slow stop beside us. The officer steps out, flashlight in one hand, the other affixed to the holster at his hip. Surprisingly, Jeff and Dick remain asleep, completely unaware of the tension building just outside the rental.

"Evening," the officer says. His voice is calm but with purpose. "Everything all right here?"

Jax takes control, his voice is steady but short. "Yes, Officer. Just taking a break."

The officer's gaze lingers from us to the two sleeping in the back seat, who now look more like two passed-out drunks rather than a pair of exhausted passengers catching up on some rest. "Can I see your license, Sir?"

All of a sudden, I feel like we're criminals under interrogation, and I'm not even sure why. We've done nothing wrong. I glance at Jax as he hands over his ID, wondering when our harmless road trip turned into a police drama. The officer studies it and then goes back to Jax, long enough to make my stomach tighten.

"Mind if I ask you where you're headed?"

"Home," Jax says, "coming from a convention in Vegas." He doesn't mention the post-9/11 delays, and I get the feeling he doesn't need to. Everyone has been on edge, and it seems the officers haven't been spared. More than likely, what sparked this little encounter.

The officer seems satisfied and nods. "All right. Drive safe and stay alert out there... Report anything that might seem suspicious."

As soon as he's back inside the patrol car, I exhale, still a little shaky as I slide into the car. Jax's hand is steady on my shoulder as I do, a subtle grounding touch.

"See?" he says. "We did nothing wrong. Nothing to worry about."

"Yeah, totally fine. Nothing. Just a minor heart attack, that's all."

He laughs, shaking his head. "I think you secretly like it when my wingman skills are being tested."

"Ahhh, maybe," I tease back. "But mostly, I like watching you look ridiculous trying to play the Mr. Calm-Cool-and-Collected."

He laughs quietly, trying not to wake Dick and Jeff, still asleep in the back seat. "You won this one. But no more bathroom breaks, and no excuses?"

"Deal." I laugh louder than I should and wink at him.

CHAPTER 15

The father-and-son snore fest in the backseat interrupts my thoughts and becomes an accidental lullaby. Between Dick's rumbling bass and Jeff's nasal harmony, paired with the hum of the engine, it's oddly soothing.

My attention returns to the front seat, and I'm ready to delve into all things Jax, hearing more stories of his life. Kicking off my shoes, I twist sideways to face him, searching for that perfect, semi-comfortable road-trip position. My legs tangle, my back finds the door, and I triple-check the lock—just in case I spontaneously fall out of a moving car. Because that happens all the time, right? One last tug. Yep, still secure. *Why am I so weird?*

Jax catches me in the act, eyebrows raised. "You're very careful, you know that? I wish I'd had some of that when I was younger."

"I'll happily donate some," I whisper. "It gets exhausting."

Once I've settled into a position that doesn't cut off circulation, I pick up where we left off, asking questions like an undercover journalist. Jax doesn't hold back.

"I live in Saddle Creek," he starts. "Population 2,003. You've never heard of it, don't worry, no one has." He cups a hand like he's sharing a secret. I grin; this playful side of him is dangerously charming.

He tells stories of his parents, who were high school sweethearts, prom royalty, lifelong teammates. They coached his childhood baseball team, rewarded wins with ice cream, and would lug them all in the back of their truck to a little mom-and-pop store called *The Brown Bag.* He talks about them with so much warmth that I can practically taste the strawberry ice cream.

His admiration for them hits me deep in my core. My mom always said, *the way a man treats his parents says everything about him.* Listening to Jax, I now get it. His voice softens when he talks about them, and I feel my chest tighten in the best possible way. I can tell he's worried about them, alone at home, with everything happening in the world. Maybe that's who he called back at the diner.

Our eyes meet. Neither of us looks away. Without thinking, I lean in and kiss his cheek. Just a small thank you. He doesn't flinch and just smiles. I turn on the radio low enough not to wake the snorers in the backseat, and we ease into a softer conversation. The uneasiness in the world outside begins to fade.

Jax tells me he's the youngest of four. He has three older sisters. Poor guy never stood a chance of scoring his allotted time in the bathroom. But it explains his steady, unspoken confidence, his respect for women, and that old-school gentleman streak that keeps undoing me.

"I remember when my oldest sister went on her first date," he says, grinning. "I was twelve, and I threatened the guy at the door. Told him I'd make him pay if he hurt her."

"You didn't!"

"Oh, I did. Didn't think about the fact that he could flatten me."

I laugh. "Every girl deserves a brother like you. I definitely could've used one growing up, especially during my dating disasters."

His eyes question me. "You mentioned your family's bad at setting you up. Why's that? Waiting for someone perfect, like me?"

"Something like that," I tease, smiling. "Mostly they just want me safe."

He nods. "Yeah, I get that. I pity anyone who hurts my sisters."

"They're lucky to have you."

When I ask about his dad, his voice fills with pride. "He started working at thirteen, painting houses, mowing lawns, building custom doghouses that matched the owners' homes."

I press a hand to my heart. "That's the cutest thing I've ever heard." Without thinking, I reach out and touch his arm, then quickly pull back, embarrassed.

"You can leave it there," he says quietly. "I don't mind."

Too late. I laugh it off, regretting it instantly. He continues, telling me how his dad framed photos of those doghouses and hung them in the entryway of his office. To remind him of the humble beginnings of the construction business Jax now co-owns with him, and is now the biggest in the Tri-State area. *I mean, who wouldn't hire a hot guy to build an addition on their home if you were able to stare at sweaty Jax with his shirt off, muscles bulging every day? I'm half tempted to get home and start breaking things just to call them for help.*

Of course he's successful. I can already picture him on a work site, shirt clinging, muscles flexing... *Lord help me.*

He tells me how his dad searched every baby store for tool-shaped rattles when Jax was born, the first boy after three girls. The story makes my heart melt. *How cute that must have been to see baby Jax in a stroller with a plastic hammer in his tiny little hands?*

Brrringgg, Brrringgg. The sound startles me and interrupts our conversation. I reach for my phone and flip it over, hoping for a signal. *Ugh, what the hell?* No service again. I shake it, thinking it somehow will help.

Brrringgg, Brrringgg. It rings again, and Jeff stirs, fumbling for his cell. "Sally? Honey? What's wrong?" His voice trembles. The conversation is quiet but heavy; I can feel the worry radiating from him.

My lips press together in a thin, sad line as I glance back at him. My silent way of letting him know I understand. His eyes catch mine, a hint of sorrow behind them. The heaviness of the past few days is weighing on his wife, Sally. And him.

"Go downstairs and heat a pot of tea. It will calm you down and help you sleep," he continues, trying to relieve her of her anxieties.

I turn back around, allowing him to talk privately with the woman he loves. Dick is unaware as he lies alongside him, still snoring. I look over at Jax, and he gives me a pitiful smile. "I feel for the guy," he says, his voice low and just above a whisper. Then reaches over and takes my hand in his, giving it a heartfelt squeeze. I smile back as he pulls his hand from mine just as swiftly as he placed it there and turns on the radio to a random country station, the volume on low. "We should give them their privacy," he whispers. "Well, whatever kind of privacy you can have in a car."

Time continues to move forward as it always does. Jeff finished his phone call and once again allowed sleep to take over. *Poor guy.*

I too, fight to stay awake, but my eyelids betray me. They are winning the war. Desperate, I rummage for the bag of gummy bears I bought earlier. Sugar, my only hope.

"Want some?" I offer, palm open.

He takes them all, his fingers grazing mine—sparks. Literal freaking sparks. My pulse quickens, my face burns, and I pray he can't *see* what my body's doing. I strategically place the bag on my lap, between my legs, so he can't see my actual vagina pulsing from his touch. *Can I get any weirder?*

I watch him as he chews slowly, and oddly enough, he chooses the same pineapple ones I love. *Of course he does.*

I nod toward the tattoo on his arm. "Why a buffalo?"

His smile deepens. "It's my dad's story."

"He found an old farmhouse with a fence that surrounded the acres of land that was home to three humongous buffalo." He laughs. The animation in his voice is endearing, and I love it. *Did I just say love?*

He tells me how his father, new to Saddle Creek as a boy, once stumbled upon a farm with three buffalo. He'd visit them daily, eventually helping the owners. Years later, when they were gone, the owners and the buffalo, the farm became a family legend. Every time they'd pass the land, his dad would sing, *"Take me home, where the buffalo roam..."*

"That's not how the lyrics go," Jax laughs, "but that's how he sang it, so that's how we remember it."

The animation in his voice is so stinkin' cute, and I love it.

"So when my buddies and I got our graduation tattoos, I knew mine had to be a buffalo. No matter where I end up, I will always have this buffalo to *take me home*."

It seems that everything Jax says or does has some sort of meaning behind it, and I love him for it. *There goes that "L" word again. I'm throwing it out there all of a sudden like it's some sort of party confetti.*

My eyes blur with tears. "That's beautiful."

He looks at me, and for a moment, everything that's happened, everything else, just disappears. The buffalo isn't just ink etched in his arm; it's a piece of his soul, and now etched into my heart. I reach out and rest my hand on his arm. This time, I don't move it.

"And so are you," he simply says.

The hum of the tires blends with the night until sleep pulls me under. I dream of tall grass, Jax and I hand in hand, a herd of buffalo, and a little boy with Jax's eyes calling me *mama.*

A gentle squeeze pulls me back to reality. I'm still not fully awake until I notice Jax's hand is intertwined with mine. Just like in my dream.

"Wake up, sleepyhead," he says softly. "You were supposed to keep me awake."

I blink away the haze, my eyes still fuzzy, and glance at our hands still joined, and smile. It feels so natural, it feels right. For the rest of the drive, we don't say a word. We just sit there, holding hands as the first light of morning breaks across the horizon.

CHAPTER 16

"Morning." Jeff's voice is husky, and if I didn't know how much he despises them, I would have sworn he smoked a pack of cigarettes last night. His body contorts in unusual ways as he stretches out the kinks that have formed throughout the night. Out of the corner of my eye, I notice that Dick, too, is beginning to stir awake.

"Good morning to you, booooooth." I smile, but it ends up turning into a yawn.

"Did you stay up all night?" asks Jeff, and he begins to slide each foot into his loafers.

"She sure did." Jax interrupts. "She's a 'trooper'!" he winks, referring to our little secret police officer scandal, and pats me on my leg. I want to tell him to leave it there, but I decide against it.

"Are you ready for me to take over the driving?" asks Jeff.

"Nah… I'm good. I'll keep going til breakfast…Then we can switch off."

The gas gauge highlighted across the dashboard agrees, along with our collective empty bellies. Mine in particular has been screaming at me.

My stomach has always been a bit "bipolar" when it comes to food. Either it's nice, content, and satisfied, or the complete opposite: grumpy, angry, and empty. In this case, it is without a doubt the latter.

The sun has risen, and the sky is already showcasing a beautiful shade of blue, holding up the puffy white clouds that appear almost weightless. Highway signs have come and gone, along with the trees, homes, towns, and the quietness in the car; a solitude we had taken for granted only hours before.

Dick chirps from the backseat. "Turn the station to Limbaugh. And turn it up so I can hear!" he demands. *Why must you ruin this?*

Given the state that our country is in and all that has transpired over the past twenty-four hours, I should be more inclined to listen to what is being discussed and take more interest in our country's affairs. But my mind could use a much-deserved break from all of the hatred, death, and sadness that the world is experiencing. Even if for only a few moments. But in the end, I falter, giving in to Dick's request to turn on the station and find his beloved radio announcer, and he gets his way. Much to my demise. *Ugh.*

A low sigh escapes me when I lean my awful bed-head hair against the passenger side window, allowing my mind to wander as I gaze out the window. It feels unnerving staring out into nothingness, not a speck in the sky for miles. Clouds are sporadic, almost as if they had been hand-painted there for effect. Aside from the occasional bird flying by, nothing else could be seen. Airplanes that once floated through the sky, delivering passengers to their respective destinations, are nowhere in sight.

On any "normal" day, the airplanes with their massive wings could be seen crowding the skies with people from around the world. Some, excited to begin their vacations at Disney World, many are off to a work conference, and others visit relatives for an overdue family reunion in another part of the country. No matter the destination, the skies have always been so full of life. I'm afraid to admit that these are not normal days. The birds even seem to sense that something is off. They, too, are scarce through the skies, and one can assume they are huddled in their nests waiting for when and if it will ever be safe for them to soar and be free. I stare out and can't help but think just how topsy-turvy the world is right now. It's like the entire earth has been shifted on its axis and everything has been turned upside down, causing chaos and utter destruction all around us. I close my eyes, a failed attempt at clearing my head, when all that keeps replaying is planes crashing. I clutch my heart, wincing at the thought, as a tear slips free before I can catch it. Given the state that our country is in, I'm not sure that there will ever be another peaceful "normal" day moving forward.

I shove away the sadness, far away, storing it for another time, and try to focus on the positive, allowing my thoughts to take me back to Jax's hand intertwined with my own, and I can't help but smile at the thought. I wonder how such a handsome, hard-working, family-based man is still single.

Hours together in the car have given me ample time to explore not only his life but also admire his impeccable physique. I am in complete awe of his gorgeous, thick brown hair, curled on its ends, poking out from the bottom of his baseball cap. A look I have always loved on a man. *Women would pay good money at the salon to have hair like his.* His striking eyes that grabbed my attention only days earlier are as blue as the sky seen above.

Working in the construction business, no doubt, aided in his chiseled arms. His biceps alone look as if he could be an avid gym goer. The flawless buffalo tattoo that found its forever home on Jax's arm appears as if it were created for only him. He seems perfect in every way, and it's hard to believe that someone hasn't snatched him up. It would be easy enough to slip off a ring while in Vegas. People do it all the time. What happens in Vegas stays in Vegas, right? But then I think of all our conversations, everything I've learned about him over the past few days. That could never be the case. Not with Jax. *I mean, he would have told me otherwise, right?*

* * *

The sweet aroma of pancakes fills the air, smacking me in the face. Butter oozes from their sides, making tiny butter puddles on the plate, and my mouth begins to salivate the moment our waitress sets down the hot stack in front of me. Memories flood through me as I think of my mother cooking her Sunday breakfasts, especially on days that the Philadelphia Eagles were set to play. Then it would surely be an all-day eating fest. A pang in my heart emerges and reminds me of just how much I miss her.

I go quiet, caught off guard by a wave of homesickness. One minute I'm thinking about Jax, the next I'm missing everything familiar, my family, my bed, the smell of Mom's Sunday sauce simmering on the stove. Just... home. It's only been less than a week since I last saw them, but right now, as I miss them, it feels like a lifetime ago. I close my eyes and rest my head against the windowpane, allowing the sadness to take over and swallow me whole.

Jax must sense the sudden change in me and reaches his hand over from under the table and places it on my thigh, rubbing his thumb from side to side. I stiffen, and my body jolts at his unexpected touch, raising alarm to Jeff and Dick sitting across from us. My face flushes, giving away our little secret. Their eyes lock onto mine, refusing to let me off the hook.

"What? They look delicious, I'm excited to eat." My hand swipes over my pancakes and alludes to the reason I am excited. I am hopeful in my attempt at convincing the two of them that my scrumptious pancakes are the obvious culprit for my elation.

"I swear... I have never met a girl who gets so excited about her food," Jeff jokes.

I turn toward Jax with a quick smile, my silent way of thanking him for knowing just what I had needed at that moment. I place my free hand and rest it on his that still sits on my thigh, and just as I do, a buzzing comes from Jax's cell phone sitting on the table in front of him. It's ringer, set to silent, but the vibration is still apparent.

"Aren't you gonna answer that?" My head nods in the direction of his phone.

He looks down at the name that appears on the screen and says, "Nah, I'll call her back when we get outside." His voice is quiet, almost guilty. He shoves the phone into his pocket, but not before I catch the flicker of something in his eyes, hesitation. Jeff's eyes squint together in confusion as he looks from Jax, then over to me.

I want to ask who it was, but for whatever reason, I decide against it and let it go. *I'm sure it's just his mother.*

Discussions about the rest of our journey home begin as we dive into our chosen breakfast entrees. A short stack of pancakes smothered in warm maple syrup, accompanied by a side of sausage links, is for me. A bacon, egg, and cheese on a bagel is for Jax, and two cheese omelets, with a side of bacon, for both Jeff and Dick.

Another round of coffee is being poured when Jeff says, "You made great timing through the night. At this rate, given there aren't any unforeseen problems that arise, we could get home sometime around midnight," he says with confidence. "If we only stop for gas and some quick food breaks, we will be sleeping in our own comfy beds tonight!" Excitement fills his voice. It's almost cute to see him so elated. I can tell he misses the comforts of his own home and, of course, the love of his life, his wife Sally.

Judging by the look on Dick's face, this too pleases him. The worn, exhausted look tells me he's had enough... done with this road trip, ready to be back in his own home, in his own bed... next to his own wife. My heart aches for him and how he must be feeling. This trip and the reasons behind it have taken such a toll not only on his mind but also on his aging body. In the seventy-six years of his life, I can only imagine the things he has seen and the world events he's had to endure. I'm sure, of all of them, nothing could be compared to being three thousand miles away from his home and soulmate of fifty-two years, all while the country that he loves is under attack. For as long as I've known him, he has always appeared to be such a strong and proud man, never showing much emotion. I can only imagine how terrifying it is for him to feel so helpless. *Poor thing.*

Out of nowhere, I reach over and place my hand over Dick's and look at him. Staring straight through to the depths of his soul, letting him know that he is not alone.

A tinge of regret begins to emerge for ragging on him like I have, in jest, throughout the drive, in particular for his awful choice of radio stations. The pitiful look on his face, as I stare at him, is tugging at my heartstrings. For the remainder of the trip, I make a mental note, promising to let up on the sarcasm when it comes to him. He can have his "Limbaugh" without another word. *For now.*

"I can drive the rest of the way until we make it home," Jeff says as he takes a bite of his strip of bacon. A drip of grease falls from it and lands on the table beside his plate.

I get the feeling that driving gives him a sense of purpose, and neither Jax nor I will disagree. The two of us have stayed awake throughout the entire night, a full twenty-four hours to be exact, and we both are in need of some well-deserved rest, even if only for a few hours. Only I've never been great at sleeping in cars, never could quite get comfortable, but I guess I'll try. Not like there is much else to do.

I'm getting more and more tired, and at this point, I know I'll crash soon – just as soon as we finish eating and hit the road again.

"The check has been taken care of... paid for by the gentleman who just walked out the door. He's a regular around here." Our waitress says, and the three of us turn to look out the window and search for the person responsible. I catch a glimpse of him as he maneuvers himself into his beat-up old pick-up truck, using his cane for stability. A 'Semper Fi' sticker affixed to the back window. "He's a Vietnam vet, and he overheard your situation, and given what has transpired over the past few days, it's bringing back a lot of unwanted memories... I think this was just a small way he could help someone," she explains. "It's good for the soul, you know?" Her voice cracks, and on the verge of breaking.

"That was very nice of him. The next time you see him, please tell him that his generosity was much appreciated... And also, please thank him for his service," says Jeff.

"I will... Acts of kindness like this have been happening here a lot since... well, you know... ever since those awful attacks," she says. "There's something beautiful about seeing kindness emerge out of hatred firsthand."

A tear escapes and falls down her cheek, landing on the hemline of her shirt. Her face reddens, and I can tell she is embarrassed by her outward display of emotions.

"I apologize for being such a blubbery mess... It's just been a lot, you know?" She stifles another outburst and sniffles. "Enjoy the rest of your drive home and stay safe. I heard on the news there is a storm heading to the East Coast," she says, then leans her head down to her side and wipes away the tears with the collar of her blouse. Then she hands us a bag of pastries to enjoy on the way home, on the house.

The weight of the tragedy looms over everyone's shoulders, yet life continues to move forward. Restaurants remain open, employees still have jobs they need to report to, and so many people are finding ways to do good, even if it is as simple as paying for a stranger's breakfast. I am grateful, and certain I will pay it forward, somehow.

Trips to the diner bathrooms are made, then once outside, the gas tank will be topped before hitting the road once more. All ensuring us there would be no stops for at least a few hours. Getting us that much closer to home.

We walk outside into the overwhelming heat with Jeff, Dick, and Jax just a few steps ahead of me. My eyes fixate on Jax's sexy back profile. His jeans fit him as if they had been stitched right to his masculine body, hugging him in all the right places. His every step exudes confidence, and his ass taunts me, begging me to reach out and grab it.

How is he wearing those jeans, though? The heat must be affecting him like the rest of us.

At the very thought, he reaches up with both hands, removes his ball cap, and replaces it facing backwards towards me. *Who doesn't love a guy with his hat on backwards?*

"Oh, good fucking Lord," slips freely from my tongue.

What was meant to be tucked into my head for my own pleasure, blurts out for all to hear. My face goes three shades of red, and trust me, it has nothing to do with the scorching sun. In rapid motion, my eyes look in every direction in fear that I have been heard. *Charlotte, you really are an idiot sometimes.*

"Did you say something?" asks Jax as he stops in his tracks and then turns to face me.

"Uhhh… yeah… sorry." I stumble on my words like a child caught with her hand in the cookie jar. "I said… Oh, good Lord… You know, because of how hot it is out here," I lie, and throw in a hint of laughter, knowing I've just been caught. "I'm sweating more than a snowman in July."

"You are not kidding, I'm hot too." Jax lets me off the hook, even if he doesn't know it.

Damn straight you are.

As I approach the car, of course, he's waiting once again, holding the door open and allowing me to enter before him.

"After you." He bends down, stretching out his arm, and gestures for me to get in. A quality in him that I don't think I could ever grow tired of. *A true gentleman.*

I take another step forward, about to make my way into the back of the car, when something slips from under my shoe, causing both of my feet to come out from under me. Suddenly, I fall forward, leaving only inches to keep my head from slamming into the door jam. In the same moment, I feel a tight grip around my arm, so tight, it almost hurts.

"Get your hands off me!" The words explode out of me before I can stop them, and I jerk away from Jax's grasp... the same grasp that just kept me from smashing face-first into the door. But at this moment, I don't know what's happening, I'm mortified and too confused.

He takes a step backward and stands dumbfounded, staring back at me in shock. It all happened so fast, and I had no control over the words that just spewed from my mouth and landed on poor, innocent Jax. It's an involuntary response that hasn't happened to me in years. It came out of nowhere.

"What-what did I do? I-I was only trying to help... I wasn't trying to hurt you." He stammers, apologizing for no reason. He did nothing wrong, but the words left my mouth at such a rapid speed that I didn't have time to stop them. Ancient insecurities that I thought were over, ones that I thought were buried and gone for good, just resurfaced and fell onto Jax. "I would never put my hands on you in anger." A look of confusion blankets his face. Like lightning, Jeff is right by my side, protecting me like I am his little bear cub in danger.

"What's going on?" His accusations are directed towards Jax, and he looks like he might hit him. I've never seen him like this before. It is now that I notice Dick standing by him as well.

"I have no ide—"

"Stop!" I interrupt; my eyes focused on Jax as I place my hand on Jeff's shoulder. "He didn't do anything wrong... He was only trying to keep me from getting hurt, and I overreacted." I plead, apologizing once again. "It was my fault... Well, in truth, it's Dickhead Derek's fault." I confess.

"Derek?" asks Jax.

Judging by the look on their faces, the three of them are baffled by the entire embarrassing situation. Three sets of confused eyes now stare at me for answers as the four of us stand alongside the Camry in the parking lot of the diner. I take a deep breath and lean my back up against the car.

"Derek is an ex-boyfriend from senior year." I begin to explain. "Long story short, he was the ideal boyfriend... The captain of the football team who got good grades, and everyone loved him. Blah, blah, blah." My eyes rolled at the thought of how everyone perceived him. "On the outside, he was every teenage girl's dream boyfriend. But what most didn't know was that on the inside, he was a narcissistic, abusive, piece of shit." I straighten and stand tall when I notice all three of them stiffen. Their bodies are like stone, and their fists are united as they all tighten into balls of fury at my confession. "At first, he was nice and polite, but it didn't take long before things began to escalate." I kick a tiny pebble with my shoe and notice that it lands next to Dick's. "He called all the shots...Where we ate, what parties we went to, and what friends I was allowed to hang out with... He started following me everywhere I went, always waiting for me after field hockey practices and after every class. I couldn't do anything without his approval." I pause for a moment before finishing. Everything is quiet; the only sound that can be heard is the cars passing by on the highway. Dick stands motionless, a look of disgust on his face and his arms crossed in disapproval. "Until one day, my team had a huge win over our rival school's field hockey team, so my teammates wanted to celebrate afterwards. We all were going to meet at one of their houses and order pizza to celebrate, but he didn't like the idea of me going without him... So, he followed me on my walk back to the school, from the field, and forbade me to go... I told him that it wasn't his call to make... That was the moment when I found out that he didn't like being told no." I say, shaking my head as I relive the entire incident. I nervously kick another pebble with my shoe, landing a few feet in front of me this time. "So, the next thing I knew, I was being called an ungrateful slut, then he grabbed my arm and threw me to the ground so hard that I later found out he had broken my wrist in two separate places."

"Jesus Christ! What a piece of shit!" shouts Jax, his teeth clenching together with such force that his jaw looks like it could break in two. I place a gentle hand on him to try to calm him.

"So, what happened to the little bastard?" Jeff asks.

"I grabbed my field hockey stick, then got back to my feet and swung it so hard against his head that it made him fall to his knees and cry like a little bitch." The memory still makes me laugh, him standing there, tears running down his sissy ass face, like a soap opera star who just found out the baby isn't his. Pathetic. "I told him if he ever so much as laid a finger on me or any other girl again, that he wouldn't get off so easily next time. Then I whacked him in the knee, hitting him once more for good measure." I still laugh when I think of him rolling on the ground, gripping his knee in agony like a damn soccer player trying to draw a foul. "So, when you grabbed my arm just then, I guess it brought back some rooted memories, and without thinking, I took it out on you." My eyes look at Jax. "I thought I was over that asshole years ago, but given the way I just yelled at you, I guess I was wrong... I'm so sorry."

"No need to be sorry... I'm the one who's sorry that you had to go through that." He grabs my hands and pulls me against his chest, and rests his chin on my head. I feel him take a long breath through his nose, then a ripple of warm air brushes against my hair, like he's breathing the horrible memories away. "Not all guys are like that," Jax assures me. "That bastard is damn lucky I didn't go to the same school as you."

"Sounds like Charlotte can take care of things herself." Jeff laughs as he swings a pretend stick through the air to help lighten up the somber mood that hovers over the four of us.

"Alright... Now that we all know never to piss off Charlotte, let's all get into the car and get the hell home." Dick interrupts, then places a hand on my shoulder, squeezing it ever so gently before walking around to the other side of the car.

We all settled into our original placements in the car, from when our journey home first began, which now seems so long ago. We each gear up for the final legs of the race, one that none of us wanted to be a part of. If Jeff's calculations are correct, we have approximately thirteen hours of "Limbaugh" left to go. *Remember, be nice, Charlotte.* I may or may not have felt my eyes roll back into my head, and not in a good way.

Seat belts are clicked, the air conditioning hums at just the right temperature, and the radio is tuned to a station that doesn't make me want to rip my ears off. We're set and ready to go. Before the break of a new day, we will be home. Jeff pulls out of the parking lot and onto the highway as an unexpected heartache washes over me. I realize at this moment, we will soon be home, and my time together with Jax could all be a distant memory. I have been stuck in this car with him next to me all this time, no escape... I have grown very accustomed to him being by my side over the past few days. I realize only now that I selfishly don't want it to end. But I know how real life works; it will continue to move forward and eventually go back to the way it has always been, long before September eleventh ever happened. The unfortunate reality is that we could both go our separate ways and live our lives apart from each other. The odds of a love formed between tragedy and loneliness could never withstand the realities of what real life can throw at you.

Negative thoughts begin to invade my mind. *Stop it, Charlotte! This time, it feels different. Jax is different.* Ignoring my pleas, I start to convince myself that all of this has meant nothing between the two of us, that once home and not confined to this compact car, our feelings will change. I have read stories of couples forming under such stressful events, only to find out that once they are back to reality, they never seem to last. Once we are all nestled into our own comfy homes, daily life will take over. This trip, which turned out to be nothing I could have imagined to begin with, will soon be a distant memory. *I won't let that happen.*

Boldly, I take control and grab hold of whatever time we may have left together and lean into Jax. My weary head rests upon his shoulder, and I close my eyes. My hand grabs hold of his, and I tangle it in mine, and in response, his lips press against the crown of my head, leaving a lasting, tiny imprint of a kiss in its place. We remain here, still like statues, motionless yet content, as we both allow sleep to take over our exhaustion. The last thought I have before sleep takes me is that I can envision every night from here on out, hand in hand, the two of us, asleep with Jax by my side, just like this.

CHAPTER 17

My eyes flutter open and close, trying desperately to regain their focus. The grogginess still lingers as they try to make out the time on the dashboard clock. I squint my eyes in an attempt to make it more visible.

"It's almost four-thirty?" I say in disbelief. "Good Lord, I slept through the entire day." I look at Jeff and Dick. Jax, too, is now stirring awake at the sound of my voice.

"You sure did," Jeff says. "You both did as a matter of fact... Dad and I even stopped at a rest area to use the bathroom, and you both slept right through it." The two of them laugh at the ridiculousness of it.

"Morning," Jax says.

"You mean, good evening?" Dick laughs.

"Holy crap." Jax looks at his watch in disbelief. "How is it this late?"

I smile at him, but my lips won't move, and my teeth are stuck to them. My mouth, all of a sudden, is drier than a Vegas martini, when I remember my half-empty bottle of Gatorade. The quickness with which I lean down and rummage through the bag at my feet lets everyone know just how thirsty I am. It takes only two seconds before the bottle goes empty.

"Thirsty?" The way Jax stares at me makes me feel like an animal exhibit at the zoo. He laughs as he continues to watch me finish off the last few sips left that linger at the bottom of the bottle.

"I guess so. Must be all that good sleep I got. I can't believe we both slept the entire day away."

"Well, I for one was very content in my sleeping arrangements." He is playful when he winks. I smile back and recall the way I felt sleeping against him. It felt so natural.

"Is anyone hungry? I was thinking we could stop in about an hour or so. Unless we find something sooner." Jeff directs his request to everyone in the car.

We all agree to wait, then settle back into our seats when an idea comes to mind.

"Want to play 'two truths and a lie'?" I ask as I open my last bag of gummy bears. I drop a few of them into his hand, one of the yellow ones slips through his fingers and falls to the floor, disappearing under the seat.

"What in the world is that? Can't we play 'eye-spy,' or something that I've actually heard of?"

"No... This is way more fun... I swear!" I assure him. "Jennifer and I used to play it all the time. All you do is think of two things that are true about yourself and one lie, and I need to try to guess which one is the lie. And vice versa." I say. "I will go first."

"If you say so." His reluctance is cute.

"Okay, here I go... My favorite vegetable is Brussels sprouts." Jax's face contorts in disgust, which tells me he loathes them, and I laugh out loud at just how cute he is. "I once got a speeding ticket by letting my boobs spill out from the top of my t-shirt after being pulled over." His eyes grow as wide as the sea. "And, once upon a time, I was engaged to be married." My face is like stone, poker-face level ten. This isn't my first game; I've got secrets and strategy.

"This is gonna be easy." He says with such confidence.

"If you say so." I throw his words back at him.

"The speeding ticket is a lie." Jeff interrupts and hollers from the front seat.

"You pipe down up front! This game is between Jax and me." The playful way I yell at him causes laughter to erupt throughout the car. *Wow... Is Dick having fun?* This adorable fact is a reminder that Jax and I are not alone in the car.

"No way... I can totally see her doing that to get out of a ticket." Jax laughs more than I expected, and I swat his arm to stop. "I'm gonna go with the lie that she was engaged to be married."

I catch a glimpse of Jeff gawking at me through the rearview mirror, his eyes boring into me. He knows the full truth about my engagement to James and the pathetic reason that it ended so abruptly. His eyebrows raise, a look of wonder in his eyes at how I might respond.

"I'm right, aren't I?" Jax asks. I pause for a moment and look away in embarrassment, and I wonder if he notices.

Three sets of eyes peer at me, waiting for my answer. I can almost feel them staring as I finally answer. "Nope... I was engaged... And not that long ago either." I finally admit. "I dumped him after I caught him cheating on me with his secretary." The reality of it all is much easier to talk about than I thought it would be. *I hope this doesn't scare him off.* Between Derek, who abused me, and James, who cheated on me, I sound like a real catch right now. *Too much baggage.* I would be surprised if Jax doesn't run as far away from me the second we drop him off.

"*Ahhhhhhh,* so that's why you said you didn't believe in the whole marriage thing." He recalls the conversation we had at the casino bar only a few nights before.

"Yupppp... He was a douche!"

"He *issss* a douche," Jeff reiterates from the front seat.

Ever since Jeff learned of James's infidelity and our breakup, he hasn't missed a chance to tell me just how he feels about him. I can still taste the yummy chocolate-covered fruit bouquet that he and Sally sent to my home after they heard about what happened. "If I had known what a weasel he was, I would have never been so nice to him at the Christmas party last year. I could have slipped a laxative into his drink for ya. That would have been fun to watch unfold." Laughter erupts from everyone in the car at the thought. My nose scrunches up at the very thought of James frantically running to the bathroom.

"Well, he sounds like a complete moron to have cheated on someone as great as you." Jax smiles at me.

Jeff chimes in. "My thoughts exactly!"

"Okay. Now it's your turn." I say to Jax and deflect the focus off of me and onto him.

Jax takes a few minutes to decide on what he is going to say. He almost seems nervous to speak. *Dude. It's only a game. It's not that serious.*

"Alright, here it goes." He pauses before he begins to speak. "I once won the title of 'Mr. Peach' in a baby contest at the local 4-H fair." His smile is wide as he bats his baby blues at me. I'm not sure how it's possible, but they seem to be an even bluer shade than they were just yesterday. If I stare at them long enough, the possibility of getting lost in them altogether is very real. "I am married." The quickness with which he spoke makes me question if I imagined it. "And I once was arrested for indecent exposure." The way he doesn't look back at me doesn't go unnoticed.

"That's too easy... I can totally see you being cute as a button and winning a baby contest. The lie has got to be that you are marri—"

122

Boom! An explosion comes from outside the car, putting an immediate end to our silly little game. Jeff instinctively taps his brakes, hard, sending the bag of pastries to soar through the air. By instinct, I crouch down, cover my head, and scream just as Jax puts his arms around me. He covers me like a soft blanket and pulls me into him for safekeeping. Visions of airplanes crashing into buildings, explosions tearing through steel and glass, people screaming and dying; they invade my every thought. I can't shut it off.

"You're good... I've got you," he whispers, calming me with his words.

The noise is followed by an annoying flapping sound, sharp and erratic, like something coming loose. The whole car starts to shake uncontrollably, like it's about to throw us off the road. I stiffen under his grasp. *Are we under attack now, too? Have we been hit?*

"What the hell was that?!" yells Dick, as he grabs hold of the armrest on his passenger side door, then sits up straight, searching out of his window for an answer. I leap from Jax's arms, which I now regret, and jump up in record time to assess where the noise is coming from. Jax follows in unison and then looks out his window, too.

It doesn't take long to realize that one of the tires has blown out, scaring the crap out of everyone in here with its explosive noise. A stark reminder of the explosions that had occurred when tragedy struck our great country, only a few days ago. It's been in the back of all our minds, lying dormant, worried that more assaults on our nation could occur. The split second between the tire blowing and understanding why it happened was enough. Enough to remind us that safety is an illusion, and maybe it always was. As a society, I fear that we might live in a constant state of anxiety moving forward. With every loud boom we hear, or a plane that looks like it might be flying a little too close to a building, we might forever be in fear that this could happen again.

I look at poor Jeff, the way he's gripping the steering wheel with such force, the pink of his knuckles now stained white, attempting to regain control over the erratic Camry. The car continues to bounce and shake in unison, but I am grateful that Jeff remains in control and safely pulls it onto the side of the road. He removes the key from the ignition, lets out a long-awaited sigh, and his body begins to soften.

"Jesus," he says, relieved to have brought the car to a stop.

A symphony of clicking fills the car as we all move in unison, unfastening our seatbelts in record time. It takes mere milliseconds for the unbearable heat to hit me, and I draw in a long breath as I open the door to exit.

"Good Lord, it's friggen hot out!" I yell out to no one in particular.

In a flash, sweat begins to form on my brow. Between my mangled hair from sleeping in the backseat for hours, my wrinkled clothes, and now sweating like a pig, I must look like a total hot mess. In quick fashion, I free the elastic band that permanently holds residency on my wrist for emergency purposes (I never leave home without one) and pull my hair into a low bun in hopes of relieving some of the heat that ambushes me.

"*Ahhhhhh,* that's better..." I reach back and rub the back of my sweaty neck, my fingers digging into its skin, trying to rid it of the multitude of kinks that have formed, a direct result of being crammed into the Camry for hours.

After a round of grumbling about the stifling heat and a much-needed stretch for our weary legs, we circle to the damaged side of the car, bracing ourselves for what we'll find. Jax scrutinizes every inch of the deflated tire, checking each nook and cranny, searching for an answer. In the end, he realizes that a two-inch screw is the culprit in the poor, innocent tire's untimely death.

"Thank god we have a spare," Jeff assures us that there indeed is a spare tire stowed in a hidden compartment underneath the trunk floor. He puffs up a little and stands taller, clearly pleased with himself, and launches into how he made the rental guy go over each and every detail of the car. "You never know," he says, like he's been waiting for this exact moment to prove a point.

I'm grateful that he did because this, without a doubt, consists of an "unforeseen" problem.

At the same time, Jax and I reach for the button that frees the trunk and the spare tire it houses. The bags and belongings are warm to the touch, the direct result of being crammed together in the hot trunk for days. We begin unloading each bag onto the dirt-mixed-gravel roadside and taking some time before we free the tire from its tomb. What would have taken me both hands and quite a bit of effort, Jax reaches in with one hand and releases it with ease, causing his biceps to bulge twice their size. The sight of them excites me, and my body heat rises ten degrees hotter than it was a second ago, giving the sun a run for its money. It's got nothing on Jax.

Poor Dick, the distressed look on his face is alarming. I notice as he unfastens the top two buttons of his unusually wrinkled dress shirt. The way he struggles to breathe is starting to worry me. Short, quick breaths escape him as he leans his frail body alongside the car, attempting to steady his balance. He begins rolling up each of his sleeves. His long-sleeve button-down is no match for the unusual September heat we're experiencing. No amount of rolling them up is going to help a seventy-six-year-old stubborn man in this awful humidity. I look at Jax and notice that he, too, is keeping a close eye on Dick's declining health.

"Why don't you three go ahead and get out of this heat, cool off, and get some dinner across the street, while I fix the flat tire," Jax says, pointing across the road. "It could take a little while. No sense in all of us being subjected to this heat."

I turn and look across the street and notice the cutest little roadside bar. The type that I would shy away from back home, not my usual, but looking at it just now, I'm not quite sure why. Perched on top of its dilapidated roof is a faded wooden, hand-painted sign that reads "Voted best burgers in the state of Ohio three years in a row." My mouth begins to salivate at the very mention of it. A burger does sound good right about now. *Who the hell am I kidding? A burger sounds good at any given time. Especially one that is voted best 3 years in a row.*

"If you could grab me a burger with fries and a large cold root beer to go, that would be great. I can eat mine in the car when I'm done, that way we don't waste any time getting back on the road... Have an ice-cold beer for me. I'll be fine."

I didn't think it was possible that he could get any hotter than he already is, but damn, I have always been a sucker for an assertive man, one who takes control of any given situation. Between his commanding little speech and the sun beating down on him, highlighting those glistening biceps straining against his t-shirt — I'm getting hotter, and trust me, it's not the weather. "If you're okay with it, then so am I," says Jeff. "I'm sure Dad could benefit from escaping the heat and enjoying an ice-cold beer to speed things along. I know I could use one, that's for sure," he says, a hint of worry behind his words as he looks over at his father. "Are you ready to go, Charlotte?"

"Go ahead, I'll stay here and help Jax. Just order me the same: burger, fries, and a root beer. The burger medium if they ask." I am confident in the fact that I do *not* want to leave Jax's side, even if it is only for a short amount of time.

Jeff gives me a thumbs up, and together they both walk away, crossing the street in silence. Jeff's hand rests on the center of Dick's back, steadying him.

Jax smiles and looks my way, "You don't have to stay, I could do this with my eyes closed. I have changed many flat tires in my life. I just wanted to get Dick out of this heat. He was starting to worry me."

"No... I *want* to," I admit. "There is no sense in you having to do this alone. Dick will be fine once he gets into the air conditioning and grabs a bite to eat." My eyes turn towards the restaurant just as Jeff and Dick enter the front doorway. "And besides," I add, unable to help myself, "someone's gotta hold your *nuts*, right?" The dirty smirk that spreads across my face is pure trouble and completely unstoppable.

His pearly whites are on full display, as laughter erupts, causing him to stumble just a little. He grabs hold of the side of the car and says, "Well, alrighty then, Charlotte."

For some reason, hearing him say my name catches me off guard. It's simple, unexpected, and it makes my heart skip a beat. It feels right, the way my name slips off his tongue, like he's said it a million times before. *His tongue can slip off me anytime it wants.* The thought alone sends a shiver down me, my breathing quickens as I imagine it gliding across my skin.

The sun is beating down in full force at this time of day, and it glistens upon Jax's face, causing salty beads of sweat to stream down his temples. I watch him as his hand reaches up and removes his hat, wiping his forehead with the back of his arm, stripping it of any dew, letting out a deep, long sigh as he begins to work on the car's flat tire.

Everything he needs is carefully placed on the ground beside him, laid out in a neat row. All it'll take is a lug wrench, the jack, one spare tire, and a generous helping of Jax's muscles to replace its sad, deflated twin. Anyone watching him could tell that changing a demolished tire is second nature to him. I have no doubt that he could do it with his hands tied behind his back and a blindfold on. *You can blindfold me anytime you want.*

Visions of Jax, tied up, flash through my dirty mind, wild and uninvited, but I don't exactly push them away. My breathing quickens as I think of him in such a way, blindfolded and exposed, leaving me to do whatever I choose with him. Without meaning to, my eyes settle on the strength in his arms. The flexing and releasing with every pump of the jack is making me hotter than an active volcano, burning the surface of the earth. I am paralyzed by his every move. I realize that I've been holding my breath; I have to wake my brain and remind it to breathe.

"Please?" I hear it in the distance. Or maybe it's just the heat? That dizzy, floaty feeling creeps in, like when you're about to faint and someone's talking to you, but their voice comes through warped and distant. Everything's fuzzy. My mind is so tangled up in lust and heat and hazy fantasies of Jax that I don't even know what's real anymore.

"Charlotte... Can you hold these for me, please?" Jax's voice grows louder. His head cocks to one side, and his eyebrows scrunched, looking at me as if I have three heads or something.

Startling me, he breaks me out of my daydream. I jolt, reflexively smacking his hand, and the lug nuts go flying, soaring through the air before hitting the ground like tiny metal grenades, bouncing and rolling into the gravel.

"Whoa!" he says, pulling his hand back as the lug nuts rain down around us.

I gasp, and in the same breath, my eyes dart to the ground in every direction. "Oh my god, I'm so sorry!" I blurt, crouching down, frantically starting my search.

He kneels beside me, chuckling under his breath. "Guess I shouldn't sneak up on you when you're daydreaming."

My face feels like it's on fire, and I don't even bother to hide it. "Yeah, well, maybe don't touch me when I'm thinking."

He leans in a little closer, his voice is low, teasing. "Thinking about *what*, exactly?"

I freeze, and my brain short-circuits. All I can think about is ropes and his smirk, and that damned t-shirt clinging to his biceps. "Changing a tire," I lie, horribly. *I'm so bad at this.*

"Right." He laughs.

We crawl around on hands and knees, brushing gravel and dirt, searching for each runaway nut like we're on some kind of twisted Easter egg hunt.

"I think one went under the car," I say, reaching blindly beneath the frame.

Jax smirks. "You know, if you're trying to distract me with all fours and denim shorts... It's working."

I shoot him a look over my shoulder. "Careful. Remember my story about the hockey stick?" I say and hold up the wrench to him and smile.

He laughs, full and warm, and for a second, the sensation melts away into something softer. "Thanks for not freaking out. I...uh...I've been a little on edge lately."

"You don't say," he teases, then his expression softens. "Seriously though... we're all feeling it... I get it."

My breath catches at the way he says it, like he sees me. And just like that, the fantasy of the two of us together doesn't seem so far-fetched.

My knees begin to ache as we both are on all fours, using our hands to comb through the rocky roadside in hopes they haven't rolled too far. With each find, we scream out in excitement.

"I found one!" I yell, breaking the tender moment, storing it away to continue for another time.

"I've got another!" Jax adds.

"Yes!!! Found another one."

We are winning in our own game of hide and seek until we are down to the last one. The lone piece of the puzzle that will get us all on the road back home. Our fate feels doomed as the last lug nut plays hide-and-seek a little too well, tucked away somewhere far less cooperative than its scattered siblings.

With each passing minute, I lose hope that it will ever be found, and I realize it's all my fault. But as luck would have it, with all its shiny glory, the sun beams down on the last one for all to see, like a diamond in the ruff gleaming in the light.

"Found it!" we both yell as the two of us reach for it at the same time, skin to skin, our hands touch, creating a sensation unlike any other.

The entire world around me spins, and it feels amazing. Out of habit, I blurted out, "Jinx!" a game my friends and I would play when two people say the same word at the same time. Laughter explodes from me. *I'm such a dork.*

The electricity generated the moment our hands touch is enough to light up an entire city block. Our bodies are only inches apart, the space between us charged, humming. We freeze, faces so close I can feel his breath against my skin. His blue eyes locked on mine, unblinking, like time itself has paused just to see what we will do next. Our hands still cling to the nut we'd just found. Seconds seem like a day, and before I know what's happening, right here on the dirty roadside in Ohio, Jax leans in and kisses me. His tender, soft lips press against mine. A warm, intense, most perfect peck that happened so quickly, I fear I imagined it. A kiss from Jax is everything that I've longed for since the moment I met him in the elevator.

But before I can even register what's happening, he pulls away.

Jax *pulls* away.

His eyes are still on me, but there's something different in them now that worries me. Regret. It's painted all over his face, and it's *not* reassuring. Panic sets in, and suddenly I'm questioning everything: Am I a terrible kisser? Does my breath smell? *What the hell just happened?*

"I'm sorry. I shouldn't have done that." He's apologizing for something that doesn't need apologizing for.

I can't think of anything more than to have his lips pressed against mine. An awkward quiet sets in with only the humming sounds of the cars passing by, no words spoken except for the untold longing in each other's eyes. Without a care in the world, I throw caution to the wind and cup his beautiful, sweaty face in both of my hands. I lean in, tilting my head to the side. My eyes close shut, my breath heaving with anticipation, and I *kiss* him.

Not a shy peck or some maybe-this-is-a-bad-idea kiss. Nope, I go all in. A long, hard, full-on open-mouthed kiss. I have no apologies, no regrets. Just a growing heat and want, and every unsaid, pent-up feeling pressed into this moment.

His lips part, inviting my tongue to slip inside, and it doesn't hesitate. Our tongues move in perfect sync, like they were made for each other. His lips, so warm and delicate, and his tongue tastes faintly of sweet pineapple, lingering from the gummy bears that he had popped into his mouth only moments before tackling the tire. I cling to him for just a second longer, my heartbeat pounds in my chest, and then reality starts to settle in.

If only this roadside kiss could last forever. But the clock is ticking, and the other two in our party will be back before we know it. Against my better judgment, and every screaming nerve in my body, I know we have to stop. This kiss can't go any further. Not now. So reluctantly, I pull away, already hoping for a sequel. And *soon.* I lean in once more and plant one last peck against his cheek and say, *"Jax,"* breaking him free from the 'jinx' that I'd placed on him a minute ago.

The sound of his sweet laughter melts me, as he knows exactly what it means. Its sound is infectious, and I can't help but smile. In this moment, right here in my tiny little roadside bubble, everything seems right with the world, even though I know it isn't.

It doesn't take long for Jax to finish replacing the deflated tire. I stand by his side observing his every move, and I come to realize that our relationship has shifted. I am changing and have developed deep and real feelings for him, even flirting with the notion that I could be falling head over heels in love with him. I smile at the thought.

"Did you miss us?" yells Jeff, and he startles me. I jump as he makes his way across the street. He's carrying a bag in one hand and a drink in the other. Dick walks by his side, carrying another drink and a folded-up newspaper tucked under his armpit. Judging by the color on Dick's face as he heads towards us, I can tell life has been restored, and for that I am grateful. He was starting to worry me. The two of them fall in line beside Jax and me, admiring the shiny new tire on the Camry, and my mouth begins to salivate as I catch a whiff of the mouthwatering aroma of the States Best Burger.

Jax replaces the tools in their home in the trunk and takes one last look at the tire, kicking it with his boot, satisfied, then claps his hands together. "All done," he says, and we all head back into the car.

Jeff and Dick hand us our takeouts, and we settle in. The aroma of grease and pickles engulf the car as I tear open the container, grabbing a few fries and popping them in my mouth as Dick begins to read the newspaper he's just purchased. Flapping it open, back and forth, until it's just right in his hands.

"Jesus Christ," He mumbles to himself. His head shakes from side to side in disbelief, and I wonder what's got him so suddenly worked up. I catch a glimpse of the headline, bold black ink screaming from the cover, taking up nearly the entire page: **PLANES SLAM N.Y., PENTAGON**. Beneath it, two harrowing photos of New York City, covered in smoke and chaos. The images hit me like a punch to the chest. My breath catches, choking me almost. Reality crashes back in. This isn't just a leisurely road trip with a sexy cowboy beside me and some happily-ever-after fairytale. The world outside the Camry is quite literally on fire. The fries I just inhaled struggle to make their way back up. At quick speed, I swallow them back down and take a long sip of my root beer, keeping them at bay. With my nose in the air, I force my eyes away from the newspaper and try to ignore the mayhem. This safe, tiny little bubble that I've created as I sit with Jax, away from the rest of the world, seems like a better place for me. For now, at least.

CHAPTER 18

The darkness has taken over, saying farewell to the light. My time with Jax is at a slow pace, and the green rectangular mile-markers on the side of the road have all but come and gone. They descend so quickly, they're barely visible. It's nearing midnight, and we aren't far from Jeff's and Dick's homes in Lancaster County. It's odd seeing this place at night. Everything looks different in the darkness. At any other time of day, these roads are full of Amish families in their horse-drawn wagons or filled with tourists admiring the simple lifestyle they lead. But tonight, as the blackness takes over, I now see Lancaster in a much different way. The roads are scarce of life, as if everyone else is hiding from something we aren't privy to. The sky is dark and ominous, like a large black hole waiting for its chance to suck us in and swallow us whole. Occasionally, the moon fights its way to peak through, letting in the slightest bit of light. There are no stars, no airplanes, and not even fireflies are buzzing around. It's as if everyone besides the four of us senses something is about to happen, and somehow it's warning us to take cover. The throbbing pain that pulses in my right ear solidifies that notion.

Whenever the pain in my ear appears, it is without a doubt followed by a drastic change in the weather pattern. A storm front is brewing; I can feel it. The pain I've dealt with over the years never fails to let me know when Mother Nature will begin shedding her beautiful tears. A downpour of rain is coming. I'm sure of it. *Of all the gifts.*

My hand cups my ear, rubbing it in hopes that the achiness will subside. Although I know it won't work. Nothing other than time will help, and I wince a little as I rub through its throbbing pain.

"Are you okay?" Jax is concerned. "You look like you're in pain."

"I'm okay... It's just, ummmm..." I stammer on my words. "I know it sounds weird, but when the weather makes a drastic change, my ear on one side begins to hurt. It lets me know that a major change in the weather is gonna happen soon," I confess, a little apprehensive as I know it sounds ridiculous. "I don't tell many people, but I'm kind of a big deal, being a human barometer and all... I'm constantly being harassed by the news stations, asking to be their weatherman, and it gets annoying sometimes." I look away from him in hopes he won't see me laugh.

"I can't, with you. You're *crazy*. You know that?"

"You almost had me for a second there," Jeff interrupts, listening in on our conversation.

"Me too," Dick agrees.

The laughter that echoes throughout the car is infectious and reminds me of the others in the car. I almost forgot they were here.

My hands swirl in a fluid motion as I look down toward the floor of the car, giving a makeshift bow for my flawless performance.

"All kidding aside, my ear pain is no joke, but I am grateful that it only happens when the weather changes. I pretty much have a built-in weather system housed in my sinus cavity. The upside is that I know the pain won't last very long," I claim. "It's more of an annoyance than anything," I say and rub my ear once more.

"Numerous amounts of torrential rainfall are forecasted for the entire East Coast over the next several hours! Causing flash flooding in some areas!" Blasts from the car radio and echoes throughout the car.

"See...What did I tell you?" My crazy intuitions are confirmed when I laugh more than I should.

According to the loud woman crackling through the car radio, a storm front is developing, set to slam much of the East Coast, along with most of its inland neighbors. By midnight, it doesn't seem that anyone in those areas will be spared. Two things are certain, at least where I am concerned. One, you can never trust the weatherman; everything, especially the weather, is always changing. They rarely are correct when it comes to a good storm. It could be clear skies throughout the night for all we know. It's one of the only jobs you can have, making a boatload of money, yet you are almost always wrong.

The second is that even though the rain can be annoying at times, secretly, I love a good rainstorm. Sitting outside under a covered porch during a thunderstorm, while sipping on a hot cup of herbal tea, with a trashy romance novel in hand, could be my favorite pastime. And that's for one reason only: when storms hit, I'm usually safe at home and in control. Being stuck in a car, miles from home, with a storm rolling in? That's a whole different story.

"Want to hear something that you wouldn't know about me?" blurts out of my mouth.

"I'm not sure, do I?" Jax side-eyes me and laughs.

"Well... While I love a good storm, sitting out on the deck of my home is one of my favorite things... Driving in one, let alone in the direct path of one as massive as this one, terrifies me. It's the same every time." My breathing quickens at the thought. "The panic sets in, causing my heart to beat a thousand times per minute, close to popping right out of my chest… or at least that is how it feels while it's happening." My palms begin to sweat. "My hands will then cramp from gripping whatever is near to grab hold, so hard. Not to mention the ridiculous, mind-blowing scenarios that will run through my crazy head. All of which always ends with me stranded alone on the side of the road and being snatched up by a psychopath. Always ending the same way, with me tied up in their basement, while they rub lotion all over my body." I explain, giving him a crazy, unrealistic, detailed scenario of what could happen.

He stares at me, probably wondering what kind of weirdo he has gotten himself involved in. "*Ohhhhh…* You're being serious, aren't you?"

"I watch way too many horror movies," I admit, then we both laugh at just how crazy I sound.

Coming off as some scared, infantile, crazy chick is not how I want Jax to view me, so I pray that the clueless weathermen and their predictions are wrong.

As we near Jeff's house, with about half an hour more to go, the rain begins to fall. At first, it comes down as a trickle. The wipers continue to swish from left to right in a rhythmic motion, and oddly, it has a calming effect on me as I watch them. The occasional annoying rubbing sound they're making, when the windshield is too dry, breaks the flow. It's an awful sound that can grate at your very soul. (God, I hate it.) Although if the rain continues at this pace, I'll gladly accept that annoyance until the end of our trip. The unnerving sound is better than the alternative, the impending thunderstorm.

Judging by the way that Dick and Jeff fidget in their seats, you can tell that we're getting close to their homes. Ants in your pants, my mother would say when I was young, whenever I was eager to get somewhere.

Jeff weaves his way through the traffic and now drives with such ease through the county he calls his home, making turns as if they're embedded in his brain and second nature to him. Without a doubt, he is beyond excited, and I couldn't blame him one tiny bit. It's been a long, exhausting few days, and we all can't wait to be home with our families, relax under a hot shower, and enjoy a warm home-cooked meal.

"I bet Sally can't wait to see you and is waiting by the window in anticipation right now," I say.

Jeff smiles at the mention of her name. "I bet... I know I can't wait to see her beautiful smile. It's been hard to make much sense of all of this without her with me and not having her by my side through it," he admits. His voice chokes up at his admission, then clears it just as quickly so I won't notice. "We literally do *everything* together."

"I bet your mother is pacing the floors behind her, waiting for the two of us," Dick says to Jeff.

Jeff laughs and agrees, "For sure. And I bet the table is filled with thirty-seven different kinds of desserts waiting for us, too."

"If it's one thing in regard to your mother, it's that when she is nervous or scared, she will bake everything she has the ingredients for." I look over to him, wanting to capture this rare moment of joy, and I can't help but notice a tear escaping from the corner of his eye.

The trip was hard for Jax and me, no doubt, but I can assume that it's been even more so for the two of them, given they both have wives and children at home to get back to. Both are such strong men, but every so often, I would catch glimpses of their anxiety in the hand we'd been dealt. That doesn't go without saying that they were also good at disguising it as well, like when the car tire had blown out. I saw the look of fear in Jeff's reflection through the mirror just as he did mine, and when our eyes locked, his demeanor all but changed. For that, I am grateful that, by good fortune, he accepted the father figure role that I needed to feel safe, even if just for the past few days. I can't imagine being so far from home during this awful tragedy, and it taking days to get back to the family you are so accustomed to taking care of and protecting. *We're almost there, guys.*

As we draw nearer to Jeff's home, his shoulders decompress, relaxing the very moment he pulls into his driveway. A weight's been lifted, and relief washes over him. I can't help but take notice as they step out into the misty night of their housing development that the two of them let out a long, deep breath that neither probably knew they'd been holding. The two men who kept me from falling apart, who made me feel safe through the chaos, are both now safe and sound. I should be happy for them. I want to be happy for them. But as the emotions I've been holding at bay start to rise, my stomach twists and turns into tiny knots. The feeling is all too familiar. It's not relief. It's sadness, heavy, aching, and impossible to ignore. From the moment this entire tragedy began, I've wanted nothing more than to get home, and now that it's happening, I feel a tinge of sadness that it's ending.

Over the past few days, I have spent every waking second crammed into a car with them. There isn't much you can hide from someone when you are in a confined space for such an extended period of time. We practically know everything about one another, and I am going to miss them immensely.

The four of us have shared something so profound that nothing could tear us apart; we will forever be tied together. I love each one of them, each in their separate ways: Dick as a grandfather, Jeff as a father figure, and Jax as my potential other half.

Together, we begin unpacking the trunk, freeing their belongings that have been stashed away for days. The rain still trickles at a slow, steady rhythm from the dark sky above, like a living metaphor, soaking our clothes just as it soaks our journey, dampening everything it touches. Each one of us is hesitant and nervous to speak, for it would mean an end to an era and to the undeniable bond we have grown so accustomed to.

Jax breaks the ice. "I can't thank you enough for offering up the ride to bring me home. It was very generous of you." He shakes Jeff's hand

and pulls him in for a hug as if they've known each other for years. Jeff promises to meet up with him for lunch soon, knowing all too well that it might never happen. Life will continue and move forward, and the three of them might never see each other again. But for now, we take solace in the fact that we all hold a special place in each of our memories, of the time the earth stood still.

"September eleventh will never be forgotten," I blurt out as I pull Jeff in for a lengthy hug that I refuse to let go of. My tears fall and absorb into his damp polo, and he doesn't pull away.

"That's for sure...The awful noises that came from you in the back seat when you slept will forever be embedded in my brain," he jokes, lightening up the mood.

"I did no such thing!" I smack him on the arm.

"Don't worry. It will be our little secret." Jeff winks.

"Thank you for taking care of me this week... I love you." And I hug him once more.

"I love you too. Just like you were my own." He confesses and kisses the side of my head. "Now let me go inside before you make me cry too."

"Where's my goodbye hug?" My head spins. It's Dick. "What am I, chopped liver?" The three of us stand there staring back at him in shock. "What? I have feelings too." His smile grows.

I walk over and hug him with such gratitude and love that I never knew was there before, "I'm gonna miss you, you old fart." The rain begins to fall at a much heavier pace now.

He squeezes me tight, kisses my forehead, and pushes me away just as quickly as he embraced me. "Now enough of all this mushy stuff. Get the hell out of here... I'm getting soaked!" he bellows.

"I love you too." I laugh, then fall into line next to Jax as we stand and watch the two of them disappear into the front door of its massive home. Two sets of anxious eyes peer out from the curtain behind the window, waiting for their loved ones.

Sadness creeps in once again, but in a flash, I push it aside, knowing our connection and the deep bond that had been forced upon us could never be broken.

Would the date of 9/11 be the next Pearl Harbor? Twenty years from now, would it be memorialized throughout our country with stories, monuments, and buildings? Will schools across the country hold patriot days, honoring the victims with children showing off their red, white, and blue? I wonder.

No matter what may happen, the four of us will always have our own similar story to share.

Crack!!!!!! Screams from the sky above, breaking me from my thoughts.

A flash of bright light darts through the sky, immediately followed by the loudest *roar* of thunder I've ever heard, causing both Jax and me to jump. Before we know it, we're being drenched, buckets of rain pouring from the angry skies above, as if the storm has finally lost its patience. It comes out of nowhere, soaking us in a matter of seconds. We don't speak, just run. Our thoughts are perfectly aligned, desperate for the car's shelter like it's the last safe place on earth. We stumble inside, breathless and soaked, the doors slamming shut behind us. For a moment, the only sound is the rain pounding hard against the roof, steady and relentless. Until my phone rings from the back seat of the car. I quickly reach back and grab it.

"Hello?" I say.

There is a moment of silence.

"Charlotte? Thank God... Why haven't you called me back? I have left you messages ever since the attacks... Are you okay?" James says and questions me like we're still an engaged couple. As if I didn't catch him cheating only a few months ago.

My heart thuds, my shoulders slump, and I glance over at Jax. I let out a sigh. By the look on his face, he can sense my despair. I feel deflated.

"I've been trying to reach you for days." He admits. His voice cracks with emotion.

I close my eyes, and for a moment, I feel bad for him. He sounds genuinely concerned. He sounds remorseful. He sounds desperate. And for some reason, I feel self-conscious.

"I'm fine."

"Thank God." He lets out a shaky breath. "I was going nuts... I couldn't stop thinking about you. About us." He declares. "I know I fucked up... But what just happened a few days ago was the wake-up call I needed... I need you."

My throat is dry, and I look away from Jax, toward the rain-soaked window. For a split second, I falter. The ache of familiarity tugs at my heartstrings. The promise of what we had. Something safe.

I turn back around and see Jax's face. His stare cuts through me, rain dripping from his brow. "Just because the world is at a standstill right now doesn't mean you need to take a step backwards... Don't settle for the past... Take a step forward." Jax says in a low but steady voice.

I smile because he is right.

"James," I say slowly and confidently, "I think the wake-up call is mine."

I don't wait for a reply, and I hang up the phone.

CHAPTER 19

Outside, thunder roars, loud and commanding, like Simba on Pride Rock in *The Lion King,* announcing his reign to the world. What started as the pitter-patter of rain, dancing on the windshield, has now developed into a steady downpour being dumped from the angry clouds above. We're soaked through, sitting in the car like two overcooked noodles. I let out a breath, chest still heaving. I look over at him, deadpan. "Well, that was fun." I say, "If this were a movie, this is the part where we either fall in love or get eaten by velociraptors."

He laughs. "Honestly, I'd take the Raptors. At least they wouldn't make me drive in this weather." We burst out laughing, because honestly, what else can we do at this point?

Strong gusts of wind shake the car with such intensity that every hair on Jax's arms is on high alert. His grip on the steering wheel is forceful, causing the veins in his biceps to pop. I don't think a crowbar could separate the two if I tried. *I kind of don't want to.* His damp shirt is almost see-through, exposing the sexy side he keeps tucked away, and I can't help but stare. *What I wouldn't give to be his shirt right now, covering his soaking wet body like a blanket and clinging to his every move.*

The overwhelming urge to touch him wins out before I can change my mind. My hand, still trembling, reaches across the space between us and lands on his arm, his bicep, firm and flexed, like it's been bracing for more than just the rain. In an instant, it relaxes at my touch.

"Are you okay? Do you think it's wise to keep driving in these conditions?" My hand still rests on him. "Maybe we should seek shelter for the night in a nearby motel until the storm passes, when it's safer to drive."

I'm not quite sure if I'm worried about our safety, or if my subconscious just wants to spend the night alone in a motel room with Jax now that Jeff and Dick are no longer with us. If I had to guess, I'd have to say a combination of both.

The awkward silence that all of a sudden fills the car makes me question what I've just suggested. Aside from the steady pounding of the rainfall outside, the absolute silence of the Camry is deafening. I'm suddenly terrified he can hear the frantic pounding of my heart, louder, it seems, than the rain outside. And just like that, horror crashes over me. *Did I seriously just ask him to rent a motel room and spend the night with me? Jesus Christ, Charlotte, you sound like a skank.*

"I think you're right. I can barely keep the car on the road, let alone see two feet in front of me. The rain isn't letting up," Jax says, breaking the awkward moment I've created in my mind.

His words barely leave his mouth when Mother Nature herself decides to entertain us with her own personal warning, as a loud crackling sound is heard from outside the car. A tree limb has fallen and landed only three feet from our car. Jax swerves to the left and avoids smashing into it.

"Jesus Christ! That was close!" I yell nervously. The grip I have on the door handle is powerful. My other hand is pressed firmly against the dashboard in front of me. The rapid pounding of my heart feels like it's beating at maximum speed, ready to explode and break straight through my chest.

He regains control over the car, his hands steady on the wheel again. I draw a deep breath, trying to steady myself too, willing my heart to settle.

Then he speaks, voice low, almost careful. "This is way too dangerous. I am not going to risk you getting hurt. I'm certain that we need to wait this out." He confesses. "We can make up the last hours in the morning."

I turn toward my window, just enough so to be out of his eyesight and smile, my insides squealing with delight. *Thank you, Mother Nature. I owe you one.*

* * *

The motel is eerily quiet, and an older woman sits contentedly behind the outdated Formica counter as we approach the courtesy desk. The worn corners of it, with chunks missing, showcase the wear and tear from its use over the years. Crowning her head is a flawlessly sculpted bun, so precise, I'd bet good money it started as a full head of shiny brown locks. Now a beautiful shade of silvery gray, hints of color are still visible in some strands around the ends. A pair of thin-wired reading glasses sits just on the tip of her nose, teetering on its edge, ready to topple off at the slightest movement. The silky white button-down that she's wearing is gorgeous with the tiny pink flowers that engulf it. Pinned to the pocket just above her breast is a stitched green name tag, likely sewn on by hand, that reads *Noreen*. It suits her. There's something steady and no-nonsense about her, like she'd keep a first-aid kit, a sewing kit, and a backup plan all in the same purse. I like her already.

She remains motionless, engrossed in the book she's lost in, and hasn't even noticed the two of us walk through the automatic entry doors. I can't help but wonder what the title is, but from the angle that she has it propped, the cover isn't visible enough for me to see. *Dang! That must be one damn good book. I really need to find out what it is.*

There's a small silver bell placed on the edge of the counter, just like a prop in the movies, with a handwritten sign alongside it that reads, "Ring bell for assistance." I can tell by the way Jax is fidgeting, he's chomping at the bit and can't wait to reach over and push it, just as the sign suggests. He stares at it with such intent, as if he can make it ring with his mind like he's some sort of telepathic superhero. His hand begins to rise. *Don't do it!*

"A-hem!" I quickly interject, and his hand lowers back down, disappointment in his eyes. I laugh a little to myself. *He's like a little boy. So stinkin' cute.*

"Oh, my!" Poor Noreen springs from her seat, startled, knocking her book to the ground beneath her, her glasses falling along in the process. *I knew they wouldn't last long.*

In quick fashion, she bends over and collects the book along with her readers, repeatedly apologizing for not noticing the two of us when we walked in.

"I'm so sorry." Sheepishly, she apologizes, then sets the book down, its cover now facing directly my way. *Yessss.*

"We would like to rent two rooms, please," Jax states, taking control of the situation and letting Noreen off the hook.

He continues to explain that we need two rooms, one for him and one for me. *Two?????*

Noreen scans through the front-desk computer, searching for two suitable vacancies, her focus unwavering. My eyes, however, drift back to Jax. Droplets of rain still cling to his face, dripping slowly down the angles of his jaw. He's soaked straight through his t-shirt, the fabric clinging to his chest, outlining every curve of the six-pack he probably doesn't even know he's showing off. I swallow hard. *Damn.* My hormones are screaming, "touch him," but my brain, the buzzkill, steps in. So, I just smile, praying he doesn't notice my internal tug-of-war.

"*Ah...* Tonight is your lucky night." The excitement in her voice is unexpected. *Oh, Noreen, you have no idea.* "There are only two vacant rooms left, and they're all yours." She boasts proudly. "It just so happens that they're adjoining. So, you have access to both rooms if you choose to do so." She looks my way, a hint of a smile peeking through. *Noreen, you naughty little woman.* I smile back. *Gotta love girl code.*

"They sound perfect. Thank you." Jax hands over his credit card. "This will take care of both rooms." he says in a flash, never giving me the chance to even reach for my purse.

Noreen's fingers fly across the keyboard at record speed. She hits the final key, exhales and reaches under the counter for something hidden from view. She returns to her upright position, holding two sets of room keys that dangle from her slender, aging fingers.

"Room one-oh-six is the best room in the house." Jax laughs along with her and takes the set of keys she holds up. "And number one-oh-seven is your lucky number, pretty little lady." Noreen winks my way and hands over my set. *Yes ma'am... It sure as hell is...*

She directs us toward the long, empty hallway behind us and says, "Straight down the hall and they'll be on your left."

I'm thankful that we came prepared, overnight bags already slung over our shoulders, packed with everything we'll need for the night. No need for either of us to dart back into the torrential downpour. Together, we thank lovely Noreen for her help, leaving her to once again lose herself in her book, alone in the lobby. We turn toward the way she has directed us, then head for our rooms.

"Oh, and don't forget that the rooms are adjoining... All you have to do is unlock the door in between for easier access." We hear her yell at us as we approach the hall. *Very subtle, Noreen.*

I turn back and look over my shoulder and wink. "I like her!"

Excitement and anticipation pulse through me, and the thought of being alone in a room with just a door between us feels downright intoxicating. The fiery heat coursing through my veins threatens to burn me alive.

It's an older, outdated motel; the hallway floor still looks like it's the original one from the opening so long ago. The musty smell of basements fills the air, dragging me back to childhood fears – when I was convinced monsters lurked below, waiting for their chance to feast on me.

Just when we find our rooms, Jax reaches into his front pocket for the key he tucked away earlier, like he knew this moment was coming. The motel is so old that it still has an actual key, complete with a dime-store keychain attached. Nothing like the electronic key cards I had days before, back in Vegas. I, too, pull mine from my pocket, turning it in the palm of my hand, double-checking the number on it. *One-oh-seven* is printed on both sides of the oval, worn-out rubber keychain attached. So tattered, the numbers are barely visible on one side; it looks more like it says *one-U-one.*

"Go ahead," he says, motioning toward the door for me to enter the room first. "I want to make sure you're safely inside before I go into mine." The compelling protectiveness he has over me is sexy. Warmth creeps up my neck. *Just unlock the door, Noreen said.*

I do as I am told and place the key into its counterpart and turn the knob, opening it in a slow manner. A familiar odor smacks me in the face the moment that I do.

"Whoa!" The unusual way Jax scrunches his nose shows his disapproval.

147

"Reminds me of my grandmother's house. She always had a Virginia Slim dangling from her lips," I say, smiling at the thought.

"Niceeeee. Did she drink whisky too?" He jokes.

"Well, now that you mention it," I push open the door wide enough for me to enter. Jax is a step behind me. *You can stay if you want. I don't mind.*

My eyes never leave him as he checks the bathroom, pulling back the shower curtain, then placing it back the way it's intended. He makes his way to the main part of the room and assures me that all is good. The two of us stand unnerved and stare at the closed door that joins our rooms together.

"Just unlock it and go through that way if you want." I nod toward the direction of the adjoining door as I set down my overnight bag on the edge of my bed. "It's silly for you to leave and go back into the hallway, just to enter your room that's literally right there," I say.

"As long as you're okay with it," he says, a little unsure.

"Totally okay."

"Great... I'm gonna go and take a hot shower. Knock if you need anything," he says and unlocks the door, pulls on the knob, then slams right into it. His entire body bounces back a few inches, and he turns back to me.

"Well, there goes that theory... Apparently, the door needs to be unlocked from the other side too." His face flushes with embarrassment as he rubs his forehead and laughs.

"Oops." I smile back at him as he makes his way over and back out the door we just came from. "Be careful..." I yell and tease him just for fun.

The next thing I hear is the sharp bang from his door closing behind him, then a clicking noise coming from the adjoining door lock. I smile at the very sound.

"That's better." The door opens just enough for his head to poke through. "I'm gonna get in the shower now. You gonna be okay?"

"Yes, of course," I assure him. "I think I'm gonna call Jennifer before I take mine."

I sit on the edge of the bed closest to the window, assessing the room from one side to the other. The room itself is nothing special, your standard roadside motel room, and without a doubt, nothing like the flashy, gaudy Vegas room I had slept in only a few days ago. It couldn't be more polar opposite, with all its glitz and glamor in every detail, the bold, bright colors of the curtains and duvet. This room quite possibly could be its evil twin, but in an odd way, just as charming.

The entire room is dim, wrapped in shadows. The only light comes from a single lamp perched on the bedside table, casting a soft glow that barely reaches the corners. It's brass with a beige colored shade and looks like something straight out of an antique store. Mauve colored flowers cover every inch of the papered walls and look strikingly the same as the ones in my parents' bathroom back home. Flowers stretch in every direction, as far as the eye can see, an explosion of prints that seem to swallow the room whole, making the room seem smaller than it actually is. The floor appears to be the only detail in the room that's been updated, for which I am grateful. Pearly white square tiles cover it from wall to wall and head into the bathroom. It shines so bright that I can almost see my reflection in it. I love a cold tile floor to place my feet on in the morning. Nothing wakes you up faster than cold feet. *And a hot cup of coffee, of course.*

Two queen-size beds take up most of the space in the tiny room, but still big enough for a small family. Thank goodness for me, no "small family" will be occupying them tonight. The only one who will be enjoying this room is me. *Unless Jax decides he could use a roommate for the night. I certainly wouldn't object.* The thought of the two of us in bed alone all night in our two-bedroom 'love shack,' excites me.

Covering each of the beds is a thick, soft, bone white duvet cover. Their crisp, clean linens blend into the floor as if they are one and the same, like a blanket of fresh-fallen snow on a cold winter morning. Completing the decor is an extensive array of pillows in every size and firmness that cover the head of the bed.

Who in the world needs that many pillows?

There's a lightning show coming from outside the window, bright lights flash through the curtain panels, making their way inside and causing the room to be brighter than it had been just a moment ago. The thunder outside is so violent, it makes me flinch at its raw fierceness.

The storm appears to be in full swing; signs of it ending anytime soon are nowhere in sight.

I busy myself with unloading some items from my overnight bag onto the surface of the bureau. On top of it holds a large, box-style television, and judging by its bulky frame, it's probably been here since the sixties. My jammies, toothbrush and toothpaste, a hairbrush, and some lotion all sit on the counter in front of me. Everything I'll need after my shower. Last but certainly not least, I pull out my razor. *Just in case a silky smooth vajay-jay is in order.*

It's faint, but I can still hear Jax's voice talking to someone through the paper-thin walls. He must be on the phone, which reminds me to call Jennifer.

I pick up my phone and dial her number. "Hello?" Her voice is groggy, and I can barely make out her words.

"Shit… Are you sleeping?" I apologize.

"I was… It's fine. What's up?"

"Oh, nothing… I just wanted to tell you that I'm in a motel room, right next to the sexy cowboy, with only a door between the two of us," I say matter-of-factly. "No biggie."

"No way! Are you fucking serious?" she screams into the phone. Instinctively, I cover it with my hand in fear that Jax can hear. *Really Charlotte?*

"Oh, and did I forget to mention that we kissed on the roadside earlier today?" I toy with her, knowing she lives for this sort of gossip.

"Shut up!" she squeals in delight. "Wait! I just realized you said you had separate rooms. Why the hell would you go and do that? Have I not taught you anything?" She reminds me of Kit De Luca scolding Vivian in the movie, *Pretty Woman*.

"I don't know… he asked for two rooms during check-in. I wasn't gonna act like some skank and object."

"Are you sure he isn't gay?"

My head shakes at the absurdity of her question. "He isn't gay, Dummy." I pick at a piece of wet lint that hangs limp from the hem of my shirt. "He's a gentleman."

"Whatever… Gentleman/shmentleman. I don't care. Just get your ass over there and have sex with the cute cowboy," she demands. "One of us needs to be having sex, and God knows I'm not!"

"Okay, Miss Bossy Bitch! Love you… I'll be home tomorrow, and we can talk more."

"And it better be with juicy details. Now go get-em, Cowgirl." Her devilish laughter grows louder by the second.

"Don't expect much. You know I'm all talk when it comes to this stuff. You're the hussy, not me."

"Then leave him for me. What's the address?" Jennifer snaps back, giggling like a sixteen-year-old girl with a bad case of hormones.

"Hell no! Get your own. *Byeeeeeee…*" I say as I hang up, her cackling still echoes in my ear.

All of a sudden, the room is filled with silence, except for the storm outside and the sound of water trickling through the pipes of this old motel. They come from the direction of Jax's room. *He must be showering.*

In an instant, butterflies come alive, their fluttering sparking every nerve ending inside me that I didn't know I had. Visions of Jax's wet, naked body consume my every thought, and I start to break out in a full-on sweat. I picture the water cascading down his body, soap tracing each carved muscle, his hands slick and purposeful as they move south, toward the part of him I already know would ruin me. With only a door standing between us, it's all I can do to stop myself from undressing right here and slipping into the hot shower with him. Sweat beads over me like a second skin, slicking my palms, trickling down my forehead, gathering in all the most inconvenient places. It's relentless, a sticky reminder of everything I'm trying not to feel. I glisten like a disco ball on New Year's Eve.

I can't shake the image of Jax, his cock slick with lather, and his hand wrapped around it. The thought burns through me, and before I realize it, my own drifts downward, settling between my thighs. I trace a gentle line over the rain-soaked fabric that clings to me, the sensation a tease, frustrating and electric all at once.

Good Lord, Charlotte, get a hold of yourself, girl.

"Damn you, Jennifer!" I speak the words out loud and laugh, even though she can't know.

With much defiance, I force my hand away and erase all thoughts of Jax's bare body from my filthy mind, just enough to finish unpacking and get ready for a shower. I make my way into the bathroom and turn on the faucet, running my hand under the water to gauge its temperature. I then turn and reach for a towel before undressing, but there's nothing there, empty. Not a towel in sight.

"Are you kidding me?" My eyes scan the tiny bathroom, and of course, none can be found. *Grrrrr.* "I'll grab one from Jax," I tell myself, confident that his room will have one to spare.

My head pokes through the adjoining door, half expecting to catch a glimpse of him. I hear the sound of the shower being turned off, then a swooshing sound, from the curtain being pulled from one side to the other. The image of his hard, wet body exposed to its fullest extent is all but killing me. *Ohhhh, what I wouldn't give to be a fly on that wall.*

"Tap. Tap. Tap." I knock on the door. "Jax? Can I come in?"

"Yeah… It's open," he yells. "Is everything okay?" he asks as I walk through the door.

The moment I do, he appears from out of the bathroom, his body glistens, still wet from the hot shower. (Ohhh, in all his glorious hotness, did he appear.) *Now that's an entrance!*

His hair is damp, tousled, and clearly the result of a lazy towel dry. No brush in sight, and honestly, it works for him. From his waist down, he is covered only by the towel that's wrapped around him, hanging low just beneath his belly button. A strip of dark hair pokes out from it. *Mmmmm, a happy trail.* I stop at the sight, gape at him for a moment, and I pray he doesn't notice.

His upper half is my favorite look by far. Bare and still moist from the steamy hot shower, my mouth falls open, hovering just above the floor, staring longer than I should. I need to remind myself to close my mouth before he notices me drooling. Each defined ridge of his abs gleams like an open invitation, and I am the intended guest. I feel like an attendee in a museum admiring a beautiful, sculpted piece of art. "DO NOT TOUCH!" the sign would say. Only, I've never been good at following the rules.

"What's up?" He fingers through his damp hair. *Good Lord, I swear he taunts me on purpose like it's some sort of game he is playing.*

"Do you have an extra towel? For some reason, mine doesn't have any."

"You want this one?" He tugs on the top of his towel, and my cheeks flush. A slow heat stirs between my thighs, sparked by the way he looks at me. "I'm just playing… Grab what you want."

Well, if you insist…

I enter the bathroom and collect a towel and washcloth. They're warm, a result of Jax's recent shower. My brain short-circuits with another round of naked Jax flashbacks. Right here, just minutes ago. *Is it hot in here, or what?* "Girl, you need to stop," I say to my reflection in the foggy mirror.

"Did you say something?" Jax yells at me from the other room.

"Uhhh... just talking to myself... I'm good." I stammer and exit the bathroom. "I'm gonna go shower now. Thanks for the towel," I say and walk through the door, purposely leaving it ajar.

My hand glides along the inside of my bathroom door, searching for the switch to activate the fan. I flip it on when an unrecognizable sound screeches from it. I'm no electrician, but it sounds pretty wonky and doesn't seem to do much of anything but make a loud buzzing noise. I leave it on without a second thought, out of sheer habit. Before disrobing, I pull back the curtain, assuring myself that there isn't someone hiding behind it, with intentions of murdering me. "Didn't I just check the curtain three minutes ago?" I roll my eyes at my ridiculousness and reach for the faucet, twisting the knob until it won't budge any farther.

I step into the scalding shower, close the curtain, and let the piping hot water work its magic.

"*Ahhhh!* This feels divine," I say to myself. "The hotter the better. Just how I like my men."

My eyes close and take in the warmth, and I try to remember the last time I had a nice shower. It's been only a few days since my last "proper" one, but as the water trickles down over my shoulders, it feels more like years. Every chance on the ride home, whether it be at a rest stop or gas station bathroom, I would take a few minutes to myself, freshening up to feel human again. Reeking like a day-old hoagie in a trash can while sitting inches from Jax? Yeah... That wasn't happening.

Needless to say, this hot shower feels like heaven on earth.

The tiny bar of motel soap sits in its dish that protrudes from the shower wall, its wrapper still intact. I pick it up and unwrap it, and I envision Jax running through the same motions only minutes before. I hold it under the water and lather it until my palms are full of tiny soapy bubbles. A bare-naked Jax, once again, invades every inch of my mind, and I'm starting to believe that it's my subconscious's favorite pastime. I begin to wash, and every time my hands meet my body, every crevice I clean, I fantasize that it's Jax's touch, caressing me. I flash back to earlier in the day, to our first kiss along the roadside—the weight of his lips against mine, the taste of sweet pineapple that lingered on his tongue. I'm falling fast, craving his touch, aching to feel his tongue inside me once more, setting every nerve on fire. It's all so fresh in my mind. So instead of pretending I don't feel it, I let the desire take over, slowly, completely, until I finally stop fighting what I've wanted all along.

My eyes close once more, blocking out the rest of the world and leaving only Jax to occupy them as the piping hot water falls, burning my skin, and I don't mind. My hands cease to exist; it is Jax's that I envision touching me. In slow and steady motion, my hand glides over my breasts and across my hard nipples, tiny bubbles gathering underneath them. My breathing intensifies as my hand makes its way over and meets its twin, giving it the satisfaction it too craves. The sensation building inside me surges, growing fast, as my hand continues to move downward. Tiny bubbles are left in its path. Lather spreads across my stomach, and my fingers trail lower, finding their way to that sweet, familiar place between my thighs, one they know all too well. They're at ease, knowing exactly where I long to be touched. A little unsteady, I regain my balance with my other hand, placing it against the shower wall, and lift my unsteady leg onto the edge of the tub. Bubbles build around me in a rush, but all I feel is the growing pressure between my legs. My fingers move in a slow, steady rhythm, each movement deliberate, coaxing pleasure with every stroke.

I continue in a circular motion, quickening the pace. Moans slip out before I can stop them, unrestrained, as my body pulses with pleasure. I freeze for a heartbeat, praying Jax can't hear what he's doing to me, without even knowing. I resume the assault on my body, my breath falling into the same steady rhythm. My head tips back, allowing water to cascade over my cheeks before streaming down my chest, gliding over firm, now tender breasts. Instinctively, my eyes close, and I fantasize that Jax is touching me. I can see him more clearly now. His strong hands push me against the wall as his tongue licks at the nape of my neck. My body can't take much more. I can almost feel the impact of his penis driving deep inside me, causing me to cry out for more. "*Ahhhhhhhhh.*" I surrender to the visions of Jax, letting them consume me, and welcome the convulsions of release as the orgasm takes hold. *I'm gonna sleep well tonight.*

My breathing resumes to a more normal speed, and I finish washing what's left of my body, being more careful around my newly tender areas. I step out onto the cold, damp tile floor, being careful not to slip. *Damn it, I should have grabbed another towel.* I begin drying my body, starting from head to toe in a sequential order that my brain has on autopilot. I give special care to the tender spot between my thighs, still sensitive and recovering from the not-so-gentle beating I just gave it.

The hotel's tiny bottle of lotion feels nice as I smooth it into my damp skin, covering every square inch of my body. The subtle notes of coconut and vanilla scents left behind not only soothe my body but also reach the very being of my soul. I pull on my pink laced panties, the ones saved for 'special' occasions. *Will this night end up being a special occasion?* I follow with a pair of thin, blue-striped men's boxer shorts, the same ones I still haven't outgrown from my high school days. *Yes, I said boxers.* Every girl in school back then wore them, especially to the pep rallies. They were all the rage for a *brief* time back in the day. Give me a pair of boxers to sleep in over a pair of expensive satin nighties any day of the week.

Next, I give some much-needed attention to my knotty blonde hair, brushing it until it's smooth, freeing it from the knots that it had endured during the road trip. I continue my nightly routine care by brushing any filth from my teeth, using my convenience-store-purchased toothbrush, leaving my breath minty fresh. At last, I pull on my favorite blue t-shirt, "I NEED YOU" written in bold white letters across my chest. The title of one of my favorite country songs.

I give myself one last glance in the mirror and can't help but smirk, realizing the words couldn't be any more fitting for tonight. *But is it a need or a want? Ahhhh, tomato... tomahto.*

"Oh well," I say to my reflection with a shrug. "The shirt doesn't lie."

I switch off the bathroom light, satisfied with my night ensemble, and enter the main part of the bedroom, which just so happens to be where I will spend the entire night sleeping next to the handsome Jaxson Lange. *Well.... Maybe, if I have anything to do with it.*

CHAPTER 20

The dividing door that separates our rooms remains open. I tap only once, giving no intention of waiting for a response, and I enter Jax's room. The television is turned down low, barely audible, and tuned to a channel that I have no idea. A woman in a bright blue mini dress, spiked high heels, and a boatload of makeup covering her face, points to a large red shaded portion of the map on the screen. From what I can gather, Lancaster County is right in the eye of the storm, bearing the worst of it, with widespread flooding and heavy damage reported. She recaps the events, giving a detailed description of where, as she points to the various colors on the map. It appears to be traveling more quickly, moving upwards towards the Northeast. The storm should subside by early morning, ensuring that the two of us can hit the road first thing.

Jax reclines against the headboard, bare from the waist up, supported by a stack of motel pillows that somehow make him look even more inviting. One leg is sprawled across the bed while the other is left to dangle off to the side. His bare chest calls to me, practically begging me to reach out and touch it. Gone is the towel from earlier, replaced by red and black buffalo plaid pajama bottoms. *Now he's irresistible and smug about it, too.* I smile. They are sexy, but wholesome at the same time, and I think I have a matching pair back home.

Jax is lost in the television, and I'm oblivious to him. He hasn't realized that I've been standing here all this time. His mind is elsewhere, maybe engrossed by the storm, or possibly the woman in the blue dress, maybe both.

"She's pretty," I blurt out without thinking.

His head turns in record time, and he finally takes notice. "Oh, hey." He pauses a moment before finishing. "Yeah, she is, but not my type."

"Oh?" I take a step closer to the bed. "And what is your type?"

His eyes meet mine, steady. "I'm looking at it." No hint of a smile, no trace of a joke. Just the truth. "She's got nothing on you... *You're* beautiful." His eyes never leave mine, and I'm left speechless with the blonde bombshell yapping in the background.

Seconds feel like days as I stare back at him.

"How was your shower?" He cuts through the awkward silence that fills the room. "After the past few days we've had, it felt good, right?"

Visions of moments ago flicker through my mind, making my cheeks flush and my skin glow, but I answer truthfully and say, "Very satisfying." He laughs a little and agrees with me, but for much different reasons than my own.

"Would you like some company?" I ask, and I don't know why, but I'm nervous.

"Of course I would," he says without skipping a beat. "I mean... You need me... soooo." He jokes, points to my shirt, then pats the space on the bed next to him.

I strode over to the vacant side of his bed, mimicking him, propping up a few of the pillows, and I comfortably sat down next to him.

His eyes make their way across my body, fixated on me, finally landing on my middle region, "Boxers, huh?" and smiles.

"Yup… I never leave home without them."

"I like 'em." His stare remains still, focused on the patch of exposed skin that's left between my t-shirt and the boxers.

I laugh to myself, hoping these boxers don't stay on much longer – especially if he's the one taking them off. I wonder if he has any idea what he's doing to me right now. Suddenly, his eyes flick to mine, questioning, but he doesn't say a word. *I swear he can see right through me.*

I smirk, imagining the playful possibilities with these boxers. His gaze sharpens, catching the look of mischief in my eyes.

"Something amusing?" he asks, his voice tinged with curiosity.

I bite my lip. "Just a thought."

He raises an eyebrow as if the unknowing is killing him.

I take a step closer, "I was just thinking… these boxers might not stay on for long."

A slow smile spreads across his face. "Is that so?"

I nod and can feel the heat rise in my cheeks. "Depends on you."

He reaches out and takes my hand, pulling me closer until our bodies barely touch. The tension is building; every breath echoes in the silence of the room. But then, he lets go, releasing my hand and scooching back a few inches, creating a distance between us. "As much as I'd love to continue this," he says, his voice steady and firm, "we should probably get some rest."

I blink, the sudden change catching me off guard. "Right," I reply, trying desperately to steady my breathing. I'm frozen, mortified by Jax's rejection. I don't want to move. I can't move. So together, we sit in silence, with the television volume on low, its sound almost non-existent.

The room feels heavy, all of a sudden, with unspoken words. I can sense Jax's presence beside me, yet there is a void between us now. *Did I misread the signals? Was I too forward?* The questions run rampant, but I remain still.

To distract myself from the waiting, I focus my gaze on the flickering images on the screen, muted like my emotions. We pretend to watch for new updates on the storm. It's clear from what just happened that his thoughts are somewhere else, far off outside of this motel room. Silence has a way of helping our minds decompress. It helps free us from the past few days and the strain our minds and hearts have endured. Stress has been at the forefront, and I can't help but let my anxiety consume me. Our country has just experienced an unthinkable, horrific act, and I wonder how we'll recover from such a tragedy. I question if any of us can overcome and move forward from such a devastating act, is it even possible? Can the damage ever be repaired? The list of questions runs wild through my mind, and I can only imagine Jax is having the same anxieties. Carrying the heavy load of the past few days hasn't been easy, especially if you've been holding in like he has. He appeared so strong and unscathed, but he's still human with the same worries and insecurities as the rest of us.

I recall our journey home and realize that with the bad, there is always some good that can be found, and it reminds me that I still have a lot to be thankful for. I look over at Jax.

"Do you believe good things can come from bad situations?"

"Absolutely." He doesn't even have to think about his answer. "Think of all the kindness we've seen in the past few days." There is conviction in his tone. "The way that stranger paid for our meal, for example."

"Yeah… I guess you're right." I never thought of it that way. "Like the way Jeff offered you a ride home when he didn't have to," I say. "On a normal day, most would have turned the other cheek, never giving it a second thought."

"Exactly! And that tiny act brought the two of us together." Jax takes my hand in his. "After that night at the bar, we probably would've never seen each other again." His head shakes at the thought. "Can you imagine? Now that we have gotten so close, to think that could have happened?" The sadness I hear in his words makes me wonder.

Listening to his words, I realize there is more to be thankful for than I thought. I gain a new level of respect for Dick and Jeff for the kindness they displayed, and for the way they took care of me as if I were their own, and I know that moving forward, we will always have a special connection somehow. The way they took in a stranger in need, without a hint of hesitation, and offered to help get him home to his family, will never go unappreciated. Those chains of events have brought me here with Jax, and I will forever hold a special place in my heart for the two of them, no matter what the future may hold.

My emotions are getting the better of me, and I find myself longing for my parents, realizing just how much I have taken them for granted. I can imagine them counting down the hours until I return, worried sick, and I vow to appreciate them more, to truly start living, not just existing. As we've all witnessed over the past few days, tomorrow is a privilege that some might never get.

The silence in the room presses in, amplifying the thoughts in my mind. A lump forms in my throat, and my vision begins to blur. I try to blink back the tears, but they escape down my cheeks in a steady stream. There's no stopping them.

"Everything's going to be okay, I promise." He turns to me, his thumb tracing a gentle line as he wipes away my tears in a single swipe.

"I know... It's just been a lot to deal with, and it's hitting me all at once, I guess." I hiccup through the sobs, and my body shivers in response. My emotions are raw, and the tears still linger. "It's all just so much... I think maybe I'll just go to bed." I say, giving in to my anxieties that have been building up. I have never felt more defeated.

"I understand." He says, his voice is low and deep. "Let's go...I'll tuck you in," he says and takes my hand, helping me to my feet. Hand in hand, we return to my room. He peels back the covers, and I slide in.

"Thank you," I say. "I'm sorry."

"Me too," he says and kisses my forehead, turns out the light, and then walks back toward his room.

"Jax?" I ask. I want to tell him that I'm an idiot and that I shouldn't have pushed so hard. I want to tell him to stay and spend the night with me. I want to tell him I love him.

"Would it be okay if you left the door open?" is all I say. *Coward.* Everything is quiet as he walks away, except for the sounds of rain crashing against the window and the sporadic booms of thunder as they continue to roll. *Charlotte, you just let the man you are falling in love with walk right out the door. Idiot.*

I watch as the final glow of light left in Jax's room fades. Darkness is all around me as the tears once again take over. Upset with how this entire night ended, I turn over onto my pillow, close my eyes, and let the exhaustion take over.

* * *

Thwack! A crash of lightning strikes down, immediately followed by the loud booms of rolling thunder, waking me out of my sleep. The light on the alarm clock flickers, creating an ominous mood in the room. Deafening blows of the heavy downpour of rain can be heard, and every few minutes, electrifying lightning zips through the sky, lighting it up like the Fourth of July. Between the gusts of wind whipping tree branches against the window and the ache that is now taking up permanent space in my heart, falling back asleep is inconceivable. The weight of the moment presses heavily on me.

Crack! Another one strikes, but this time, right outside my window, and my room goes black. The motel has lost power. The only light that can be seen is a red glow peeking from under the door, coming from the emergency exit signs that hang from the hallway ceiling.

I lie here in the darkness, and all I can think of is Jax and the countless stories we shared about our families, our likes, and dislikes. Even down to personal ones of his father's upbringing. I realize for the first time I'm happy, and it's all due to Jax's presence in my life. I've finally found what I had been searching for all this time, my soul mate. Without anyone else's help, we found each other on our own, the way it's meant to be. Fate may have had a little to do with it, but either way, I feel complete, and it feels right. Sitting here alone, I realize I am undeniably in love with Jaxson Lange. *I hope it isn't too late.*

I pull back the covers, and my feet hit the floor. The coldness that shocks them doesn't faze me, as I have only one thing to focus on. I walk through the door and pause for a moment, and stare at him. Jax lies peacefully asleep, oblivious to the storm outside. The flash of light casts shadows across his face, and he remains undisturbed. I walk over to the empty space in his bed and slip under the covers beside him, closing any available space between us, and feel the warmth waiting for me.

He begins to stir and turns in my direction, our faces only inches from each other. The heat from his breath warms my skin. Between the glow against his face, the romantic thunder roaring in the background, and the fire ignited inside me, I lean over and place my lips against his, allowing the warmth of them to take me back to the roadside. To our first kiss.

His eyes flutter open, trying to focus on what's happening, and they struggle to adjust to the lack of light left in the room. The look on his face is one of uncertainty, and he probably questions if it's all a dream. I smile and lean in to kiss him once more, hoping to give him a little more clarity.

"Charlotte... We really need to talk... I don't think this is a good..."

Before he can say another word, I close the space between us, pressing

164

my lips to his in a kiss that silences his words.

At first, they're tender kisses, delicate and sweet, until our mouths part, allowing our tongues to find each other. Our bodies respond in unison, and our mouths become one, as if they've done this so many times before. He tastes of sweet peppermint, the lingering trace of toothpaste still fresh on his lips. So cool and crisp, and I crave more of it. In one swift motion, with his arm around me, he rolls me onto my backside, all while still kissing me, his lips never leave mine, our rhythm never skipping a beat. Our tongues twist together, and I feel myself wanting more.

"*Ahhhhhh.*" A moan escapes me, and right away, he pulls back.

"I need to talk to you about something," he begins, his voice firm.

But I can't let him finish. Before he can say more, I kiss him again, silencing any further conversation. There is no time for talking. Not now, whatever he needs to say can wait, because right now I can't.

My hands reach up, cupping his cheeks, and like a scene straight from a movie, our eyes open and lock on each other, staring as if we can see straight into each other's souls. The desperate need we both have is evident, even a blind man could see. The lust we feel for one another couldn't be tamed if we tried. Time stands still as we're lost in each other's gaze, the look of desperation in his yearning eyes sets every nerve ending I have on fire. I kiss him with every breath I have, and whatever reservations he might've had, whatever confessions he's been holding back, have all but vanished.

The need for him becomes more intense, stronger, and I fear I might break, yet I can't think of anything I desire more. With gentle hands, I press against his chest and push him back from me. Our eyes meet, and in that charged silence, I reach down for the hem of my shirt, raising it above my head, exposing my bare breasts to him. A silent gesture, letting him know that if there was ever a doubt, it is okay for him to take all of me. "Are you sure?" His eyes are so intent as he asks. I smile in return, reassuring him, and pull him back on top of me, covering me like a soft blanket. His body is weightless on top of me, as if we are suspended in the air, floating. Once again, our lips meet, as if they are the only ones each other has ever known, perfectly in sync, and we both know there's no turning back now.

His hands are calloused, rough, but in a sensual way as they caress my inviting breasts. The sensation is exhilarating, and I hunger for more. The yearning I feel for their touch is overwhelming, every inch of me aching to be held. I've never felt this way about anyone. His lips part, trailing a path of tender kisses down my chin and along the curve of my neck. My breast is still cradled in his hands; their warmth ruins me as I arch toward him, seeking more. A wave of pure ecstasy builds within me, igniting every nerve as he continues his descent. Each brush of his lips is deliberate and with purpose, until he finds one of my breasts. He takes it into his mouth, and a low, primal moan escapes me. The sensation is intoxicating. My nipples harden as he teases them with his tongue, licking and sucking with such intent that I can't hold it in.

"Ohhhhh!"

My hands reach up and tangle through his thick, soft hair, tugging at it ever so gently. My breathing quickens, and I draw in air as I arch farther, exposing all of myself to him. The firmness of his erection pressed against my thigh, igniting a spark, sending a heat coursing through me. A surge of desire rises within me as I yearn for the closeness only he can provide. Right now, nothing else matters, only the undeniable sexual chemistry drawing me to him, the unspoken connection that deepens with every heartbeat. I release my hands from his hair, slowly sliding them down across his bare skin, as I caress and tickle along his backside. The tips of my fingers trace just above the waistband of his pajamas, gently pushing them down, just enough for my hands to cup around his firm, irresistible ass. His breathing quickens, sending shivers through both of us, stirring a reaction that surprises us both, as he bites my nipple.

"Oh God!" I cry out, begging for more.

He pauses, flashes a devilish smile, then resumes the tongue-lashing he's giving me.

Jax shifts his attention, giving my breasts the reprieve they need, as his tongue glides along the nape of my neck, alternating between soft kisses and tender licks across my shoulders. With each touch, they leave their own erotic sensation that I can't seem to get enough of. My body yearns for each and every one.

Without a moment to spare, I pull his bottoms further down, freeing his erection and exposing all of himself to me, as I demand into his ear, "I need you inside me now!"

My hand drifts to him, fingers grazing his warmth, caressing around him, and I feel him stir, growing beneath my touch. He exhales, a low, aching sound that wraps around me, and a surge of erotic sensations shoots through me, causing every inch of me to burn. His hips shift, and he reaches down, his fingers slip beneath the edge of my boxers, slow and methodical, and draws them down past my thighs. He doesn't rush, as if he is unwrapping something he's longing for, something fragile that he doesn't want to break. With a gentle hand, he caresses my sweet spot, finding the tender center of me, sending shivers coiling up my spine. At the same time, his mouth finds my earlobe, his tongue warm, teasing me, his lips stealing it with slow kisses. Another moan escapes as my body braces for what's to come. *"Ohhh."*

With him still cradled in my hand, I shift just enough to shimmy out of the boxers tangled at my hips, kicking them away until they fall to the bedside. My grip tightens, the strokes growing bolder, my way of telling him that I'm teetering on the edge and won't last much longer. I'm unraveling beneath his touch, and there is no space left for waiting. I need him, now and completely.

My hips thrust toward his, pushing into him and pulling him in closer, closing any vacant space between us. For if there is any left, I couldn't bear it. It is in that heightened, breathless moment that our eyes meet, his gaze locking with mine, deep and unwavering. It's as if he can see through me, reading every naughty, unspoken thought I have. I've never felt so exposed… or more importantly, ever seen. His eyes never leave mine, captivated in each other's stare, he slides himself into me, and without thought, our eyes close shut. His air feeds my lungs along with my beating heart, as I let out my own labored breath. *"Ahhhh."* The rise and fall of my chest quickens, as soft, gentle thrusts push and pull inside me, sending every nerve ending in my body to heighten to a level I've never known. My breath falters, and I gasp for air.

Between the intense emotions of the past few days, coupled with the overwhelming love I suddenly feel for Jax, a single tear escapes me, sliding down my cheek and disappearing into the pillow beneath me. So many mixed heartfelt emotions, good and bad, pent up, in desperate need of an escape.

Our lips once again find each other, and our tongues rejoice in their reunion. Our breathing becomes more urgent with each passing moment, quickening its pace while our bodies move in sync, with every thrust into me. We hold this rhythm for what feels like eternity, and I don't object. I let myself feel everything. I don't rush and let the suspense build inside, knowing the fall will be worth the wait.

I'm not quite sure how it's possible, but my body needs him closer. I lift my leg, crossing it above his buttocks, and pulling it against him, deepening the sensation. The low whisper that escapes him tells me his approval.

"Hmmmmmmmmm."

Outside, the storm is subsiding as the moon's glow begins to peek through the motel curtains, Jax's beautiful face now gleaming in the light for my own personal viewing. I could look at his gorgeous face for all eternity and never grow tired of it. His eyes still wide and focused, never leaving mine, I whisper, "I love you."

At the sound of my words, or maybe just the weight of the moment, I can feel his body quiver, just slightly, but enough to know he's right there with me, trembling with the same electric need.

My body can sense what's next, and it sends pulses throughout it, heightening every inch of me. I tense underneath him. And then, when our bodies become one, it's like something inside me breaks loose. Jax lets out a sound so raw, so full of everything he is feeling, it sets off something in me. A domino effect. My release crashes through me, not stopping, like it's been waiting for this moment, waiting for *him* to finally let go.

He gently collapses on top of me, feeling weightless, his warmth still inside me, while his head falls into place next to mine. His eyes stare into me, as if he can read my every thought.

"I love you, too, Charlotte... I have since the moment I met you on the elevator," he confesses.

My heart swells at his words, growing two sizes. I smile, unable to help it, and somewhere deep inside, my body makes its own quiet confession, one he can't hear, but somehow, I get the feeling he already knows. I have finally found my happily ever after. I kiss him once more, preserving this moment in memory. *What could possibly be better than this?*

CHAPTER 21

The bright light of morning beams through the curtains of Jax's tranquil motel room. The harmonious sounds of birds joyfully sing outside the window, now that the threat of the storm has passed. They soon will break from song, swooshing in puddles that have formed from last night's downpour, just as I had when I was young after a storm, tiny little red rain boots on. I could be found splashing in them for hours, giggling the entire time.

My eyes flicker, still adjusting to the light, half-wondering if the night before was all just a made-up dream. My subconscious is playing nasty tricks on me. I roll over onto my side, the sheets catch beneath my arm, and there he is, Jax, wide awake, his eyes staring back at me. He's smiling and content, and it feels right to be seen like this. It finally feels good to let him.

"Good morning, beautiful," he says and leans over, closing the space between us, placing a tiny peck on my forehead.

I continue to smile and place my hand on his chest, leaving it there as its new resting place. Not another word is spoken as we lie, gazing at each other, my mind reminiscing about what occurred just hours before. A few moments seem to linger before he breaks the silence.

"Would you like to go to breakfast?" he asks, and it reminds me of the fact that our little adventure will soon be ending. Once we leave this room, our next destination is back in our separate homes, taking us back to a harsh reality.

"Sure." A somber tone is left in its presence.

Of course, the answer would be a yes, I mean, I freaking do love food. I would have said yes to robbing a bank if it meant I could spend more time with Jax. But the sudden dread of having to pull myself from him and get dressed to leave is holding me back. I can already feel myself missing him, and I haven't even had my morning coffee yet.

"On two conditions," I say, my mood begins to perk up.

"Oh yeah? I can only imagine." He chuckles at my demands.

"First… I will go to breakfast with you, but only if we can go to the Waffle House. There isn't one too far from here." I place a peck on his cheek and smile.

"Waffle House? *Seriously?*" He questions my strange choice of restaurant. "But wherever you want is fine, though… as long as I'm with you."

"Yup…There is something about those buttery waffles that turns me into a different person." I laugh. "Kinda like *you*," and I kiss him on the lips this time. "Which leads me to my second condition."

"Let's hear it."

"That you promise to make love to me once more before we go," I say, and waste no time as I pull myself onto him.

"Wellllll… If I must, I guess." He laughs, and before I can respond, he's kissing me again, all fire and intent. In one seamless motion, he rolls on top of me, pulling the covers over us. That devilish grin is back on his face, and I know my waffles are gonna have to wait.

* * *

Jax is in the shower, and I decide to do the same and head back to my room. Yet my body is paralyzed as I lie in Jax's bed, relishing in the love we just made for a second time. I wait until the last minute and muster up the strength and rise, dreading the thought of having to leave this room and return to reality in just a few hours.

I make my way across the room and head to my own just as Jax's phone screen lights up to life, as it sits alone on the dresser. Its settings are set to silent, because it never rang. I watch as a tiny green bubble pops up on the screen, reading "missed call from Joanna." *Joanna? His old girlfriend, Joanna? Why would she be calling?* A moment passes, and I contemplate yelling out to him through the bathroom door, informing him of the missed call. But instead, I refrain, knowing that in just a few minutes he will see it for himself. To put it more bluntly, I don't want him to assume that I am snooping through his phone and invading his privacy. I mean, I may have just had sex with a man I met only three days ago, but come on, I am not a complete psychopath, stooping as low as to snoop through his phone. I have standards.

* * *

It takes longer than it should before I leave my room for the last time, and my craziness kicks in as we pack up our belongings. I get down on all fours and check underneath the beds, inspecting the dresser drawers for the umpteenth time, ensuring I haven't left anything behind. Jax laughs at me while he stands in the doorway, waiting, watching me as if I am some kind of lunatic. *He's not wrong.*

For some unknown, ridiculous reason, I take time to make the bed, knowing all too well we will never return. Satisfied with the room being cleaner than when I arrived, Jax opens the door, leading me out first, leaving me only with unforgettable memories of last night, as the door closes behind me.

I feel the familiar touch as his hand finds mine; the two now fit together as one. Hand in hand, we walk to the lobby. Noreen is still at the counter, shuffling around some papers and straightening them into a pile. She looks up, taking notice of the two of us walking towards her. I can't help but notice the way her eyes zoom in on our hands, now entwined with each other. Such a difference from just one night.

"What are you still doing here?" Jax asks. "Don't you ever leave?" He says in a playful way.

"I might as well take residence in one of the rooms," she jokes. "As a matter of fact, I'm getting ready to leave, just finishing up a few things," Noreen says as she takes both of our room keys from our hands. "How was your stay?"

We look at each other, a guilty smirk painted across my face, "Everything I hoped for." Truer words have never been spoken.

"I *seeeee*." The not-so-subtle wink she gives me is mischievous.

We say our goodbyes to sweet Noreen and walk outside, hand in hand once again, solidifying the end of our perfect first night together, hopefully the first of many.

Outside looks like a war zone, and for a split moment, I want to turn back. Branches are scattered everywhere, and even whole trees have been uprooted, leaning on their sides. One has been broken completely in half and lying right in the middle of the parking lot, with a stroke of luck, just missing our rental. Birds dance through the morning light, splashing in the shallow puddles left behind by the night's relentless rain. The world feels fresh and new, like even nature is pausing to enjoy this moment. The heat wave, sweltering across most of the country, seems to have finally broken, and for that I am grateful. Aside from the obvious debris that looks more like a battlefield, it's quite beautiful out.

The skies are ice blue with endless miles of white fluffy clouds floating throughout. Such a stark difference from when we arrived last night.

A block away in the distance are emergency vehicles. Police cars, ambulances, and firetrucks, all with their flashing lights spinning and blinking like the inside of a dance rave. The only thing missing is the loud music. As we walk nearer to our car, I can see that an accident has occurred involving three separate cars, the reason for all the commotion.

"Oh wow… That looks bad… I hope no one's hurt." I crane my neck, trying to get a better look, and take a moment to pray for everyone involved. "I bet some of the roads are still bad from the storm."

"I know a thing or two about that." His eyes squint, and his head shakes from side to side, trying to assess the damage. I notice when he does, he reaches up and touches just above his eye.

"What do you mean?"

"When I was seventeen, right after getting my driver's license, I hydroplaned during a rainstorm, smashing into a telephone pole. Totaled my parents' car," he says, wincing at the memory. "Broke my left arm and leg. My head hit the window so hard that I got a concussion." *No wonder he wanted to get off the road last night.* "I have a scar to prove it." He rubs his thumb against his temple, where a thick patch of skin, an inch in length, is left in its place.

"Oh geez… That must have been scary." I say, thankful that he made it out okay. "Knock on wood, I've never been in an accident, and I hope I never will." We approach the car, and I'm not sure how, but Jax is already waiting for me. *How does he do that?* He pops the trunk, and we stash our bags for the last remaining hours. The quiet attentiveness, the gallant gestures, it all reminds me so much of my dad. Always the perfect gentleman. Jax does the same, crosses to my side of the car, and opens the door before I even reach for the handle. It's effortless for him and instinctive, and I love him even more for it.

It only takes a few quiet minutes before the iconic black and yellow sign comes into view, towering high above the roadside to our left. My stomach, clearly just as excited as I am, lets out a loud rumble. Jax chuckles at the sound and grins. "Guess someone's ready for breakfast," he teases, and I don't even try to deny it.

"Well... I mean, I did work up quite the appetite," I tease back.

The annoying *ding, ding, dinging* of the turn signal continues as we sit in the line of cars, waiting for our moment to cross the road. The light changes from red to green, giving us the go, safely crossing the street, and into the first vacant spot we find. Heaven awaits, and my mouth begins to salivate. I can almost taste the yummy goodness of the warm, buttery waffles inside.

Jax rounds the car to open my door again, "After you," he says with a playful bow.

Inside, it's warm and smells like bacon and fresh coffee, and I am greeted the same way I have so many times before.

In unison, the entire staff yells out, "Good morning," as the two of us walk through the smudged glass doors.

"It is now... Good morning." The excitement I have can't be hidden.

A young woman wearing a blue collared shirt, layered with a black apron and a yellow name tag that reads 'Violet,' seats us in the last available booth. Through the window, the view makes me smile, a quaint little hotel across the street, shaped like an old-fashioned steamboat, complete with a faux smokestack and paddlewheel painted bright red. It feels like it belongs to a different time.

"Welcome to Waffle House, my name is Violet... Can I get you something to drink? Coffee?" she asks politely.

A wave of nostalgia hits me as memories of my dad and me eating at the counter flash through my mind, him sipping hot coffee and chatting with the staff while I sit beside him, lost in a plate of syrupy goodness. Our love of breakfast items is something the two of us have always shared, especially ones from the Waffle House. Ever since a young age, it's been a dream that the two of us would someday open one up together. *I wish.*

Violet hands each of us a menu. She doesn't know it, but I haven't needed one in years, so I placed it down on the table beside my napkin.

"Are you ready to place your order?" she asks, noticing right away that I've set down the menu.

It wouldn't matter if I frequent this place at two in the afternoon or two in the morning, my order is always the same. I've never strayed from it; I have no reason to, it's perfect, and I could order it in my sleep.

"Yep… I will have a waffle with a side of hash browns smothered and covered, a hot coffee, and a small OJ, please." I recite it like a familiar ritual, just as I have so many times before.

"Geez, you weren't kidding when you said this was your favorite place. What is smothered and covered?" Jax questions me, clearly enjoying the game.

"They're hashbrowns with cheese and onions, aka, smothered and covered."

"Need a job?" Violet jokes.

"That sounds good. I'll have what she's having." He doesn't bother to look at her, and his eyes never leave mine.

Violet turns to stand on the usual spot, a small square tile behind the counter where the orders are given, and she begins to shout, "Drop two smothered covered and plate two waffles!" *Ahhhhhh, the sweet sound of yumminess.* Next, she pours our hot coffees into mugs, each branded with the iconic logo on them, then follows with the OJs and sets them down in front of us. I add a tiny container of cream to the cup along with 2 packets of sugar and take a long sip. It's borderline orgasmic. Instantly reminding me of a few hours earlier, my eyes close without meaning to, and my head falls back as a sigh of quiet satisfaction slips from my lips. *"Ahhhh."*

Why are the first sips of a coffee always the best? Just like the owl says, the world may never know.'

We sit in comfortable silence, sipping our hot mugs of Joe, and I take the moment to let last night sink in. I can't help but smile.

That all stops when I catch a glimpse of steam floating from the piping hot waffles in Violet's hands, and my mouth begins to salivate at the very sight. The aroma of the sweet buttery waffles is almost illegal, and I start to fidget in my seat. I take no time to spread the container of soft butter onto it, covering every inch, then douse it with a heaping dose of syrup, its handle still sticky from its previous owner. Every little crevice of each tiny square is filled and spilling over to the sides, and I am dying to sink my teeth into them. In true "Charlotte" fashion, I eat nearly three-quarters of it before switching to the crispy, golden hash browns, saving the last few bites of syrup-soaked waffle for the end, just so the sweetness will linger on my tongue.

I look over at Jax and notice he's barely made a dent in his.

"Do you not like your breakfast?" I ask, baffled at such a ridiculous thought.

"Yeah… Why?" He's puzzled by my accusation.

"Oh… I don't know, you only took a few bites."

"Charlotte…You do realize the food just came three minutes ago, right?" His head shakes as he takes another bite of his waffle.

I throw both hands in the air, palms up, my eyebrows and lips lifting right along with them as I laugh with him. *Ain't no shame in my Waffle House game.*

We sit for a moment in silence as I savor my last few sips of coffee. I watch him fiddling with his last bits of waffle, pushing them around his plate, taking bites every so often. He seems off. Something about him is different, ever since we left the motel, but I just can't figure out what, or why.

"Is everything okay?" I ask, concerned. "Did I do something wrong?"

"I'm fine," he says, without a hint of feeling behind it. *What happened?*

His monotone response confirms my suspicions that something isn't right, and it's obvious that it's weighing on him. His mind seems elsewhere, somewhere far off in the distance. Thoughts of last night swirl in my head, and like always, I jump to the worst-case scenario: that he regrets it. Once again, I get the unnerving feeling that he is holding something back and needs to tell me something. *Maybe it has something to do with that phone call?* In a desperate attempt to free him of whatever internal battle he's fighting, I reach over, spear a piece of his waffle with my fork, and pop it in my mouth.

He laughs. "You cannot still be hungry?" Then he points to my two empty plates and raises an eyebrow.

"One can never have too much of a good thing." I wink back, teasing him, a playful mischief look on my face.

"Well, I guess I can't argue with you on that one." He laughs, but I catch him inching his plate closer, like I might steal another bite.

I ask Violet to refill my coffee, giving Jax more time to finish his breakfast, but more selfishly, I want more time with him. I sip on my freshly filled cup of brew when a familiar song begins to play in the background. My eyes go wide, my mouth right behind them, as Jax stares at me like he can't believe what he's hearing.

"Did you do that? Did you play this song?" he points behind me.

Over the speaker, a certain song plays from the jukebox in front of the window. "Home on the Range" blares throughout the diner. I mean, what are the freaking odds that this particular song would be playing at this very moment, where Jax and I sit enjoying our breakfast?

"No! I'm just as shocked as you are."

"What are the odds?" He shakes his head in disbelief, side to side, as we both start singing along, right up until the very last note. We're lost in the overwhelming emotion of the ironic song choice, and I realize we will be "home" in a few short hours. At warp speed, my singing begins to crumble at the gloomy thought. Jax notices the sudden change and reaches for my hands, cradling them in his, but not before wiping a tear that escaped from the corner of my eye.

Jax pays for our meal, then we make our way back to the car, each taking our sweet time and not wanting it to end. His pace quickens like usual, and he opens the passenger side door and gestures for me to get in. Just as I do, he leans in and kisses me on the forehead. *I'm starting to get used to this.* He makes his way around the front of the car and over to the driver's side; my eyes never leave him.

He takes a moment before sliding the key into the ignition and starting the engine. After a few moments of silence, he shifts into drive and pulls away. The unavoidable ending is just beginning. It won't be long now before we land where the buffalo roam, and where we will say our goodbyes. Then it'll just be me, alone for the final stretch of the journey... my home.

Sadness washes over me, heavy and overwhelming, as the weight of our ending settles in. Tears stream at a steady pace, down my cheeks, dripping off onto my lap, as I stare out into the passing blue skies. Cotton-ball clouds float across the sky, perfectly placed, as if hand-painted by Constable himself. Jax reaches over, gives my hand a gentle squeeze as we ride in silence, just at the very touch, more tears begin to flow.

CHAPTER 22

Time passes, and soon the huge green signs for the bridge come into view, and I find myself wishing I could somehow turn back time. They remind me of the fact that Jax's house is getting close. I remember during one of our talks, he mentioned his home was just past the bridge, maybe twenty minutes or so. My heart aches at the thought that it won't be long now.

I glance over at him, memorizing every detail of his face, soaking in everything that I can, trying to capitalize on whatever time I have left with him. I know this isn't goodbye forever, but part of me fears it won't feel the same. We've spent nearly every second together over the past few days, and the thought of waking up alone in my bed tomorrow suddenly feels... foreign. *Why can't we just stay in our little bubble together forever?*

His face is stubbled now, long overdue for a shave, and I'm starting to get used to the look. It suits him – rugged, unpolished, and, if I'm being honest, ridiculously sexy. He looks so serious with his sunglasses covering his beautiful blue eyes, blocking them from the radiant sun shining in. We drive in silence, the only sound is an old country tune playing softly in the background, "Eastbound and Down" by Jerry Reed, which couldn't be more fitting given our situation.

An overwhelming sense of pride for my country fills me as we make our way across the bridge. The entire length of it is lined with what must be thousands of American flags, a quiet, powerful tribute to recent events. It's breathtaking to witness. Our country may have been ambushed and rattled, but we can never be fully broken. We will continue to rise, and we will always, and without a doubt, bleed red, white, and blue. And if all this talk of war really does come to pass, I have no doubt our military will lead us through it, with strength, with honor, and with everything this country stands for.

"Wow!... I've never seen so many flags flying in one place. It gives me goosebumps." The hair on my arms stands at attention, and instinctively, I rub them as I glance over at Jax.

"It really is... I don't know who is responsible for the attacks, but I'd bet that they're shaking in their boots right now and will be sorry they messed with the U.S.A."

"Sounds like a country song." I laugh, just as we descend from the bridge and cross into New Jersey.

The ease with which Jax drives these country roads lets me know we are close; it's clear he doesn't need directions.

"Right down there, about a quarter mile, is a hidden driveway back to an open field." Jax points down a dirt road off to his left. I notice a stray cat runs across the road and disappears into the trees. "Everyone would head there on Friday nights after a football game, most with a bottle of Boone's Farm in hand... Only the lucky ones would end up 'making out' by the huge bonfire that we would set." He laughs and reminisces about his high school days. With every story he shares, I feel a little closer to him, as if I am reliving the moments with him.

His voice lights up as he talks about Cream Valley, his favorite ice-cream spot, and I catch a glimpse of the way he was as a kid. He used to go there with his friends after school. His order never changes: a simple twist on a cake cone with rainbow jimmies. (Yes, jimmies, we're from Jersey, sprinkles are for cakes, remember that.)

"I know you won't believe this, but that's literally my same order." My mouth can't help but salivate at the very mention of it.

"Seriously?" He doesn't believe me.

"Seriously." I laugh, shaking my head at his doubt.

I take in the beautiful scenery as Jax continues to drive. We pass by corn fields, all lined in perfect rows, ready to be harvested, as it's nearing the end of the season. Roadside stands are plentiful with tables full of apples and pumpkins. We've passed four of them already, and we're just a few miles past the bridge into New Jersey.

We pass an old wooden tavern off of Route 40, and according to Jax, it's the hotspot to be on Saturday nights.

"Get there before the place fills up, they'll teach you some country line-dancing moves. Just try not to step on anyone's boots,"

"That sounds like it would be fun." I imagine myself dancing the night away in a pair of cowboy boots with Jax spinning me around, just like in the movies.

"It is. I mean, I'm not good at it, but I bet you would look great out there dancing." He says. "We need to get you a pair of cowboy boots." He smiles at the thought.

He no sooner says that when something catches my eye, up ahead in the distance, a tall, gargantuan statue in the shape of a "cowboy" standing close to two stories high, alongside the road, holding a rope that dangles from his hands. Directly past him is a billboard that reads "COWTOWN RODEO Saturday nights at 7:30 May 28th- September 24th." On either side of the script, a painting depicts a bronco rider on one side and a bull rider on the other.

"So, this is the rodeo that I've heard so much about," I exclaim, my voice is higher with surprise.

The fact I live only forty-five minutes away from here, and I've never gone, not once, is actually wild. Even my parents have gone. The stories of the barrel racers and insane cowboys riding bulls, eating peanuts in the shell, then tossing them to the ground, all sound like a fun night. As we pass by, I make a mental note, storing it in memory to get there one day, hopefully with Jax by my side.

"Have you never been to the rodeo before?" *I swear he can read my mind.* "If not, I think it should be our first official date. I mean, if you want to, that is." He stumbles on his words.

I smile, reassuring him that he's said nothing wrong.

"Funny, I was just thinking the same thing. Sounds like it would be fun... Although, according to the sign, it looks like next week will be the last of the season." My voice deflates. "I hope we don't wait until next year to go on our first date."

"Well then, if that's out of the question, then I guess we'll have to settle for McDonald's."

"Deal." I smile. He may be joking, but I wouldn't mind; you can never go wrong with a Big Mac and fries.

"I'm gonna stop at the gas station really quick. The tank's getting low, and I want to make sure you have enough gas to make it home." His concern for my safety is thoughtful. I'm getting used to Jax and the way he protects me. It makes me think of the god-awful choices I've made in past relationships. *It's about time I found a good one.*

"Charlotte?" He interrupts my thoughts, bringing me back to the moment.

"Oh... Okay... Sounds good." I smile back and agree because it slows any time I have left with him, even if only for a few minutes.

The next thing I know, Jax pulls into a small, old-fashioned gas station with enough bays to fuel two cars at one time. He pulls the car to a stop beside pump number two and turns off the ignition.

"It's nice to see Sean isn't price gouging like some of the ones we stopped at on the way home." He shakes his head in disbelief, a silent refusal to believe it.

"Yeah... My brain just can't comprehend someone benefiting from such a tragedy." I look toward the window and out to the sky. It's hard to believe that anything is wrong in the country right now when it looks so picture-perfect outside. "People can be screwed up to take advantage of someone in need. Especially after what this country has just gone through." Sadness creeps in, swallowing up the Camry, and without hesitation, Jax reaches over and calms me with his gentle touch.

His free hand pushes the button on the door, and magically, the window begins to open, and his eyes never leave mine. I forget where we are for a moment as I am lost in my thoughts. "Fill it regular, please," Jax says, not even bothering to look at the gas station attendant who's just crept up beside his window.

"Jax! Buddy... You made it home!" The excitement in his voice tells me he and Jax are close. "I didn't realize it was you from the type of car." He says, bending down to get a better look at Jax, then reaches in and grabs his shoulder, giving it a little tug, like he's checking to make sure he's real.

"Yoooo... Sean... What are you doing out here pumping gas? I haven't seen you work in years," he jokes. "I didn't know you had it in ya." Jax lights up with a bright, huge smile and is elated to see him.

He's good-looking, and those mesmerizing dark gray eyes stop me in my tracks. The smirk he flashes when he spots me says it all; he knows exactly how handsome he really is. He reminds me of a male version of Jennifer, and probably the reason why I feel like I already know him.

"He thinks he's a comedian, doesn't he?" laughs Sean, directing his question to me. "I just so happen to own the place... Did ya pick this guy up hitchhiking on the side of the road?" he continues to joke. I laugh but say nothing in return.

"Sean, this is Charlotte. The one I told you about in Vegas." He admits, casually, but there is honesty to it. "The girl from the elevator." *He told his friends about me.* "And Charlotte, this is my obnoxious best friend, Sean." *Aw, they're so cute together.*

"Well… well … well, so this is the mystery woman you wouldn't shut up about on that last night of the bachelor party?" admits Sean. "We all thought you were full of shit and made her up." He jokes once more. "You look familiar, though." his eyes go to the side as if he is searching every crevice of his brain, trying to find out where from. "Wait!!! You're the girl from the airport… Aren't you??? With the book."

I'm shocked, "Holy crap! Yes!" excitement fills my voice. "What a small world." Jax looks back at the two of us, a mix of confusion and wonderment in his eyes.

"This is the guy I was talking about!" He smacks Jax on the chest a few times, and now I'm confused. That's when it hits me… Jay, is the letter J… short for Jax. Instantly, I'm taken back to that day in the airport, an inebriated Sean telling me that his friend 'Jay' would be perfect for me. I never gave it a second thought. Why would I?

"This is just crazy!" I am completely floored, stunned by what he's just said.

"Must be fate," Jax claims with a grin, then squeezes my hand. I can't help but smile at the whole encounter.

"Joe came in yesterday and said that you would be home last night." Sean breaks the moment. *Joe? Jax never mentioned Joe.* "Are you just getting home now?" The concern he has for his friend is eminent. "Did something happen?"

"Yeah… We got caught in that nasty storm and spent the night in Lancaster." He winks at Sean. "You know me. Safety first."

"I sure hope so… Safety was never your strong point, buddy." Laughter explodes from him, but I'm not sure why. I notice Jax's shoulders tense and his hands gripping the wheel a little tighter than before.

"Alright then… We're gonna go now," Jax says with a nervous tone in his voice. "I'll call you tomorrow."

"You bet… And Charlotte, it was nice to put a pretty face to the name we all heard so much about. Glad you both made it safely home." Sean's tone is more sincere.

I lean over, lean my elbow on Jax's leg so I can see Sean more clearly through the window, "It was nice to meet you, too," I say, and mean it.

Once again, he looks at Jax, "Tell Joe and your parents hello for me." He waves goodbye and walks to fuel the car that just pulled into the other bay.

Jax pulls out of the gas station and back onto the road we had just come from. The mood throughout the car begins to shift as we draw nearer to the end of our journey home.

"My house is just a few minutes away from here… Well, technically, my parents' house, but mine is on a piece of the same land behind it." Killing the mood altogether.

"Oh…I just assumed you lived with your parents. I didn't realize you owned your own home," I say, not giving it a second thought.

He says nothing.

Sadness crept in as I secretly thought we could stay on our little adventure together, closed off from the rest of the world, forever. I've grown accustomed to having him by my side twenty-four-seven, keeping me company. I say nothing more, force out a half-hearted smile, then lean over and lay my head on his shoulder.

A few short-left turns and then a right, past one of the many cow farms we'd passed along the way, and Jax pulls the car to a stop in front of the two-story white farmhouse. Black shutters frame the windows, and the house is wrapped by a large white porch, stretching around its entire front. Rocking chairs sit on either side of the front door and look like a picture out of a home improvement magazine. Beautiful purple and pink myrtles, still holding some of their color, are all planted throughout the yard.

I imagine myself living here with Jax, or at least in a house just like it. Quaint and small, a perfect place to raise a family. The only neighbor I see is off in the distance and is equally charming. It must be Jax's, probably built by him and his father.

The humming of the car engine slows to a stop, and before turning it off, Jax turns to me.

"I have been trying to talk to you. There's something that I've been trying to tell you... but haven't been able to find the words or the right time to say it." The anxious tone in his words is alarming. And the way he keeps looking away, not making eye contact with me, doesn't go unnoticed.

There is a tension in his voice that wasn't there before, and it's beginning to unnerve me. We've been together in the car for the past few days and have talked about everything. Whatever he needs to discuss, he's had more than ample time to do so.

"Whatever you have to say, just say it. You know you can tell me anything, Jax. I'm sure it's nothing anyway." I attempt to ease his mind.

"I'm not so sure abouuu–"

Bang! Bang! Bang!"

He's interrupted by a tapping on the driver's side window, startling both of us, causing me to jump from my seat. Jax looks toward the tapping sound and then back to me. And just when he does, he slumps down into his seat, a look of defeat now plasters across his face.

"No..." Jax says barely over a whisper, and I get the feeling it was meant for his ears only.

Standing just outside the window, there are three very anxious people, all waiting patiently for Jax to open the door. But for some reason, before he does, he looks at me. Worry blankets his face, then turns back to the door, frozen for a moment before cautiously opening it. A little apprehensive, I follow his lead and do the same. *I'm so confused. Why does he suddenly look so terrified?*

Nervous, I exit the car and walk around the front, over to where Jax is waiting, and stand quietly by his side. Long-awaited hugs and a few stolen kisses are already being exchanged by the time I reach him, my heart thudding with every step. The undeniable relief shines brightly over their faces, now that they finally have their arms around him: Jax is home. Tears stream from the older woman's eyes; my only guess is his mother, that I've heard so much about. I have seen the look of a mother's love so many times before, especially on my own. She's a natural beauty, aging with such grace, without a trace of makeup on, and could easily pass for ten years younger than what she is. Her auburn hair is pulled back in a low bun, her cheeks are stained pink, probably the result of being out in the sun. She wears a simple, flowy pink sundress with tiny flowers covering it. Perfect for this warm September day.

She's the first to be introduced. "Charlotte? This is my mom, MaryEllen." The words still linger on Jax's tongue when she pulls me into the biggest, most grateful hug, whispering her thanks for bringing her baby boy home. I laugh, knowing I had very little to do with it, but I squeeze her back, not realizing just how much the hug was needed and ignoring the fact that I don't even know her.

"Of course. I'm happy to be a small part of getting him back home. You've raised a true gentleman." I smile and look back at Jax. "I'm not sure how much help I was, though, unless talking his ear off for three days counts," I joke, and she hugs me once more, for good measure.

"And this guy right here is my dad, Michael." His face beams with pride.

"It's a pleasure to meet you, Michael." His name slips off my tongue with ease, almost as if I've known him my entire lifetime. *Maybe we can name our firstborn after him.* I laugh at the ridiculous thought of a man I just met three days ago. "I've heard so many wonderful stories about you. Jax puts you on a very high pedestal." I admit. Now that I see him with my own eyes, there's no doubt, he's exactly as Jax described, through and through. He's just as I imagined him, tall, strong with salt and pepper hair, and with the same striking blue eyes as Jax. It's like seeing into the future, twenty years from now, what Jax will look like. (The thought of us together, years from now, growing old together, has a calming effect on me.) He pulls me into a hug too, stronger, deeper, as if he's done it a thousand times before. It takes my breath away, not only from the force of it, but from the strange, unexpected desire to never let it go. I feel comfortable with him, as if he were my own father. Pure love emanates from the two of them, and it warms me how much I can see just where Jax gets his strong family values from.

Jax then turns to the young woman standing quietly next to his mother, one of his sisters, I assume. She's beautiful, with long dark waves and a figure that turns heads, but something about her feels... off. I can't quite put my finger on it. She is quiet and doesn't say a word. I smile at her to break the awkwardness that lingers in the air between us.

Jax hesitates, just for a second, barely noticeable, but there's an obvious, nervous tremor to his voice when he introduces her. "This is Joanna... My wife..."

For a moment, everything is quiet, still, as if the earth has somehow been knocked off its axis and stopped turning. And just as quickly, it hits me.

Gasping for air, I take in a deep breath, and, without warning, I feel as if life itself has been sucked from me; in an instant, my belly twists in knots like a soft Philly pretzel. *What the actual fuck?!?!* The sudden ache I feel is comparable to a punch in the stomach by Mike Tyson himself, and I can't breathe. The world as I know it has just been turned upside down. *What is happening right now?* I can't speak, shocked by what Jax has just blurted out, and I'm unable to move, motionless, and just stare at her. No smile, no greetings, not a single hug, no other emotion other than pure shock spews across my face. When I look at Jax, the heartbreak in my eyes meets the fear in his. He doesn't say a word, and somehow, that says everything, and in no time, that pisses me off. Anger builds within me, molten and fierce, and my tears threaten to erupt like Mount Vesuvius. I fight to hold them back.

Breaking the deafening anger inside me is his wife, "Hi Charlotte, it's so nice to meet you. I have heard so much about you from Jax…I feel like we're already friends." She heeds with extreme caution, and the way she says my name makes my skin crawl.

This greeting is different from the others; she doesn't reach in for a hug like his parents did, and for that, I am grateful. Her hand meets mine, steady, while mine trembles, and that's when I notice it. No wedding band. Nothing at all. For a moment, I question myself, that maybe I had heard Jax wrong, that somehow, I mistook his words. But how could I? They flew out of his mouth so freely, cutting me like a knife in the process. In the same mouth, I had my tongue in just last night. *What the hell is happening right now?* Everything starts to spin, and a wave of dizziness washes over me. I grab the side of the car to steady myself. Maybe I'm dreaming, still sleeping in the back seat, caught in the middle of a terrible nightmare.

Quick as a whip, I pull myself together and muster up a fake smile. "Hi…" I answer, our hands remain connected, but I notice mine are still shaking.

Michael and I make eye contact, briefly, but enough to feel the weight of everything neither of us is saying. Hurt and confusion radiate from me, no matter how hard I try to hide them from everyone else.

"Let's go inside and let Jax gather his things and say goodbye to Charlotte," he says, and I can't thank him enough. The three of them walk off and disappear into the house, but not before Michael gives me a pitiful smile back.

With everything that's transpired in the past few minutes, I can feel the pain swelling inside me, a storm trapped beneath my skin, desperate to escape. I fight hard to keep it all together and refuse to break down in front of Jax. The pain is still there, sharp and consuming, but it gets shoved aside as anger begins to creep back in. The heat rises, climbing my neck like fire I can barely contain, fury pulsing through my veins, and I'm absolutely livid.

Everything I've been holding in since the moment we stepped out of the car comes pouring out: the anticipation, the hurt, the anger, every jagged piece of pain I've tried to swallow. It hits all at once, one raw, aching rush. My tears are simmering, a slow, steady boil just waiting to spill over.

"Married????" My teeth feel like they might shatter as I scream through them, clenched tight with rage. The death stare I give him speaks louder than my scream, leaving no doubt just how furious I am. "Are you fucking kidding me right now with this? Married???? How? Why?" I shout at him in one long, exhausted breath. I scream so loud I wouldn't be surprised if his family could hear from inside their perfect little home. "Why would you make love to me knowing you had a wife at home?" Now I'm hollering, each word filled with anger, and I can't hold it in any longer. "Why in the hell would you play with my emotions and tell me that you loved me? Was I some kind of sick joke to you?" I'm not finished, giving him no room to speak. "On the countless hours over the past few days, you couldn't find five fucking minutes to tell me something as important as you being married? Like before we slept together. *TWICE!*" My ongoing rant continues, the back of my throat becoming sore from the constant screaming. "I mean... I know the meaning behind your tattoo... but I don't know the fact that you're fucking married? Is that a lie, too? Is anything you told me true?" I barely finish when a migraine slams into me, sharp and sudden, blooming straight out of the ache in my broken heart.

"I'm sorry... I meant every word... I tried to tell—"

My hands raised to him, "That is enough! I do *not* want to hear another word!" I yell. "I've heard enough lies from you. I'm not sure what the truth is anymore. Get your damn bags and go into *Joannaaaaa*, I'm leaving and going home!" My face goes cold, like stone, a silent shield against the storm brewing inside me.

Once more, he tries to speak, and again I shut him down before he can. I'm trembling. I'm so furious, my hands shake as I lean against the car, staring at the house that sits in the distance, Jax and Joanna's happy little fucking home. I bite at my fingernails, a nervous tic I developed in high school, as I wait for the sound of the trunk hatch to close. I'm not sure what's taking him so long. He needs to hurry so I can leave and drive as far away from this dreadful nightmare. Because being this close to him, even for one second more, is more than my shattered heart can take.

"I'm sorry..." he says, from the back of the car as he still fumbles with his bags. Sadness is embedded in his pathetic attempt at an apology.

I can't bear to be out here for even one second longer, so I climb into the car and slam the door shut, leaving his apology as the last thing I hear. I can still hear the rustling of his luggage being removed from the trunk, then silence, no more movement. Time stands still, dragging on this horrible nightmare as I count down the seconds til the trunk closes.

"Whack!" at last it does, and in the side view mirror, I see him heading straight for my window.

"Finally!" I say out loud, meant for no one but myself. It hits me all at once: I'm alone again. Truly, and this time, quite literally.

I scramble through the center console for what seems like days, searching desperately for the car keys. Every second here feels heavier, and I can't leave fast enough. As if someone heard my silent prayer, my hand finds the keys. I jam them into the ignition, but then I spot Jax. He's standing right beside me, a thin sheet of glass between us, bags in hand, blocking my escape.

"Can you please roll down the window and let me explain?" He spoke through the windowpane, his shoulders slumped, his eyes pink and starting to swell.

Silence...

"I tried to tell you... I really did... It's not at all what you think... Can you please just listen to what I have to say?" his voice is low and urgent.

Silence...

"I'm sorry." He says one more time, and those are the last words I let myself hear. They tear through me like a dull, jagged knife.

I don't give him the chance to say another word; he doesn't deserve it. With a sharp jerk, I shift into gear and speed away, leaving Jax and every lie he ever told me in a thick cloud of dust. In the rearview mirror, I see him standing there, watching me go, fading from my life, for good this time.

Just a few miles into the drive, it hit me. The missed call from Joanna. I'd seen it on Jax's phone this morning. I should've known. He was acting off at breakfast, guilt written all over his face. My stomach knots, bile rising in my throat, and suddenly I feel sick.

"I feel like we're already friends!" I scream out loud, repeating Joanna's odd choice of words. *Like what the actual fuck? He told her about me. What the hell kind of marriage do they have?* Memories of last night are rushing back, each one burning a hole deeper inside me. "Did you tell her we *fucked* too? *Asshole!*" I scream out into the universe, as if the world itself could offer me an answer and make sense of all this.

I think of our conversations, personal stories of our lives, and the beautiful love that I naively thought we shared. I feel every one of them, each emotion, every touch, come to a head like a scalding pot of water, ready to boil over. Like a leaky faucet that can't be fixed; my tears flow, they won't stop, and I fear they never will. It's uncontrollable, and I don't try to fight it. I know it won't help. I feel utterly useless; the pain is just too much. So, I do what any heartbroken woman would do: I welcome it all, the pain, the lies, the heartache, and allow the floodgates to open.

My body, drunk on its own tears, leaves my vision impaired. Between that and my hands that won't stop shaking, I'm forced to pull over before I get myself into an accident. I need a moment to regain my wits, enough at least to be able to drive more safely.

The next forty-five minutes become a complete and total blur. Like I'm flying a plane on autopilot, I'm driving, but still not quite sure how. I don't recall a single thing, not a stop sign, turn signal, nothing. My head's clouded with the most hurtful words said by Jax…*"my wife"* a thousand times on repeat. I relive the hurt over and over, torturing myself with the soul-crushing truth: he belongs to someone else. And all this time, he always has. *How can I be so stupid?*

By the time I pull into the driveway, the tears are gone, just dry, salty crust left clinging to the corners of my eyes. My face is a puffy, swollen mess, my nose red and raw from blowing it with scratchy gas station napkins I found crumpled on the backseat floor. I sit in the driveway, giving myself one last moment alone to breathe before I head in. I pull the keys from the ignition, readjust the rearview mirror, and give myself one last look, assessing the damage. It's worse than I imagined. I'm a complete and total miserable, hot mess.

"Enough is enough, girl…You need to pull your shit together and get ahold of yourself!" My pitiful reflection in the mirror stares back at me.

"You are a grown-ass woman! You will be fine!" I preach it to the empty car, as if saying it out loud might make it hurt less.

"You will forget all about that coward in a month or two… And laugh about this someday!" I desperately try to convince myself.

I refuse to let my heartbreak win. I hike up my imaginary big-girl panties, climb out, and make my way to the back of the car. My fingers tremble as I fumble with the key fob, releasing the trunk door and exposing everything that's been left behind. I grab hold of my suitcase, then set it onto the driveway beside my feet. As I reach to grab the last of my belongings, something catches my eye. *What the hell is this?* Poking out from the side pocket of my bag is a small piece of paper. It's the Waffle House receipt from this morning, and on the back is a message from Jax.

Handwritten in blue ink, it says, *"Please let me explain. I'm sorry. Call me so we can talk, it's not what you think. I love you. Jax. 856-555-7373"*

I loved you, too, asshole, and look where that got me.

I draw in a deep breath, a useless attempt to calm myself. Without a second thought, I crumble the receipt into a tight ball, the paper crackling before I shove it into my pocket. He doesn't deserve that. I gather my bags and walk into my family home like nothing happened, as if not only an hour before, my whole world hadn't just caved in on top of me.

"Charlotte????? Is that you, baby?" My mom's voice screeches from the top of the stairs. The moment I see her, I collapse, dropping my bags and any confidence in keeping it together, right along with them.

CHAPTER 23

The past month, since getting back, has been hard to say the least, but I am grateful that I didn't have to be thrown right back into work. I needed time. In light of the catastrophic events that brought our country to its knees, Jeff generously gave the entire company a few weeks off, allowing us to stay home with our families. The 9-11 attacks have rattled the entire country, leaving everyone in it on edge. Jeff thought that spending some time at home might help settle our nerves, maybe even help us feel a little more safe, before sending us back to work. He couldn't have been more spot on.

The first few days back, after discovering Jax's lies, not only mentally drained me but physically as well. The toll it took on me hit with the force of a Mack truck. The two weeks practically flew by; I swear I slept through most of it. I don't know what came over me, but one thing's for sure: my exhausted body needed it. On the rare occasion that I wasn't asleep, no matter how much I tried not to, my thoughts were consumed by Jax.

Being back at work has been incredible. Calling it a great week doesn't even begin to cover it; it's done wonders for my mental health. While the idea of having those initial few weeks to myself was a thoughtful gesture, sitting at home thinking of Jax with another woman overwhelmed me and drove me insane. I couldn't take another minute lying in bed, wallowing in my pathetic misery. I desperately needed a distraction, and returning to work, keeping busy, was just what the doctor ordered.

My customers surely haven't complained. Now that I'm back, I'm making more cakes than I ever thought possible. Seriously, though, it's enough to feed the entire U.S. Army. I'm cranking them out like a woman possessed.

If I were scheduled to decorate a hundred cakes for the day, I would kick out two. This week, one manager seriously asked me to leave because I'd iced way too many; they had nowhere to store them. We ended up having to stash them in the back room's ice cream freezer for future use.

Just yesterday, I was in the zone, locked in, before I realized I never stopped to eat, so I grabbed a donut to satisfy the craving. Big mistake, my stomach was so out of sorts that I'd made myself sick. I barely made it to the bathroom before throwing up. Turns out my stomach wasn't that empty after all, judging by how fast I filled up a toilet bowl. Just the sight of it made me hurl once more.

It was the second time this week. It's like I'm stuck in a never-ending loop. If I'm not working, I'm getting sick, and if I'm not getting sick, I'm so exhausted that I'm passed out on the couch before I can even kick off my work shoes. Coming back after those few weeks off is kicking my butt harder than it ever did before. And now I'm starting to wonder if I'm coming down with something, because the nausea is just plain next level. Lately, certain smells that never used to bother me are setting me off like crazy. I grabbed fries and a burger the other day, and the scent was so overwhelming I had to stick the bag in the trunk until I got home. Totally weird.

Rumors of a new strain of flu are circulating, and now, as my symptoms persist, I'm certain I'm coming down with it. If I don't feel better soon, I'm gonna call the doctor, because my body can't take much more of this. *I* can't take much more. *Hopefully, they can figure it out, and it won't last too long.*

CHAPTER 24

May 4, 2002

"Mom! It's time!" I gasp into the phone, my breath in short, frantic bursts.

"Are you sure, honey?" she asks, but doesn't bother to wait for an answer. "Okay... Dad and I will meet you there!" she says in a panic. "I can come get you and drive you if you want!" She is now in full panic mode.

"No, Mom, I'm already here... Come to the hospital," I plead.

"Oh... You are ready, I guess." She reiterates what I just said, and my head shakes when she does. *Maybe this wasn't such a good idea.* "Be careful and be strong, you are going to do great," Mom says matter-of-factly. Yet I can hear a distinct, familiar tone in her voice; she is worried about her baby girl.

"I love you, Charlotte," Her voice is much calmer. She doesn't want to worry me.

"I love you, too, Mom. See you soon."

The contractions are coming fast, about every four minutes now. Just a few short hours ago, at work, they began slowly and sporadically at first. I was in the middle of piping "Happy Anniversary" on top of an ice-cream cake when the first one shot a pain straight through me, causing me to jerk, messing up the wording. Its result was more like "Happy Annive_-=r="y)." Boy, did it piss me off, too, because I then had to scrape off the entire top of the cake and re-ice it. (One thing I despise is having to do double work.) One minute, I was fine; next, I was gasping for air, pain shooting through me, and ruining cakes in the process. It came from out of nowhere, but thankfully not another one for some time after. So, I continued decorating, but pushed any piping of words to the other decorator working beside me. It wasn't until the contractions had become more frequent that I finally decided to leave and head for the hospital. But of course, not before a McDonald's run. I've heard countless stories from women, hours of labor, stuck in a hospital bed, and all they're given is a few inadequate ice chips. *I'm no dummy.* I scarfed down a Big Mac and fries in record time, washing it all down with a fizzy fountain Coke. If I were going to have this baby tonight, I wouldn't do it on an empty stomach. *Nope... not gonna happen.*

It was with careful intention that I waited as long as I did to call my mother and tell her I was in labor, both for her sake and mine. Waiting was my only option; it would give her less time to worry, and it would ensure that my sanity would stay intact for as long as possible. I love my mom more than anything, but she would drive me crazy, worrying with each and every contraction. So, I knew exactly when I would need to call her.

Not only did she insist on being in the delivery room with me, but I wanted her here, too. She's gone through this before, when she delivered me, and God knows, I have no idea what to expect. Not to mention, her first grandchild is about to be born, and since Jax clearly won't be here, she is the obvious next best thing.

"You should try and rest a little bit in between contractions, save your strength for when it's time to push... Is your mom on her way?" Nurse Joy asks.

I nod my head, gritting my teeth through the pain, answering her without even saying a word.

The hospital room is dimly lit; the only light comes from the window, shining into the far corner of the room. It features a beige rocker with an attached footrest, likely intended for the father-to-be to relax and put his feet up, but mine remains empty. Jax will never get that chance. He won't get to experience any of this. *I wonder what he's doing right now?*

I often imagine that if things were different, if he hadn't been married to someone else, he'd be standing right here by my side, talking me through each painful contraction and calming me with his kind and thoughtful words.

Against my parents' wishes, I refused to tell Jax about his baby. Jennifer, too, agreed with them, pleading with me on multiple occasions, trying to convince me that a baby needs its father. Throughout this entire pregnancy, I've been adamant about keeping it a secret from him and raising the baby all on my own. Jax has a wife, and it's not me, end of story. No amount of pleading or nagging was ever going to change that undeniable fact.

But don't get me wrong, I'm grateful for the continued love and support from my parents, Jennifer, and even Jeff. They mean well, always wanting what's best for the baby and me, but keeping the pregnancy from Jax has always been my decision, and mine alone.

Jennifer's been my lifeline through the past nine months. She's kept me grounded, and anytime that I've wanted to quit, she was always there to kick me in the ass. With Jax out of the picture, I needed her more than she could ever know.

Of course, I couldn't have survived this pregnancy without my parents, too, but a best friend is different and takes it to a whole other level. She has this uncanny ability to step into whatever role that's needed. In the moments I broke down, she was always there with a shoulder to lean on. Don't tell her, but I may have wiped my nose on the sleeve of her shirt more times than I can count. If my nerves were wrecked and I was desperate for a glass of wine, she'd step in like a champ and polish off the bottle for me. (I'm pretty sure I didn't need to twist her arm on those occasions.) Or when my hormones played nasty tricks on me, and I'd tell myself I was the size of a whale, she wasted no time telling me I was nuts.

"You look just as beautiful as you did thirty pounds ago," she had said that day.

"I never said I was ugly... Dummy... I said I was fat," I said, annoyed, but then we both laughed until we couldn't breathe, and when she snorted, there was no turning back. We laughed so hard I had to clamp my legs together, torn between worrying I'd pee myself or that the baby might just slide right out of my vagina.

When my belly became so ginormous, and I could barely see my toes, she painted them, even with tiny little flowers on them. (That proved she loved me, because that girl *despises* feet.)

And every time that I would say I hated Jax, she never hesitated to join in and hate him right along with me. One time, early in the pregnancy, I hit a low point and threw myself a full-blown pity party. Going on and on, questioning how I was gonna get through the pregnancy without Jax's help, whining about anything I could dream up. She never asked a single question, just showed up an hour later with ice cream, some candy, and a box of old mismatched dishes.

"What's with the dishes... Dummy?" I remember laughing as I questioned her.

"Don't worry about it... these are for later... Stupid." It all was so mysterious, something for the life of me, I couldn't figure out.

(*'Dummy' and 'Stupid'... our pet names we've had for each other since middle school. She's not actually a Dummy... welllllll, maybe just a little.*)

Later that night, she started a fire, and the two of us sat on the back patio, stuffing our faces with bowls of ice cream. One by one, we smashed the plates against the concrete, letting each porcelain shard break away the pain.

The list goes on and on, but one thing is certain: I'll always be grateful for our friendship. It's deep and unwavering. I love her like the sister I chose. *But I have a Jennifer.* When the time comes for baptizing the baby, she'll be the obvious choice with the honor of being the baby's godmother. I can't think of a more deserving person. Between my parents and Jennifer, this baby that's about to be born is going to be extremely loved. And of course, spoiled as hell.

* * *

I lay my head back, doing as Nurse Joy suggests, and close my eyes. Knowing full well that my overwhelmed mind will never let it rest, always running at warp speed, but I do as I'm told and try.

Of course, my mind wanders to where it always seems to these days, a beeline straight to Jax. Reflections of our journey home only nine months ago now feel like a lifetime has passed since then. Memories of the love we made on that stormy September night consume my thoughts. I remember every detail, the roughness of his hands on my body, a heat that still burns straight through to my soul. The sweet, minty taste of his tongue against mine is still embedded in my mind. But like always, the sting of that fateful day finds a way to creep its way back in, bringing me back to the harsh reality that my baby's father is married to another woman.

I recall the countless phone calls he made to my house, days and weeks later, begging my parents to persuade me to answer, to give him a chance to explain. Often wondering how he ended up finding out my phone number in the first place. Sure, it could've been found in any phone book, but I can't shake the sneaky suspicion that Jeff was the one who reached out and gave him my information, thinking he was helping somehow.

Jeff isn't one to pry, so he never came right out and asked, but it was obvious that he assumed the baby was Jax's. He witnessed the attraction between us on those long days riding together in the backseat of the car. Jeff's a smart guy; he did the math and could tell that something horrible happened on that last day of the trip, causing things to end between us. For weeks, my daily routine at home and work was walking around like a depressed zombie. I guess he couldn't stand to see me like that, so one day he finally broke down and asked.

"Charlotte, I know it's none of my business, but if you want to talk about what happened between you and Jax, I'm a good listener," he said. "You seemed to hit it off so well, and I thought he could have been the 'one' for you." His concern was genuine.

"I'm okay... Thank you... But I'm not ready to talk about it yet, it's just too painful," My voice cracked as the words left my mouth that day.

Then, of course, I reacted the way any betrayed woman would; I ran out of the bakery and cried in the produce aisle. I laugh about it now. But that day will be forever etched into my memories. I felt so bad for him. He was just trying to be supportive, but yet soooooo out of his element. Dealing with a crying, hormonal pregnant woman was definitely not penciled in on his agenda planner that day. He was a frantic mess searching for me throughout the store. I can still picture the panicked look on his face when he found me sobbing next to the asparagus display. Just embarrassing. *I was pathetic.*

"There you are. How about you go home and take the rest of the week off?" he had said to me, in a tone like speaking to a five-year-old. "I can get Liesl in here to cover you. Just do me one favor before you leave, will ya?"

"What's that?" A sob caught in my throat as I tried to push back tears. I remember the way the other shoppers looked at Jeff, with burning eyes, thinking he was the reason for my tears. *Poor thing.*

"Go down to the freezer aisle and pick out a few gallons of your favorite ice cream. On me," he pleaded. "Ice cream always does the trick for my wife, Sally, when I've done something to piss her off."

I gave him the biggest hug, then thanked him and went on a search for my ice cream hunt.

Ever since that day, I have vowed to put any energy I had left into my work, along with the tiny human that had been growing inside me. I decided after that embarrassing outburst that I wouldn't let my emotions determine my fate. I would work right up until the birth, unless my doctor instructed otherwise. I'd be the best damn single mother I could be.

CHAPTER 25

A nother contraction rips through me, and I scream out in pain. *"Christ all mighty... how do women go through this more than once?"*

Just as fast as the pain hit, it vanishes, and suddenly I'm laughing. A random memory from when I was pregnant pops into my head, and I can't help it. Nurse Joy gives me a look, like she's not sure if I'm losing it or just overly tired. Could be both.

One time, when I was around four or five months pregnant, my belly was at the point where it was starting to show. The annoying "in-between" stage of pregnancy where you could fit into normal jeans, but only if they weren't buttoned, and hid it with a large shirt. Otherwise, I needed those god-awful maternity jeans that were annoyingly more comfortable. Strangers were never sure whether to congratulate me or keep their mouths shut in the unfortunate case that I was just an overachiever in the eating category. Most of the time, I would just go with it, but sometimes I would mess with people's minds, just to help lighten the mood. Like the one time I was standing in line at my local coffee shop, down the street from my house, called 'The Mug Life.'

"How exciting... When are you due?" an elderly woman asked me. I can still see the way her face lit up at the sight of my belly. It was apparent that she loved babies.

"Huh?" I answered her.

"The baby... When is the little bundle of joy due to arrive?" The excitement in her voice was genuine as she reached over and placed her palm on my swollen midsection. (She was sweet and all, but why on earth do people, let alone strangers, think it's acceptable to touch a pregnant woman's stomach?)

"Oh, I'm sorry... I'm not pregnant," I said to her, my face was like stone, giving nothing away. "I just can't say no to those lattes and have been packing on the pounds." I pointed to the barista behind the counter, who was finishing up my order.

The poor woman looked mortified, turning five shades of crimson at her "blunder." I'm ashamed to say, I enjoyed that a little more than I should have. *She really was sweet.* I probably should have confessed and absolved her of her embarrassment, but instead, I grabbed my latte and walked out the door, laughing the entire walk back to my car.

But not before saying "Have a nice day! Enjoy your latte!"

Being pregnant is nothing short of a miracle. Every day, I marveled at the fact that I had a tiny human growing inside me. Even on the sick days, I absolutely loved being pregnant. The glow of my skin was a bonus, and the fact that I had no problem giving in to every craving I'd had was a great perk, too. It was an instant excuse for indulging in midnight snacks without the guilt attached. My favorite time of the day was bedtime; it was always the moment I would lie down. It was the baby's favorite time as well, tossing, turning, and stretching inside my belly until it was just so, finally allowing me to drift off to sleep.

One night, I remember balancing the television remote on top of my growing midsection as I lay there, still as a cucumber, while the little pickle inside me practiced gymnastics. I was in awe of the way I could recall every hand or foot as it moved throughout my belly, then knocking the remote clear off onto the bed. Like something straight out of a Hollywood sci-fi movie where aliens and humans somehow make babies together. I felt so connected to the baby in those quiet moments, just the two of us.

But with all the unforgettable, beautiful moments, there were many that I wish I could forget. The numerous visits to the OBGYN come to mind. What should have been an exciting time, getting the chance to hear the baby's heartbeat, measuring my weight, and progress of the pregnancy was always a reminder that I was doing it alone.

Fathers would sit beside their wives, hand in hand, sometimes feeling her belly just as their baby kicked. They would look at me with excitement, convinced we shared a bond, or so they believed.

"I take it the baby's father couldn't get off work today?" They would ask while I sat there alone. "I don't know how I would do this without him." Then, like always, they would turn to their husbands and kiss them on their cheeks and smile.

I never wanted anyone to feel uncomfortable, and to save myself from any embarrassment, I would always lie and make up a story. The 'mystery father' would either be at work, or getting dinner ready, or at home putting the baby furniture together. All seemed like reasonable excuses as to why I was alone on such important, monumental appointments.

"Yeah, unfortunately, he couldn't make this appointment; he was so disappointed to miss it. He has made all the others up until today." I would tell them.

CHAPTER 26

"Holy, fuckkk!" I scream out, as a searing pain rips through me when another contraction hits. This one is different, more intense, and lasts longer than the others. My mom walks in, her face as white as the hospital sheets I lie on. Judging by the look on it, she must've heard me screaming and cussing like a certified truck driver from down the hall. She's pale like she's just seen a ghost, and she seems more than terrified. *Maybe having her here wasn't such a great idea.*

I can't imagine having a baby girl of my own, and then one day having to witness them in such pain without a damn thing you can do to stop it. It must be gut-wrenching. One day, I could be in her shoes, and I don't envy her.

"Such language, Charlotte... Who raised you?" she says, lightening the mood. A much-needed distraction from the pain that feels like it's splitting my insides in two.

She walks to my side and kisses my forehead, whispers that she's here, and tells me that everything will be okay. I believe her.

When the contraction is over, she walks over to the empty corner chair, Jax's chair, and sets down her purse when the next one hits. Like lightning, she's frantic and runs to my side, grabs hold of my hand and doesn't let go until my stomach relaxes.

"Charlotte, Daddy is right here!" my dad yells from the other side of the door, in the hallway. "You've got this, Honey, you are the bravest girl I know! You're my superhero!" He reassures me, his voice filled with love, calming me with every word.

I smile, even though I know he can't see, when tears begin to spill from my eyes, landing on the hem of my hospital gown. My dad's always been my biggest fan, forever cheering me on and telling me that there's nothing I can't do. He would move heaven and earth for me. I can only imagine that this entire situation is killing him right now, like a dagger being stabbed through his heart, knowing that he can't rid me of my pain. I can almost see him out in the hallway, pacing the floors, trying to come up with a plan to do so. I am the true definition of a "Daddy's little girl."

The two people that I love most in the world are the very ones who brought me into it, and now, they're here to help me bring *my* baby into it. The three of us have come full circle, one shaped by love, united from this tiny baby inside me about to be born. A wave of emotions blankets me, and just as it does, the sudden urge to push from deep down within begins to emerge. Panic sets in.

"Alright, Charlotte... The nurse tells me that the baby's head is crowning and it's almost time to push." Dr. Morris declares, appearing out of nowhere. "I hope you're ready because this little one sure is." He jokes and puts on a fresh pair of sterile gloves. A smacking sound echoes throughout the room as he fits them into place.

He's like some sort of ninja, because I hadn't even seen him walk in. *Where did he come from?* Within seconds, nurses I've never seen before begin filing in like a well-oiled piece of machinery. Each has its role to play in the delivery process. The fluorescent lights above me light up the room like it's the fourth of July, and I squint, allowing my eyes to adjust. At lightning speed, my bed is changed from an ordinary hospital bed to a delivery bed, all while I remain in it, as if it's some sort of secret Autobot transformer bracing for a battle.

My mother is magically clothed in drab blue hospital scrubs, complete with sterile gloves covering her tiny, aged hands. *When did that even happen?* Everyone in the room, except for me, seems to be ready for this delivery to happen. I grow more nervous by the second, knowing the baby will be here soon, and wonder if I will ever be ready. I look over to my mother, still clenching my hand, and can only hope that I could be half the mother she's been for me.

An overwhelming urge to push rises within me, and with it, an unbearable pain makes me feel like my insides are being torn apart, piece by piece.

"It's now or never, Charlotte… Are you ready?" asks Doctor Morris. It was more of a statement than a question, and there is no way to escape it. I have to do this. "It's time to start pushing." He says, and panic begins to rise within me.

"It's time? Are you sure? I… I don't think I can do this?"

"Honey… Everything is going to be okay. Just think about holding your baby that you already love so much…You are so much better at this than I was." My mother says as she grabs hold of my hand once more. "I was a wimp when I was delivering you. I cried during the entire process… You've got this." She assures me, and I believe her.

"On the count of three, I want you to push from deep down in your bottom. Understand?" I brace myself and grab hold of the bed rails, shake my head in silence, as the agonizing pain strikes once again.

"One! Two! Three!"

"AHHHHHHHHHHHHHHHHHHHHHHHHHHHHHHHHH!"

An ear-piercing scream echoes throughout the room and in an instant becomes silenced by the sweet sounds of my precious newborn baby's cries.

"It's a Boy!" Dr. Morris shouts out in excitement.

I look at my mother, tears of joy engulf her as she watches the doctor hand her first grandchild over to me, and I cradle him on my chest. A moment that neither of us could ever forget, etched into our hearts, tying us together in an unshakable way.

One long, painful push is all it took. The agony I just went through quickly fades, knowing it was all worth it for how I feel in this moment. I'm a mom now, and I couldn't be happier. Lying across my bare chest, skin on skin, is a tiny, slimy, beautiful, perfect baby boy. A full head of brown curly locks covers his head, reminding me of the terrible heartburn I had throughout the entire pregnancy. *I guess the old wives' tales are true.* Looking back, I should have purchased stock in antacids with the amount that I would consume in a day. I'd be a millionaire.

His tiny eyes are closed shut, covered with some gel-like goo, but I imagine him having the same icy-blue eyes as Jax's. He may only be a few minutes old, but I can already see the multitude of resemblances to him. The shape of his tiny chin, the slope of his cute little button nose, all remind me of Jax. Michael Leonard Evans (Michael for Jax's father and Leonard for mine) is perfect in every way possible, and he's all mine. As I lie here, captivated by his angelic, innocent face, I already know I would give my life for him. The love I already have is more than I ever dreamed possible, and I promise to be the best mother I can to him, even if it means having to do it all alone.

I can do this.

* * *

After what felt like an eternity, Baby Michael is given a clean bill of health from the on-call pediatrician, allowing my dad to come in and see his new grandson for the first time. A cluster of blue balloons clanging together in one hand and a box of blue cigars made from bubble gum in the other. *When the heck did he have time to get them?* Pure joy emanates from him at the sight of his new grandson. Seeing my father gently take care of baby Michael brings a sharp pang to my stomach, and instantly, I find myself thinking of Jax. As I look at him loving his only grandson, feelings of regret for Jax begin to surface.

Withholding the truth from him and ultimately denying him the joy of seeing the birth of his child, a son he knows nothing about, suddenly feels wrong, especially as I watch my dad's face light up. Guilt creeps its evil head, knowing all too well that Jax would make a wonderful father if only he were given the chance. I question myself if I've done the right thing. What would the news of a baby do to his marriage? So many questions run through my mind, and the heavy weight of regret I'm feeling begins to pile on. I'm having second thoughts, and it's clouding my mind.

But now isn't the time. I think to myself, just as I catch a glance of my dad kissing baby Michael's forehead before handing him back over to me.

"Your mother and I are going to run to the cafeteria and grab a few coffees, then to the gift shop. Would you like anything?"

"No thanks... Pop-Pop." I say, and smile at the way his new name rolls off my tongue.

His eyes light up with pride as he hears the words. "I like the sound of that." He boasts with joy, and the two new grandparents walk out the door, leaving just me and Michael completely alone together, for the first time since he was born.

I look down at my son, who has only been on this earth for a short time, but already resembles his father in so many ways. My heart hurts for Jax once again. *What have I done?*

"I'm sorry, Michael. I'm new at this, just like you." He sleeps against my chest, I marvel at his tiny, innocent face, and silently question the choices I've made. "I'm afraid I made a mistake." He stirs in my arms. "I didn't tell your Daddy about you, and I'm sorry he isn't here right now... His name is Jax, and he is beautiful just like you are... I have no doubt he would love you with all his heart." I blink back the tears rising in my eyes. "But mine is still broken, and right now, it hurts too much." I barely finish before the floodgates break loose.

For now, I need some one-on-one, mother/son time with baby Michael, to prove that I can do this motherhood journey alone, if it does indeed end up staying this way.

For all I know, I could tell Jax about his baby, and he could deny him and choose not to acknowledge him as his own. When I hear myself say it, I know it's absurd. Because if Jax knew there was a beautiful baby boy out there that was his, he would do anything in his power to be a part of his life. Which is why I can't tell him. Because he can never be part of mine.

CHAPTER 27

September 11, 2002

Michael is four months old. Time is flying by so fast, my head spins. So many milestones have already been reached, and still so many more to come. He's smiling, cooing, and so close to rolling over. (I think he could be a child prodigy) I know the moment he masters this last feat, I can kiss my sanity goodbye. He'll be scooting over every inch of the house and getting into mischief, just like my parents had warned me.

"Karma," they say on too many occasions, as if they're enjoying it a little too much.

Sitting down for a moment's peace would be a thing of luxury for the next few years.

I pour cream into my coffee and catch a glance of the calendar on the refrigerator, and am reminded once again what day it is. On the first anniversary of the 9/11 attacks, our country is, without a doubt, on high alert, in fear that copycat events could occur. The entire world appears to be on edge, and for good reason. Me included. Not only for the anniversary of such a heinous act, but also for the fact that almost a year has passed since I last spoke with Jax or had any form of contact at all. Not that I don't wonder about him, because I do. A lot. Especially now that Michael's been born. No matter how busy I am, he's always lingering in the back of my mind.

More than once, I've caught myself taking Michael for car rides, only to somehow end up an hour away, subconsciously driving through Jax's hometown. In hopes of catching a glimpse of him driving past me in his truck or possibly coming out of the local Wawa convenience store, coffee cup in hand. But never once, on any of those trips, did I see him, until that last time, when I decided to drive past his home, testing the limits.

It was just last week, over Labor Day weekend, when Michael had been unusually fussy. I decided to take him for a drive and promised my parents that we would be back in plenty of time for the fireworks that night. I purposely bought a pair of noise-canceling headphones for him so the loud "booms' wouldn't damage his tiny, sensitive eardrums. A recommendation from his pediatrician.

Off we drove, and again my car was set on autopilot, driving straight through to Jax's hometown of Saddle Creek. I made the turn onto his street, heading straight to his home. I hadn't thought it through, still uncertain of what I'd do or how I'd react if I saw him that day. I distinctly remember just how much my anxiety was getting the better of me. I became fearful that he might spot me, and I decided it was best to turn back. My nerves had taken over and ultimately became in charge. I slowed the car to a stop on the side of the road, ensuring no traffic was coming in either direction, and I made a "Uie." Just as I was about to speed up, a truck approached from the other side, then slowed to a dead stop, positioning itself right next to me in the middle of the road. It was

Jax.

I never really expected to see him. I'd made the drive so many times and always came out unscathed. So needless to say, when I did, I was shocked. Frozen and unable to move, I didn't know what to do. In that brief moment, our eyes locked, and that's when I noticed his window beginning to roll down. *Jesus Christ! What do I do?* I remember thinking.

After months of being torn on whether to tell him the truth about his baby, in the end, I'd come to the realization that Jax needed to know. All this time, I was so desperate to see his face, talk to him, and most importantly, introduce him to Michael, who slept peacefully in the back seat. Everything I knew I needed to do became clouded as visions of his wife, Joanna, came crashing through my mind. The very sight of him brought back every ounce of ache that fueled my decision in the first place. Bile began to surface in the back of my throat, and my stomach felt woozy. My vision blurred, a direct result of my tears. I remember staring forward as I pushed my foot down on the gas pedal and drove as far away from him as the car would allow.

I vowed to stay strong, to never go back, no matter how much I missed him or how wrong it was, keeping his son from him.

Until this morning.

It's deceivingly peaceful as I sit alone in the backyard of my parents' home, enjoying my coffee. A slight breeze blows, swaying the branches of the Oak trees as the clouds float in swift motion through the blue skies above. Notes of autumn are visible everywhere I look. The leaves are turning beautiful hues of red, orange, and yellow. Every roadside stand is filled with freshly picked apples and pumpkins. Bales of straw sit on every front porch with scarecrows peeking out from behind them. Everything screams fall, except for the temperature outside. It's only 8:30 in the morning, yet it's already warm, and it feels eerily identical to how it was on this exact date last year.

One year ago, the attacks on our great country occurred. For so many reasons, this date will forever be embedded in my soul. The most important reason can be found lying peacefully, sleeping upstairs at this very moment. A constant reminder every time I look into Michael's blue eyes.

I sit here savoring the subtle notes of cinnamon in my morning coffee while I listen to the birds sing. Beside me sits a makeshift side table, nothing more than a wooden tree stump, cut by my dad's bare hands, holding the receiver to the monitor connected to Michael's nursery. The soothing sounds of his breathing float through the machine, and I wonder what he could be dreaming of.

Reminiscing, my thoughts drift back to that fateful day just one short year ago. It feels like only yesterday the uncertainty we faced was what scared me most at the time. I think back to Jeff, Dick, and, of course, Jax. Each of them played their own crucial role without even knowing, not only safely getting me home, but easing my fears while doing it.

Not in a million years, from when I woke up that September morning, did I think I would be forever tied to those three in such a way. Let alone be the mother to one of their children. A child that was conceived from one night of lovemaking, a baby that he doesn't know exists.

The regrets I've been having these past months continue to pile up. Wondering whether I did the right thing and if I'd made the right decision. Dreams of the three of us together consume my nights and show glimpses into a life that I didn't know existed. I can envision the two of us hand in hand, walking through the park, Michael asleep in a sling strapped to my chest. I picture the future vividly, hearing the roar of the crowd as his teammates swarm him with high-fives after he scores the winning touchdown in pee-wee football. I can visualize my parents' faces as my mother proudly records him, tears of joy flowing as they hear him singing his tiny little heart out in the school musicals. An entire future version of the three of us plays out before me as if watching an after-school special.

Missing Jax has been constant these past few weeks, because deep down, I know I'll never find a love like the one I had with him. It's the kind that I've never felt for anyone, nor have I since. Sadness overwhelms me, certain no man could ever come close. Tears fill my eyes at the thought of a love so deeply lost. I cry for the love that's now just a memory. *Maybe it's time we talk.*

Brrrinng... Brrrinng... I fumble through the pocket of my robe and pull out my phone, along with it, a tissue, and a binky, so I shove the latter two back in.

"Hello?" I say, never bothering to look and see who the call is from.

"I hope I didn't wake you... I just felt like I had to call you." Jeff says. His tone is somber. I can almost feel the weight of the day carried through the sound of his voice.

"Aww... good morning... and no, you didn't wake me. I've got a four-month-old, I never sleep." I laugh. "As a matter of fact, I'm out back enjoying my coffee and was just thinking of you."

"How is that little butterball doing?" His mood improves when he asks about Michael.

"He's upstairs still sleeping..." I pause for a moment. "Jeff..."
"Yeah???"

"I think I'm ready," I confess, and can feel a weight being lifted as the long-awaited words leave my mouth.

"For what it's worth, I think you're making the right decision. I'm proud of you, Charlotte," he says, knowing exactly what I'm referring to. "Today certainly puts everything in perspective, doesn't it? There's no guarantee that tomorrow will come, and telling Jax about Michael is the right thing to do."

"Thank you... I love you, Jeff... You really are the best." Once again, tears well up inside me, as he always knows just what to say.

"Maybe mention that to Sally the next time you see her," he jokes, lightening up the mood. *See what I mean?*

"I'll see what I can do." I wink, although he won't see.

"Alright. Now it's time to call Dad... Wish me luck."

"Hahaha... Good luck with that... Seriously though, tell Dick hello for me and that I am thinking of him today... and tell him I miss him too." Which I do. He may be a crabby old man, but he is a crabby old man that I have grown to love. Considering all we've been through and the reasons behind it, how could I possibly not? Like Jeff just said, it puts things into perspective, and I'm beginning to see things through much clearer eyes. Especially from all the stories of the 9/11 victims being retold over the past week.

On every radio and television station, there's been a constant reminder for all of us to "never forget." So many heartfelt articles, all paying a special tribute to the nearly three thousand innocent people who lost their lives that day. Intimate stories, giving us personal insights into each one of their lives, their work, hobbies, and of course, their loved ones. I make it my purpose to truly listen to each and every one of them, paying private tribute to all who have perished.

I pull out the crumpled-up tissue from my pocket and wipe the steady stream of tears that falls from the corners of my eyes. If there is one thing I've learned from this past year, it's that tomorrow is never promised, and from all the interviews with family members of that day's victims, I've never been more reminded that love remains the most powerful force in the universe.

It's time to talk to Jax and listen to what he has to say. I love him, and right now, love is all that matters. I can't dismiss it so easily anymore. I think to myself.

I can hear movement coming from the kitchen. My mother, a creature of habit, will be pouring herself a mug of coffee right about now, I can almost guarantee it. But not before brushing her teeth, wiping down the bathroom sink, and making up her side of the bed. It is the same daily routine, and it has been for years. *Gee, I wonder where my OCD comes from?*

I have the sudden urge to get out of here. *I need to clear my mind.* I figure I can escape for a few minutes and head to the bakery for some goodies, then swing by the post office and save my mom the trip. It's only a short drive away, and she can look after Michael when he wakes up. Today is going to be all about distractions, if I have any chance of getting through it unscathed.

I grab the monitor and my empty mug and dump any remnants into the grass before I go back inside. Confirming my intuitions, my mother is in her fluffy white robe, sipping from the same mug she has been drinking from since I was a toddler. "World's Best Mom" is written on its side, for the world to know that she is indeed just that.

The aroma of fresh-brewed coffee smacks me in the face, and I instantly crave a refresher. Her coffee will always be my favorite recipe. She still thinks it's her little secret, but what she doesn't know is that I have seen her make it dozens of times: she adds a pinch of cinnamon and a dash of Himalayan salt to the grounds, leaving it tasting like a warm hug in a mug.

"Hi, sweetie. Is Michael still sleeping?" she asks.

"He is… Like a baby." I laugh at my corny joke and pour myself a refill. "I need to get out of here for a bit, some sort of distraction, I have a lot going on in this noggin of mine." My finger taps on my head. "Jeff called this morning, checking in on me. He says it is going to be our 'thing' and will call me on this date every year." I say, my tone is reflective.

"That was very thoughtful, and heartbreaking at the same time." She drops a spoonful of sugar into her cup. "You know how lucky you are to have a boss that you actually like and genuinely cares about you?"

"Ever since I got off the phone with him, I've been an emotional mess, thinking about this day and of course Jax," I sheepishly admit. "I was thinking I could run to the bakery for some fresh bagels and donuts, then swing by the post office for ya on the way back. If that's okay with you?"

"Of course."

"I won't be long," I promise.

I run upstairs to my childhood bedroom and throw on my trusty old red, white, and blue sweatshirt. Worn and tattered from years of use, purchased over Memorial Day weekend down the shore, my senior year. Memories of that weekend flash through me and now feel like a lifetime ago. So much has changed since then. I pair it with some cutoff jeans and my very favorite not-so-white "Chuck Taylor" sneakers. Before heading back down, I stop and peek in on Michael and marvel at the ability he has to sleep without a care in the world. My heart is full and ready to burst at the seams at the very sight of him. I blow a kiss into the air, whispering, "I love you," just softly enough to float into the universe, but not enough to wake him. I tiptoe down the stairs and back to the kitchen, saying goodbye to my mom before heading out the door.

I turn on the radio station to 92.5 FM, to drown my mind with some good-ole country music. An attempt to block out the past year as I drive to the local bakery. It's an amazingly beautiful day out, perfect for a relaxing drive and donuts, of course. Almost too perfect. My mouth begins to water at the thought of enjoying a donut on the back patio with little Michael on my lap when I return.

The sweet aroma of freshly made donuts and warm baked bread permeates the air the moment I walk into the bakery. The brilliant colors of red, white, and blue are everywhere, overpowering everything else the bakery has to offer. A flag is hung by the doorway just as I walk in, and behind the counter is an impressive array of patriotic donuts, cookies, and cakes on display. Most covered in red, white, and blue sprinkles, candies, and icing. All to show their pride and patriotism for our great country and to "never forget" the victims and their families affected by 9/11.

National pride has been on full display everywhere I go, with everyone showing off their red, white, and blue, each in their own special way. *God, I love this country.* I think to myself as I soak it all in and walk up to the counter.

"I will have a dozen assorted donuts, with at least three of them powdered cream, and also a half a dozen assorted bagels as well, please." The bakery owner behind the counter is already putting together my order before I can finish.

He hands me two boxes, each wrapped with a patriotic ribbon. I handed him a twenty-dollar bill in exchange, insisting that he keep the change. Reluctant at first, but in the end, he agrees to drop it in the donation bucket on the counter. A repurposed bucket used to store icing, now used for donations to go to the victims' families of 9/11. *Pay it forward, he asked.* I recall the man in the diner who paid for our meal.

The Post Office is not much different from the bakery and the rest of the country, proudly showing their patriotism. The man behind the counter sports a red button-down shirt with blue and white stars covering it. He waves to me and says hello, just as he has so many times before, as I unlock my box and retrieve the contents of our mail. My purse is bursting at the seams with God knows what, barely enough for an extra pack of gum, but I shove the stack of mail in anyway, then head out the door. I intend to sift through the contents when I get home. *Maybe clean out my mess of a purse while I'm at it.*

I place it on the passenger side seat, alongside the pastries that have been taunting me with their yummy goodness, and head for home. *No one will notice one missing, will they?*

"Courtesy of the Red, White and Blue (The Angry American)" by Toby Keith blasts throughout the car the moment I turn it on. It's become my favorite song these past few weeks. Written in response to the 9/11 terrorist attacks, he sings every word we as Americans all feel in our hearts, making it so fitting for today. Singing along, bits of crumbs sputter from my mouth like confetti, but the sweetness fades when memories of this day last year, and memories of Jax settle in. Pulling out of the parking lot, the pain follows me, carrying them both with me the entire way home.

CHAPTER 28

Edith Evans

Sesame Street plays in the background, its volume turned low, as I rock Michael on the living room glider. It was given to Charlotte as a baby shower gift, purchased from her godmother, Peggy, and is the perfect addition to our existing furniture. He lays against me and snuggled tight into my arm, sucking away on the bottle I just prepared.

Charlotte has gone out and left me here to take care of baby Michael. Out for a quick drive to the bakery and then to the post office, and not quite sure in which order. I wasn't expecting her to be this long. I have my own errands to run when she returns.

I take a glance at the clock on the wall, made from wood, cut from my father's bare hands. The minute hand goes tick-tock as the clock reads ten forty-five. Worry begins to creep in, as an hour has already passed since Charlotte left.

"Mommy should have been home by now," I say to Michael. I try to shake the worry from my mind, look down at him, and smile. "She will be back soon, sweetie. I'm sure of it." I whisper to him, rocking him in my arms.

I'm not quite sure who I'm trying to reassure, him or myself. Overcome by the instinct to hold him closer, I give in and kiss his forehead. The scent of baby powder covers his precious little body, reminding me of Charlotte when she was just an infant. It seems like just yesterday that I was changing her very own dirty diapers, and now she has a baby of her own.

"The days are long, but the years are short," my mother would always say.

When I was young, I never understood its meaning until I grew up and had Charlotte. No truer words have ever been spoken. I swear I gave birth to her, blinked, and the next thing I knew, she became a grown woman. Even though, no matter how old she gets, she will always be my little girl. The same one who stood on my kitchen stool beside me, helping me bake my famous chocolate chip cookies. Cracking the eggs into a bowl was her specialty, one by one, so careful not to let any of the shells fall in. She's always had a love for baking from the time she could stand, so it's no surprise that she grew up to be a baker herself.

Bang! Bang! Bang! Echoes through the room, startling me, causing me to jump and scaring poor Michael. He begins to wail as the banging continues. Knowing Leonard is out back in the yard and impossible for him to hear, I instinctively run to the door. Michael cries out louder and carries permanent residency on my hip. *It has to be Charlotte.* I can almost see her with hands full of pastries, unable to turn the knob on the front door and kicking it with her foot.

Shushing Michael, then shifting him from one hip to the other, I reach for the knob and turn it. I ready myself to relieve her of her load, a small trade-off, as I extend my arms with Michael still cradled in them.

Looking very similar to Rafiki holding up Simba in Disney's The Lion King.

A burly, middle-aged man in a policeman's uniform stands before me. In an instant, worry swallows me whole.

"Sergeant Washington" is affixed to the name tag on his chest. I can smell the scent of his rich, masculine cologne, reminiscent of fresh pine in the great outdoors.

I freeze and nearly drop Michael straight from my grip, but thankfully, my maternal instinct kicks in as I pull him in closer to me, almost to the point of suffocation, then ease up on my hold.

"Is this the home of Charlotte Evans?" Sergeant Washington asks, his tone firm but kind.

My mouth feels like the desert sand, and when I try to speak, no words come out. Every inch of me goes numb. If the movies have taught me anything, it's that a police officer at someone's home is rarely a good sign.

I feel as if I'm the leading role in my own horror movie, and it scares the living daylight out of me. I try to respond, but my voice refuses to cooperate. It's reluctant, but my brain finally takes notice, my head shakes in an up and down motion, signifying that it indeed is Charlotte's home.

"There's been an accident, ma'am. Charlotte has been airlifted to Cooper Trauma Center in Camden." His voice is low. The concerned tone hidden beneath it doesn't go unnoticed.

"Oh my God!!!! My Baby!!!! No!!!!" I cry out. "Is she hurt? Please tell me she is okay!" My screams rip from my throat. So loudly I startle poor Michael, scaring him once again as he begins to wail, mimicking my horror, though he is too young to understand why.

Leonard comes barreling in from the backyard, wondering where the screams are coming from. My knees go weak, feeling like a bowl full of Jell-O, and I stumble back a few steps, bracing myself against the stairway for support.

"What the hell is going on?" Leonard comes in yelling, wondering where all the shrieks are coming from. By instinct, he grabs Michael from me, keeping him safe from being harmed. His eyes lock with Sergeant Washington's, and all the color drains from his face.

"She appears to have suffered severe brain trauma and is unresponsive at this time," says the officer. "I assure you, the doctors at Cooper are top-notch and are doing everything they can to help her."

"Jesus! Is he talking about Charlotte?" Leonard releases the stare he has on him and looks at me, nothing but fear in his eyes as he pulls Michael in closer.

From that moment, and the ones that followed, meld into a single continuous blur.

CHAPTER 29

T he steady sounds of beeping and clicking engulf the room, echoing from every corner. Doctors and nurses walk back and forth with frantic looks masking their faces. Leonard and I stay quiet as we sit on the cold emergency room chairs, scared, oblivious to what is going on with Charlotte. Her head nurse has already briefed us on the multitude of tests that have already been taken: bloodwork, CT scans, Ultrasounds, and MRIs. If there is a test, Charlotte has been given it.

Her left arm has been broken and shattered in multiple places, along with her left leg. A huge gash on the side of her head has already been stapled shut and covered with bandages to help it heal.

From what we've been told, a truck drove straight through a stop sign and then slammed straight into the driver's side of the car. Charlotte was directly in its path. She is broken, cut, and bruised, but thankfully, all of that is an easy fix. According to the doctors, the main concern right now is her brain, and they are still waiting for the results from her scans. Fears that there could be some internal bleeding or swelling on the brain loom over all of us. The fact that Charlotte still has not awakened, not only scares the hell out of her father and me, but the looks exchanged between the many doctors that filter in and out of her room show they're worried too.

I think about my grandson. He was still crying even as I left him with Jennifer. It's as if he could sense that something had happened to his mama. Immediately after the officer broke the news of Charlotte, I called Jennifer, asking her if she could watch him. The moment we handed Michael over to her, we rushed to the hospital to be by Charlotte's side. Dark thoughts begin to creep in and consume me. *What if, God forbid, she doesn't make it? Would Leonard and I raise Michael? Should I reach out to Jax and tell him he is a father?* A flood of terrible outcomes overwhelms my mind, and I must stop them before I drive myself mad.

Positive thinking and lots of prayers are all that is needed. I keep praying for her to wake, and the fact that there isn't a damn thing I can do to help her do that is just about killing me inside.

Doctor Nordone walks out to greet us, his clipboard dangling from his hand, knowing all too well that it holds the story of Charlotte's fate.

"Mr. and Mrs. Evans?" Both Leonard and I nod in agreement without speaking a word. The two of us are afraid too, for if we do, it might feel more real to us.

"We've received all of Charlotte's tests back, and I have some news," says the Doctor. "Every test that we could run has all come back negative. No visible trauma to the brain, and by God's good graces, there is no bleeding on Charlotte's brain. That, in itself, is promising news and very reassuring." The way he speaks sounds encouraging. "With that being said, Charlotte still has yet to wake and has not responded to any of our treatments thus far. Unfortunately, we have no way of knowing just how long she will remain this way, if not forever," he says, lowering his voice on the last bit, and it was barely audible, that I almost didn't hear. "All we can do now is wait. You both can go back with her and stay for as long as you like… Visiting hours are non-existent in cases like this."

With everything that Dr. Nordone just said, "In cases like this," struck me the most. Straight to my very core.

Leonard is already up and on his feet, waiting, but my legs are struggling and fighting against me. They feel like lead bricks attached to my hips, keeping me from moving and weighing me down. I try willing them to move, but they remain frozen, in a state of shock, just as I am. I want nothing more than to go to her and tell her that everything will be okay. Tell her that her Mommy is here, kiss her wounds, and make everything alright. It's what I have always done; that's what mothers are supposed to do, but truth be told, I am scared. I'm frightened at what she might look like, banged up with bruises, cuts, and tubes coming from every orifice of her body. Most of all, what haunts me the most is the awful thoughts I have of her waking and not remembering anything, and forgetting all about me. *What if she remains this way and never gets the chance to see her precious baby grow up?*

I am scared for so many reasons, but what I am most terrified of is losing my precious baby girl. My whole world begins and ends with Charlotte, and stepping through those doors that lead into her room is going to make all those unthinkable possibilities a reality. God's honest truth is, I am not sure I can handle it, but as her mother, my one job in life is to be there for my daughter, no matter what. If the circumstances ever arise, I will take a bullet for her, and if I am strong enough for that, then I am strong enough to walk through those doors and face whatever is on the other side. She's my baby girl, and I will do whatever it takes to bring her back to us all.

The beeping, clicking, and suction noises are the same from the emergency room, but these are solely for Charlotte. The moment we walk into her room, the harmony of clatter all collectively plays together to aid in Charlotte's health, in hopes of healing her. She is covered in a blanket up to her chest, and aside from some bruising and stitches to her face, she appears to be asleep. If she were anywhere else, lying in a bed, you wouldn't know a thing was wrong with her.

A familiar weight sets upon my shoulder; a calming touch I have felt so many times before. Leonard rests his hand on it and lets out a low, labored breath. His free hand reaches over to hold Charlotte's, and his presence, along with his touch, reassures both of us that somehow, everything will be okay. His belief that things always work themselves out, no matter what the circumstance, might as well be his superpower. No matter what doubt I've ever had, he's always been the one to counteract it. He will forever be my rock, although in this particular circumstance, I wonder if he believes it himself or if he is just being strong for the sake of my sanity. Either way, at this very moment, he calms me, and I am grateful for him, just as I have been all these years. If he says Charlotte is going to be okay, that is all I need to hear, and I will trust his words.

I walk alongside the front of her bed and reach for her free hand, placing mine in hers. Before I do, I reach up on my tippy toes and kiss Leonard's cheek, silently thanking him for being my forever rock.

"I love you."

CHAPTER 30

Charlotte's hand is warm, soft, and heartbreakingly fragile as I hold it in mine. I squeeze it ever so gently, afraid that anything more might break her. It's been way too many years since the two of us have held hands with one another. I close my eyes, reliving all the special moments we shared hand in hand, ones that I've taken for granted. I recall the many times I walked her to and from school each day, together with her tiny hand in mine.

"I still think of her as a little girl." The words catch in my throat as I confess to Leonard. "Remember all the trips to the Cape May Zoo? The way she would laugh at those tiny monkeys when they would swing from vine to vine. I can't remember what they were called," I say, breaking down into a fit of tears as I remember her little hands encased in mine at the zoo.

"I think they were Tamarins, right?" he answers, unsure of himself. "Whatever they were, she asked if she could have one for a pet every day for at least three months after." A sound comes from him, a sad attempt at laughter, trying to lighten the mood, but it comes out more like a deep smoker's cough. Only Leonard hasn't smoked a day in his life. I've been by his side more than half my life and know him like the back of my hand. I can tell by the twisted look on his face that he is trying to hold back his emotions, but his big-ole-heart is refusing to let that happen.

"Remember how contagious her laugh was?" I attempt to bring light into the room, relieving him from a full-on breakdown. "Is," I quickly corrected myself. "Like the first time we took her to the beach."

Memories of summers spent down the shore in Ocean City drift back, her sand-filled hand clutching mine as she jumped the crashing waves, both of us unaware of how quickly those days would slip away. How things can change in an instant.

I now wonder when the last time it had been, trying to pinpoint an exact moment that we'd held hands together. I search through every stored memory, and it fails me, deepening the sorrow even further. That's the thing about life and motherhood, no one ever tells you when the last time, in fact, will be the last.

How I long for her to be a young child again, so carefree, with me being the most important person in her life, the one she would reach her hand out to. And so, I sit beside her, helpless, watching her lie still in a cold, sterile hospital bed, waiting, because I would wait forever if that's what it takes.

I close my eyes, and in my own silent way, I begin making deals with God, the Devil, my deceased Grandparents, and anyone else willing to listen. I beg anyone who will hear my pleas, offering anything, everything, just to have her back, no matter what price I have to pay. Charlotte is my whole world. I love her more than life itself, and I will give up mine in a heartbeat if it means her waking and being okay. She has an entire life still left to live, one that involves raising her little boy.

If making a deal with the devil will help her achieve that, I would gladly give up my soul to him, hand it over on a shiny gold platter.

While I bartered with the heavens, I didn't notice the tears escaping through the cracks of my desperate, praying hands. I wipe them with a tissue, found in a box that sits on Charlotte's bedside table. Through the sting of my salty tears, my eyes flutter back open when something catches my attention, something I almost missed. In the far corner of the room, a chair that sits beneath the window. I wipe away the last of my tears with the back of my hand and force my eyes to focus. It's Charlotte's purse, worn, familiar, and heartbreakingly out of place.

I've all but seen it a thousand times before, constantly hanging from the stairway's landing post. An unspoken spot she claimed as her own. It used to drive me crazy, seeing her purse hanging where it didn't belong, and I never missed a chance to tell her so. I like things put away, nice and tidy. Now, I'd give anything to see it there again. From this day on, that landing post is hers, a quiet place where her purse waits for her, ready for whenever she decides to leave the house again.

I wonder how it got there, sitting by itself on the chair. Just the thought of a stranger handing it over to someone else makes my stomach twist into knots, the accident settling deeper inside me. I wince at the thought of the carnage left behind in the wreckage, her purse abandoned on the roadside, torn from the car at the point of impact. I can almost see Charlotte, lifeless, still strapped to the twisted metal, and the bile rises in my throat, choking me with the weight of it.

A maternal instinct pulls at me to hold it, as if cradling it could somehow bring me closer to her. Or at the very least, rifling through it might piss her off enough to wake up and yell at me for going through her personal things. The risk of her being furious with me is one I'm more than willing to take if it means she opens her eyes.

Half-heartedly, I pull my hand from hers and let go, leaving that task to her father as I walk over to the chair and pick up the purse. It's bulky and heavy in my hands, and curiosity prevails as I wonder what's inside.

"Good lord, what the heck is in here?"

Purses have always been a waste of space for me; I never carry one. Any essentials I have are stuffed into the back pockets of whatever pants I'm wearing. Not because it's the smartest place, but because it's what I've always done, easy to reach. If whatever I'm wearing doesn't have pockets, my husband's the next best resting place for whatever I need to carry.

"Get a purse like every other woman in the world, why don't ya?" He always gripes, muttering about being turned into a pack mule, but he never actually says no.

I always respond in the same way, "But I'm not like every other woman in the world." And bat my blues at him and laugh. Then into his pockets they would go. So, every time Charlotte would leave the house with her "suitcase" slung over her shoulder and walking with a slight limp from its weight, I always shook my head at her reasoning.

I pick up the purse and hold it close to my chest. The moment I touch it, I inhale the sweet scents of her that still linger, and it soothes me, even if just for a second. I take in another faint scent, one that brings a rush of memories: the day Charlotte gave birth to Michael. It lingers in the air, soft and comforting, like the warmth of that moment.

It feels like it was just yesterday. Charlotte asked me to go through her purse and fetch a hair tie so that she could pull her hair away from her face.

"I'm sweating like a pig!" she yelled at the time. "Can you grab me one of the hair ties from my purse, please?" she had asked, but it sounded more like a demand. "I think I might die if it gets any hotter in here!"

I remember laughing quietly to myself back then, thinking she was being so dramatic, but loving her all the more for it. But now, as she lies in yet another hospital bed, under much dire circumstances, I long to be able to hear her complaining about the heat just once more, or anything for that matter.

The moment I sit, I waste no time and open it up. Inside, the first things that come into sight are a hairbrush and three tubes of Chapstick (strawberry, mint & vanilla). *Who needs these many Chapsticks?* I spy her wallet, a pack of baby wipes, a binky with a piece of lint attached to its end, a crumpled-up granola bar wrapper, and a myriad of random items sitting on the bottom. Poking out from the inside pocket is the mail that she had picked up this morning.

She must have made it to the post office before the accident.

Out of habit, I pull out the stack and begin sifting through it, automatically separating the junk from the bills like I've done a hundred times before. In the middle of the pile, hidden between a realtor flyer and a coupon book, is an envelope addressed to Charlotte. I notice that it hasn't been opened. *She hadn't seen this one.* It's handwritten in black ink with a return address that reads Jaxson Lange, his address just below it.

Just seeing his name sends a surge of curiosity through me. I know it's probably wrong, but I can't help myself. I need to know what he's written. I try to ease my guilty conscience, reminding myself that with Charlotte in the state she's in, maybe it's not just okay, it's necessary. *You keep telling yourself that, Edith.*

I open it with great care, not wanting to risk tearing what's inside. In a flash, the letter is set free, and I begin to read.

Charlotte,

I want to start by saying, I miss you more than you know, and again, I am sorry. I need to explain. Given that you haven't answered any of my phone calls over the past year, I thought writing to you was my last and only option. I even drove to your house once and saw you and another woman in the backyard. As I walked toward the back, all I could hear was the smashing of something onto the ground and your voice cursing my name while doing it. I chickened out that night and turned right around and drove back home.

I can't apologize enough for not telling you sooner about my marriage.

Believe me, I tried so many times but could never bring myself to hurt you. Now realizing that's exactly what I did.

My ex-wife, Joanna (yes, Ex), and I grew up together as best friends, then dated throughout high school. All of that was true. Towards the end of our senior year, she became pregnant, and we decided to get married, thinking it was the responsible thing to do. While everyone else was at the prom, doing what every other senior was supposed to be doing, we got married with our parents by our sides.

But a few months later, she suffered a miscarriage. Losing our baby boy was devastating for both of us, unthinkable, and as you can imagine, put a strain on our marriage, a marriage that only came to fruition because of that baby boy in the first place.

Over the years, we tried to make it work, but in the end, we both knew that our high school crush was never meant to be anything but just that. We tried doing what we thought was right, but it just wasn't meant to be.

When you asked me the reason I was in Vegas, I told you that I was there for a bachelor party. That part was true, but I was scheduled to stay a few days longer, to be alone and prioritize my life and the end of my marriage. Giving us both a little time to digest the decision to get divorced. We were set to do just that when I returned from that trip. And then I met you...

When we shared that drink that first night in the bar, and our conversation talked about marriage, it spooked me, and it was the reason I left so fast. Never in a million years after that night did I think I would ever see you again.

Until I did, then I spent the days after falling head over heels in love with you.

Joanna had already known about you before we made it home that day. I talked to her on a few of our stops, telling her that I met you and my feelings for you.

After you left that day, we signed the papers and ended on very good terms and are still close, but just as friends.

I have a history with her, but I want you to be my present and future.

I love you, Charlotte. I knew from the first time I met you in the elevator that we had a special connection. What we had in those few short days was real for me; it was nothing short of a miracle meeting you, and I hope for you as well.

In my last attempt to ask you to forgive me and be with me, I say this.

I will be waiting by the entrance to the Cowtown rodeo this upcoming Saturday night, the place where we were supposed to have our first official date, in hopes that you will meet me. I hope you can forgive me. But in the chance that you don't, I will take that as your answer and will let you get on with your life, promising to never bother you again.

I hope you can find it in your heart to forgive me and remember that no matter what, I will love you forever.

Love always, Jax

Tears blur my vision as I refold the letter just as it was meant to be, tucking it gently back into its envelope. Deep down, I already know what must be done.

CHAPTER 31

Jennifer Riley

"I thought your mommy was tougher than this?" I ask Michael. "She needs to wake the fuck up!" I say. "Shit... When you learn to talk, don't ever repeat either of those words."

I've been taking care of baby Michael since hearing the news about Charlotte and her car accident. It still doesn't feel real. One minute we were talking about getting our nails done, the next I'm changing her son's shitty diapers.

On a normal basis, "Auntie Jenn," yep, that's what he'll call me, whether he wants to or not, would be all over his baby snuggles, weird songs, and making up stories about how his crazy hair looks like he might be a rodeo clown. But this... is different. I hold him, and my chest squeezes so tight it's hard to breathe. Every time I look at Michael's chubby, squeezable face, all I see is Charlotte. My best friend. My person. Lying unconscious somewhere.

I talk to him because I don't know what else to do, and I don't want him to realize his mom hasn't come back. This is the longest he's ever been without her. I tell him about how his mom once threw a piping bag across the kitchen because the buttercream wouldn't cooperate. And how she hates bananas but makes banana bread for my birthday every year because she's a stubborn little cupcake like that. I even told him how the two of us would lie to our parents, tell them we were sleeping over at each other's houses, then would sneak off to senior parties and drink warm beer out of red cups like we were invincible. We were in the tenth grade, and we thought we were cool. Charlotte once puked in a bush behind the Village Deli and made *me* promise to marry the cashier if she didn't survive. *And she says I'm the dramatic one.*

Michael gurgles and kicks like none of this is wrong. And I wish I could believe him. *He needs to be right.*

I hear a knock at the door, and glance at my phone, it's almost nine. It's Charlotte's parents, here to pick up Michael. Edith wants him to sleep at home, in familiar surroundings, with his night light shaped like a horse and that creepy stuffed tiger that freaks me out. She says it's important to keep things as normal as possible for him. Like anything about this day has been normal.

I kiss the top of his head, whisper to him to never tell our secrets, then hand him over. Mr. Evans gives me an awkward nod instead of words. I tip my head and nod back. It feels weird, but I do it anyway. I don't trust my voice, not to crack.

The two of us discuss what I will need to say when I arrive at the hospital. Mrs. Evans tells me I'll have to lie and tell the front desk that I'm Charlotte's sister and there to switch out with *our* parents. A little white lie is an unfortunate necessity to ensure access to Charlotte's room. Of course, only immediate family is allowed in after hours. But I've watched enough *General Hospital* with my mom to know a thing or two about sneaking into places I don't belong. All those afternoons on the couch, watching fake doctors have fake affairs in a fake broom closet, are finally paying off.

Before leaving, Mrs. Evans pulls me aside and slips a torn, already-opened envelope into my hand. "We need to talk... after you read this," she says. The secrecy of it all makes me feel like a private detective, unveiling an important clue. I stash it in my overnight bag and assure her I'll read it, just as soon as I get settled into the hospital room for the night. I can't help but wonder what it is and who it might be from. Judging from the urgency in her voice, I figure it has to be serious. The suspense is killing me. To say I am intrigued is a fuckin' understatement.

* * *

As I drive to Cooper Hospital, it feels as if time has come to a standstill. Twenty minutes alone in the car at night is basically a mental obstacle course. One second, I'm thinking about parking validation at the hospital, and the next, I'm spiraling about my best friend in a coma and a suspicious envelope that has a *Lifetime movie* written all over it. My brain's in hyperdrive, doing flips, and not the fun kind.

Somewhere around Exit 32, my mind decides to go back to the time we tried hot yoga and Charlotte passed out mid-downward dog. I thought she was just Super-Zen until I realized she was unconscious. I freaked out and flung my water bottle at her but hit the instructor instead. She screamed out in pain, Charlotte woke up, and we both got kicked out. We laughed until we almost peed our pants, promising never to do yoga again.

And now she's in a coma. For real. And I'd give anything to hear her make fun of my aim again.

A tear slips down my cheek as I flip on the radio, desperate for a distraction. Pop, rock, and gospel all blare through until a twangy voice comes through the speakers, *not* the good kind, either. Not like Johnny

Cash or Dolly, but the fake country that's all trucks and beer and no soul. *Country rock.* Don't get me wrong, the new sound is great, with some pretty damn hot country singers too, but old school is what I will always prefer. Good for your soul music. I twist the knob once more and find a familiar station.

Home on the Range is playing as I switch it on.

"Wow… I haven't heard this song in forever," I say out loud to myself.

There's something weirdly familiar about it. I can't quite put my finger on it, but it itches the back of my brain like deja vu. It's ironic somehow, and I just don't know why. It feels so familiar.

As the lyrics play on, it finally hits me.

I remember, clear as day now, this time last year, during one of our infamous men-bashing sleepovers, Charlotte told me about Jax. Well, that particular time, I was drunk, she was sober. She'd just found out she was pregnant but hadn't told anyone yet. We were lying on her bed, half-buried in blankets and junk food, when she started rambling about their road trip home.

Something about a buffalo, a tattoo, his father, and this very song. She had gone quiet and soft, like she was remembering the exact moment she'd fallen for him. And now this song is playing in my car, like a nudge from the universe.

"Is this a fucking sign or something?" I yell out loud. My voice echoes throughout the car. "Seriously? Of all the songs in the world, this one? Jesus, Charlotte, if you can hear me, you'd better wake up soon because I cannot handle the universe trying to be cute right now."

I recall the many sleepless nights that we'd spent together on the phone. She told me all the memories she shared with Jax, the way he made her laugh, the way he listened, the way he *saw* her. She said she didn't think it was possible to love a man like that again.

He hurt her, that much is true, but as much as I wanted to hate him for causing Charlotte so much pain, I still couldn't bring myself to do it. She's my best friend in the entire world, and no matter how much she pretended to hate him, I know she never stopped loving him. She couldn't, even if she tried. And believe me, she *did* try.

She was just hurt. And I could never hate a man she loves, not truly. Not when he gave her something no one else ever could. The heart knows what the heart wants. Unfortunately for her, it wants a heart that belongs to another woman.

I used to tell her she needed some kind of closure. Maybe just answer one of his calls, hear his side of things… something. But every time I brought it up, she shot the idea down quicker than I could finish the sentence. Letting me know that it was absolutely not up for discussion.

I can't help but wonder if things had been different, if the idiot she fell for wasn't married and the two of them were together. In all likelihood, I wouldn't be on this fucking drive right now. I'd probably be babysitting while they were out on a date night, me sitting on the floor with Michael, playing peek-a-boo and making ridiculous faces until he giggled.

But obviously, none of that is the case.

My stomach twists in knots, tighter with each mile that passes as I get closer to the hospital. Closer to my stupid best friend.

I pull in through the emergency room entrance, parking my car in the first available spot I can find. Traditional visiting hours are long over, and the main lot is closed for the night. The only way in now is through the ER entrance, sliding glass doors, fluorescent lights, and a burly security officer at the door.

The sterile scent of antiseptic hits me the moment I walk through the doors. It all but singes my nostril hairs, and my nose scrunches in disgust. That smell always makes me a little nauseous, like my body knows something bad is about to happen.

At least I know it's clean.

I've always been a bit of a germaphobe. And hospitals? They're the worst. Giant Petri dishes full of sneezes, coughs, and microscopic heebee-gee-bees. Just walking through the doors makes my skin crawl; I can practically *feel* the germs hitching a ride with each step I take.

But Charlotte needs me. And given that she's my best friend and all, I'll deal with it. Even if every cell in my body wants to run and bathe in a tub of hand sanitizer.

"Suck it up, buttercup," she would always say, laughing whenever I would catch her sneaking a sip of my drink, knowing full well how much I *hated* sharing.

It always ended the same way: me yelling at her, telling her how nasty she was, and her grinning like she'd won first prize in a baking contest. And honestly? She had. She annoyed the shit out of me in the most infuriating, sisterly way possible.

"You are so gross, I don't know where your mouth has been or who you have been kissing," I would say.

She'd laugh even harder, then lick the end of the straw, on purpose, knowing I'd never drink from it again. Beverage sabotage. It was her drink now, and she knew it.

"Bitch!" I would always call her and then laugh right along with her. Honestly, it was genius. And I kind of loved her for it.

* * *

A large, crotchety-looking woman sits behind the desk, planted smack in the middle of the floor, like a troll guarding the bridge to the ER. Her graying hair is piled into a loose bun, held together by a cheap plastic claw-clip with a sparkly butterfly glued to it, giving the distinct impression that it could flutter right off her head.

"Can I help you?" Her tone is rude and sour. The attitude hits me like a brick, and oh, do I want to throw one right back.

Remnants of white powder cling to the corners of her mouth, evidence of the cream-filled donut she clearly just demolished. I'm guessing the attitude is from me interrupting her late-night donut break. Which, honestly, I get. But still… she didn't need to be so bitchy.

"Room seven-o-four to see Charlotte Evans, please," I say, "please," trying to play nice.

She doesn't look up as she pounds her fat, stubby fingers at the keyboard, like it isn't part of her job or something. "Are you a relative?" she asks, each word coated in powdered sugar-fueled annoyance.

"Yes. I'm her younger sister… I'm going to be staying the night with her," I say with enthusiasm, just to agitate her a little bit more, because her unwarranted attitude is starting to piss me off at this point.

She doesn't even look at me when she slaps a visitor's badge onto the counter and points a powder-dusted finger past my shoulder. "Seventh floor. Make a right."

I grab the badge, gingerly, like it's diseased, and turn toward the elevator.

"Enjoy the rest of your donut," I threw over my shoulder, sarcasm dripping from every word as I walked away toward the elevators. *Bitch.*

Just as I reach them, the doors slide open, allowing me to enter. Out of habit, I use my elbow to press the button for the seventh floor. No way am I touching anything in this germ-infested building if I can help it. Especially not an elevator button. Probably crawling with a shit-ton of bacteria.

"My God, you are crazy," I admit to myself and laugh.

I already know the first thing I will do when I get to Charlotte's room is make a beeline straight for the bathroom and scrub down, destroying any filth that could've been collected along the way.

The elevator doors open with a ding that sounds way too happy for a place like this. I step out and follow the signs down the hall. Everything is quiet except for the hum of the machines and the squeak of rubber soles on the tile floor. The hallway lights are dimmed for the night, casting everything in an eerie glow. Beeping sounds echo from every direction, constant, rhythmic, and unsettling, like a heartbeat.

I turn right like the powdered-sugar-troll told me and finally reach Charlotte's room.

I take a deep breath in, pause for a moment, not knowing what to expect, then push open the door. The germs I was obsessing over a second ago just got shoved to the ground, knocked out by something much worse.

At first glance, Charlotte looks like she always does when she sleeps, peaceful, calm, like after a long day of drinking mimosas. The only thing missing is her snoring.

But then I notice the tubes, and just like that, my illusion of her is gone. The wires. The way her chest rises and falls in sync with the machine beside her. I draw in a deep breath and walk to the foot of her bed, noticing her entire left side, completely shattered and mangled. She is in bad shape, and we all know it. The longer she stays like this, the more nervous I get. That she might never wake up. That this could be it.

The thought of losing her, a world without her, hits me like a brick, and before I can stop it, the tears start. My body trembles, and I'm crying in that ugly, helpless way you do when you feel hopeless, and everything around you is crumbling.

I wipe my face with my sleeve and move closer to the bed, wrapping my fingers around Charlotte's. Hers are different from mine; hers are cold.

"Hey Dummy... Guess who's here? It's your bestie," I say through muffled cries. "If you needed some attention, I could have given you some... You didn't need to crash your damn car to get it," I joke, thinking that maybe our usual banter might help somehow. "Seriously, though, did you need to be so *extra* and end up in a coma? You're always so dramatic." I look at her, really look at her, and the tears return, bringing on more of them, a steady flow, without an end in sight.

"Whatever... If you're gonna be stubborn and ignore me, then I'm gonna sit here all night long, bugging the shit out of you until you talk." I lick my finger, leaving a smacking sound lingering as I pull it out from my mouth. "How about a nice wet willy? I bet that would wake your ass up."

Silence...

I sit in the empty chair at her bedside, giving my feet the rest they need. I'd spent most of the day standing, holding Michael, who had been glued to my hip like a koala with separation anxiety. The poor thing is too young to understand what's going on, but he knows something is wrong; kids always do. He needed me constantly today. And now, here I am, just me. No Michael in my arms. No nasty diapers to change or childish pop-up books to read. Just the deafening quiet of this room, and Charlotte lying still in that bed.

I rest my hand gently on her arm, careful not to disturb the IV that pokes out from just beneath the crease of her elbow. But what I *want* to do is shake her, jolt her ass awake, drag her out of this hell that she's trapped in.

She makes me nervous, just lying there so peacefully. Too peaceful, like she's not even trying to get back to us. Like she's getting *comfortable* there. Although I know that could never be the case, not now that she has Michael to take care of.

"You're scaring me, you know that?" I confess.

"You're one stubborn bitch," I whisper, brushing my thumb over her arm. "And I usually love you for it." My voice waivers. "But not now... Right now, you need to fight...You don't get to give up."

Charlotte and I share everything with each other, and talking to her so freely is second nature to me. I decide on another tactic, using Michael as bait.

"Michael needs you to wake up… He needs his Mommy." The desperation in my voice is killing me. "Besides, you don't want his first words to be Auntie Jen, do you? I mean, I may or may not have practiced saying it with him all day long today." My voice cracks through every word, no matter how hard I try to hold it together. Normally, I don't beg. But I'm begging now, because I don't know what else to do.

"Please, Char," I whisper, "Just wake the fuck up."

I search her face for any sign that she can hear me. I study her eyelids, her fingers, her toes, *anything*. But there's nothing. Just that awful, steady rise and fall of the ventilator. At this point, I'd do or say anything if it meant getting through to her. And then I remember the letter.

Fumbling with my bag, I pull out the torn envelope from Mrs. Evans. My hands are shaking when I catch sight of who it's from.

My jaw drops the second I see the return address. My mouth hangs open wide enough to catch flies, like a damn Venus flytrap, just waiting to snap shut.

Of all days, he picked today. The exact day one year ago that they met. *Of course he did.* Jax has a flair for timing, I guess. Whether it is perfect or catastrophic is still up for debate.

I look over at Charlotte, still unmoving, still quiet.

"Hey, Dummy, looks like the cowboy is a romantic," I whisper, holding the letter a little tighter. I'm desperate to say anything to try and wake her. "Well, since you're in no position to protest… I'm gonna read it… Actually… either way, I'm gonna read it."

Is this wrong? Reading a letter meant for my best friend while she lay there motionless? Fuck it!

"If you would wake your skinny little ass up, you could be reading this yourself," I say.

"Now let's see what the guy you've yapped about all year has to say. The suspense is killing me. I'm dying." I force out a tiny laugh. "Uhhh, maybe a poor choice of words for right now… Sorry, Dummy."

And with a deep breath, I begin to read out loud, just enough for Charlotte to hear. (I've heard stories of patients in a coma being able to hear their loved ones as they lie there, lifeless.) I lean in close, my elbows on the edge of the bed, teetering, holding the mysterious letter between both of my hands. My chipped fingernails, currently in desperate need of attention, are on full display as I hold the letter. They remind me that Charlotte and I have an appointment scheduled for this Saturday morning. Our usual nail salon catch-up session, where we'd complain about life, pick out colors with ridiculous names, and drink mimosas. I make a mental note to call the salon in the morning and cancel. *My God, I hope we get to reschedule someday.*

As I continue to read, I search for a twitch of an eye or a slight movement of her hand, and cross my fingers, in hopes this letter will somehow wake her from this horrible nightmare, but there is none.

The letter gives me a different perspective, one I wasn't expecting. It's beautiful, honest, and full of things I didn't know.

For the past year, I've only ever heard Charlotte's side, her heartbreak, her anger, her stubbornness. But now, reading this, I can almost *hear* his voice. He's broken and pleading for forgiveness. *And damn it... It's working.*

My emotions begin to shift, and my voice catches as I continue to read. I try to push through, but the sincerity of his words chokes me.

There's no denying it; he loves *her*. Every word screams it. And as much as she hates to admit it, she loves him just the same.

Unfortunately, by the time I reach the end, nothing has changed. Charlotte's body remains still, untouched by its words. No flutter of her eyelids, no twitch of her finger. Just silence.

I fold the letter carefully and slip it beneath her hand, letting her fingers rest over it.

And then... from the corner of my eye, I swear I see a tear falling from her cheek. Like lightning, I jump from my seat, my heart beating at a rapid speed, searching.

But there is nothing. My mind's playing tricks on me. I have nothing left in me, and with nothing more I can try, no words, no prayers, I reach for my phone and send a text to Charlotte's mom.

CHAPTER 32

"Jennifer...You seriously are not wearing this... You look like an idiot." I stare back at my ridiculous reflection in the mirror as a large cowboy hat flops to one side of my head, half covering my right eye. "Who knew these hats weren't one-size-fits-all?" I rip it off and toss it onto the floor, landing in the corner of the room.

Clothes and shoes are haphazardly spread throughout my bedroom, on the floor, over the bed, and spilling out from my dresser drawers. It looks like a department store has thrown up here. Decisions have never been my strong suit. It usually takes me fourteen outfit changes just to settle on the first thing I tried on. I don't know why I'm such a nervous wreck; this shouldn't be this hard.

"What the hell do I wear to something like this?" I say out loud to no one, but half expecting an answer. "How should I wear my hair? Hat or no hat?"

These are the questions I ask myself.

I feel like I'm going on a blind date, and I'm nervous and uncertain. But one thing is for sure, I don't want to be the one to screw up. This plan that Mrs. Evans has cooked up is our only hope.

Five days have passed since Charlotte's accident, and still not been a single change in her. As I try on yet another hat, I tell myself that if this doesn't work, then nothing will, and fear begins to creep in. The thought of Charlotte being stuck like this forever and leaving Michael without his mother is becoming more real with each passing minute.

Everything needs to be perfect.

Time's ticking, and at the risk of being late, I finally settle on something casual: jeans, a plain white shirt, and a tattered FORD hat that belongs to my brother.

"I've got this." I try to convince myself as I take one last look in the mirror.

CHAPTER 33

Jaxson Lange

"Dang... It's muggy out tonight," I say to the woman checking tickets, giving her a polite nod as the rodeo fans file in. Even with the sun about to set, it's still eighty-seven degrees out. Beads of sweat are already forming along the hairline on my forehead. The unbearable heat takes me back to this time last year, when I first met Charlotte. I still can taste the sweat on her lips when we kissed on the roadside, when it was just us, thousands of miles away. I wish we were still there.

The aroma of freshly roasted peanuts and deep-fried funnel cake mixed with the unmistakable scent of cow and horse manure wafts through the air. Crowds begin to gather early, eagerly lining up for tonight's sold-out show. People are decked out in their red, white, and blues, some in camo, all in honor of the fallen. Tonight's rodeo is paying a special tribute to all those affected by the 9/11 attacks, as well as to all soldiers and servicemen. *I still can't believe a year has passed since the ambush on our country.* The atmosphere feels heavier tonight, like everyone is carrying a little more than just excitement for the show.

I turn back around, lean up against the entryway fence, and look at my watch.

It's seven-thirty on the dot when the last few stragglers, in a drunken stupor, walk through the gates. Cowboy hats on top of their heads, worn-out boots cover their feet, and igloos full of cold beer cans hang from their hands. Cowgirl "wannabees" strut around in their twenty-dollar hats, probably bartered from the flea market this morning, acting like they've ridden more than a carousel horse.

The boys argue on which bull rider will last the full eight seconds, placing bets like it's the Super Bowl, while the girls complain about the long lines forming at the porta-potties.

"I need to pee soooo bad!" the one with the shiny pink hat yells, then stumbles, grabbing her friend in the process, trying to steady herself. It's a failed attempt; they both collapse to the ground, giggling like little kids. Their uncontrollable laughter definitely tells me they've had one too many.

"Oh my God, look at the line already!" fancy-white-cowboy-boots-girl replies as she gets back to her feet. "It's going to take forever... We might have to go behind one of the trucks!"

It all sounds so familiar, but tonight I'm not here for the beers, horses, or eight-second rides. I wait here, hoping that the letter I sent to Charlotte has reached her and that, somehow, she's forgiven me. And desperately hoping she's just running late and on her way.

It's crazy to think that just one year ago was the last time we were together. I remember the conversation we had as we drove by this very place, her smiling in the passenger seat. I told her that I wanted to bring her here for our first real date.

Funny how things don't always go the way you plan... but God, I wish they had.

It was only minutes later when my world crumbled to pieces, much like the world around us had at the time.

So much has changed in the past year. My marriage to Joanna ended, something that should have happened long before it did. But in the process, I lost the love of my life. Charlotte. I've spent every day since trying to reach her, in hopes of reconciliation. Hoping she'd see the truth behind it all. The unfortunate thing is that life is never that simple. None of my calls were ever answered, not one. In the end, the letter felt like the only reasonable way to reach her, to show her that what I feel for her is real. And that I can't let another day pass by without her in my life.

So here I stand, against the rickety old fence, biding my time until she gets here. If she gets here. Waiting for what might be the most important moment of my life. This could change everything, and I'm trying to play it cool, but my mind is running wild with every way this could go wrong... or right. I have no idea what to expect. Will she show up and forgive me, and pull me in for a kiss? Or will she come here out of frustration, just to cuss me out, then slap me across the face? The latter haunts me in my dreams at night. But the thought of her ignoring my letter altogether and deciding I'm not even worth her time is a strong possibility that I try not to think about.

I push the negative thoughts away and continue to wait, as I turn my focus back to the stands. Nervousness begins to creep in as I catch myself checking the time on my watch for the hundredth time tonight, shaking my wrist to make sure it still works.

From what I can make out over the loudspeaker, the barrel racing is about to start. Which means enough time has passed since I asked Charlotte to meet me, and I'm starting to lose hope that she's coming.

I look back at the crowd, trying to buy myself some time. The stands are packed, shoulder to shoulder, filling every inch of space. All kinds of folks, different backgrounds, different stories, brought together by the same love for the rodeo. They holler and cheer with every tight turn around the barrels.

Above it all, hanging high over the arena, is a massive American flag, waving in the wind with pride. I don't think I've ever seen one so big. Red, white, and blue, stronger than ever. A symbol of freedom, and right now, it feels like it's watching everything, like it knows just how much is riding on today. It's impressive and has always been one of my favorite sites to see.

I check my watch again, even though I already know what it will say; it's later than last time, and that's all that matters. I exhale, slow and heavy, defeated. My shoulders sag. My head drops. And the fact that she didn't show settles in.

She's not coming.

And just like that, like a rider being bucked from a bull, I have to face what I've been trying not to admit: she's done. With me. With us. With whatever I thought we were meant to be.

"Jax?"

At the sound of my name, every hair on my body stands at attention. My heart... shit, it's pounding so loud it might as well be a drumbeat. *Ba-boom. Ba-boom.* I can't stop the grin that spreads across my face.

I can't believe it. She's here. *She got my letter!*

Her voice is different, though. Almost unrecognizable. It's been a year since I heard it, but it feels like a lifetime. The sound of her, the warmth of it, hits me like a bull.

I can't wait to see her face again, to look into those baby blue eyes that have haunted my thoughts for the past year. Anxiety builds in my chest as I turn to see her. But fate has other plans.

"What the?" My mouth falls open in shock. I blink, trying to make sense of it.

This isn't Charlotte; instead, another woman I don't recognize stands staring at me. She is tall, pretty, and wearing a baseball cap with long blonde hair falling from it, and it's obvious she knows who I am. For the life of me, I have no recollection of her. Panic sets in as I start flipping through memories, fast, but there's nothing. She's a beautiful stranger saying my name like she knows me. And the way she looks at me, worried, with hope in her eyes, it's freaking me out.

"Are you Jax?" she asks, her voice filled with hesitation.

"Yeah?"

"Ummm, Hi." Her voice wavers, like she's not sure what to say. "You don't know me... but I've heard a lot about you... I'm Jennifer, Charlotte's best friend." She pauses, studying my face for a reaction. I can feel the blood draining from it. "Charlotte's been in an accident."

Her words cut through me; my legs feel unsteady. I grab the fence without thinking.

"What?" I yell. "An accident? Where is she?" The sounds of the rodeo are fading out with the thumping in my chest. My heart is beating faster than it should, and it feels like it might explode. "What happened? What do you mean by accident?" I don't wait for an answer. "I need to go to her... see her!" *How could I be losing her all over again?*

My legs take off before my brain can catch up, running on instinct. But I have no idea where to.

"Jax, wait!" A hand grabs my arm. Jennifer catches up and pulls me to a stop.

"Okay... first... calm down, and I will explain," Jennifer says in a calming voice, snapping me out of my panic.

She begins to explain, giving me a detailed description of the past week. Going on about the horrific accident, my letter, the coma, and the scheming between her and Charlotte's mother. All of it led her here to me.

A heavy wave of guilt sets in. *If I hadn't lied to her, we would still be together, and she never would have gotten hurt.*

"This is all my fault," I say, not directed to anyone but myself. Jennifer doesn't say a word. Maybe she already knows it.

I don't care that the past year's been hell. None of it matters, not the mistakes, not the silence, not even if Charlotte never wants to see me again. All that matters is getting to her. Now.

I need to see her, be there, no matter how broken things might be between us. She's the love of my life, and nothing, not fear, not regret, not even her anger towards me, can keep me from her now.

CHAPTER 34

Once again, my legs take over. I bolt for my truck parked at the far end of the lot. Dodging trucks, horses, and people, dirt kicking up under my boots. I can't get there fast enough. Jennifer's footsteps are a few feet behind me, but I don't slow down for anything until I hear her shout.

"Wait! Jax... Wait up," screams Jennifer. "Calm down... We don't need you getting into an accident, too," she says, and she is right.

"If I let you go like this... and you get hurt and Charlotte wakes to find out... she will kick my ass." She laughs, trying to lighten the mood and calm me.

It starts to work, her voice, her words. I take a deep breath, forcing the beating in my chest to calm down enough so I can think. Jennifer nods, catching her breath too. And we come up with a plan.

"I'll drive," she says. "You follow me to the hospital."

I nod back. "To Charlotte," I say, because she is all that matters.

Unfortunately, I've made this drive a few times before, and none have brought good memories. While they may be bad, the drive is not. The hospital isn't that far, about a thirty-minute drive, but as I speed down I-295, it feels like time has slammed on the brakes. Every mile stretches like a lifetime.

Finally, the neon lights that read COOPER HOSPITAL shine high above the top of the building. Relief washes over me, knowing that Charlotte is near and it won't be long before I am with her. The deafening wails of sirens pierce through my ears as an ambulance screams past me, lights flashing like a warning. But I don't mind, because it reminds me, I'm close.

We reach the car lot, and our cars drive at a snail's pace as we search for available spots, finally claiming two of our own on the fourth floor. I put the truck in park and hop out in record time. The air is heavy with an unpleasant odor. It's one of car fumes mixed with urine, and my nose scrunches in disgust.

"You okay?" asks Jennifer, not waiting for an answer as she is already a few steps ahead, heading toward the elevator doors. I follow her lead as she knows the way to Charlotte's room.

We walk in silence, which is odd. I can remember the stories that Charlotte told of her, and being quiet was not one of them. In fact, she said, out of the two of them, Jennifer is the outgoing and talkative one. The fact that she hasn't spoken a word since exiting the car is a concern. Not a single word has been spoken, even as we continue to walk through the parking lot and into the hospital. She seems off. *But why?* Something tells me she's hiding something. Something important. Something I should know. And the closer we get, the heavier the silence feels.

She seems nervous, almost, and for the life of me, I can't figure out the reason why. *Maybe things are worse than what she's told me?*

Once we're in the hospital, Jennifer heads straight for the elevators and presses the button for the seventh floor. We ride up in silence. When we reach the room, I find myself standing in front of a large wooden door, the only thing separating me from Charlotte.

I pause for a moment, my hand rests on the handle, and I look at Jennifer. "Is there anything else I should know before I go in?"

Her fingers start to fidget, and she avoids eye contact with me.

"Ummmmmm, let's just go in, okay?" Her lack of an answer doesn't go unnoticed and confirms my intuitions. *What the hell is she not telling me?*

My heart races, and my feet refuse to move. I'm stuck. It's as if I'm grounded to the floor, ankles trapped in quicksand, gravity dragging me down. My chest rises and falls, heavy and ready to explode. I draw in a final, shaky, not-so-courageous breath, then push the door open.

At first glance, Charlotte looks like she's just sleeping, so beautiful, so peaceful. Just like the morning after the storm. I can remember how her blonde hair spread across the pillow, a few strands clinging to her cheek, and I just lay there, watching her breathe, soaking in the scent of her shampoo.

You would never guess that she's ever been hurt. That is, until I walk a little closer, standing by her side. Stitches cross her once flawless face, faint purple and yellow bruises forming around them, early signs of healing. A patch of her hair is gone, shaved clean by her doctors, exposing pale skin and the gash left by the impact. A neat row of staples holds it together.

The beeping of her heart monitor is deafening, drowning out the constant buzz of the fluorescent lights overhead. They cast a harsh glow over her still body. Even with bruises, cuts, and broken bones, she's still beautiful. Just as perfect as she was a year ago. It's hard to imagine her ever looking anything less than stunning, even on her worst days. And this, without a doubt, is one of them.

I take her hand in mine and close my eyes, focusing attention on the feel of her skin against my own. I've longed to hold her for months. I just wish it didn't have to be like *this*.

When I turn to Jennifer, I realize we're not alone. I'd assumed it was just us. I was so caught up in the sight of Charlotte that I didn't even notice the others in the room.

Sitting in the far corner is an older couple, Charlotte's parents, I assume. Jennifer stands beside them. All three are watching me, their eyes tracking my every move.

Aside from the hum of the machines, the room is still. No one speaks. Not them. Not me. The air suddenly feels heavy.

The older gentleman sits silently, his glasses resting in his hands, folded neatly in his lap. The woman beside him cradles a small boy, not more than a few months old, on her knee. A baby rattle is wedged under her leg, teetering on the edge of her seat, ready to fall. A diaper bag sits on the floor at her feet; a bottle filled to the brim with milk is peeking from one of its side pockets.

Judging by the little hat on his head and the matching pajamas, I can assume he's a boy. Our eyes lock, and an odd feeling washes over me like I know him. Which is impossible.

And yet, those are my eyes staring back at me.

It sounds crazy. But it's as if he recognizes me, too. He smiles, a soft, innocent grin, and something inside me shifts. We've never met, but somehow at this moment, we already know each other.

The more I look at him, the more familiar he becomes. Every feature he has, the sharpness of his jawline, his nose, and his eye color, is a striking resemblance to me. His smile isn't mine. It's hers. That distinct, heart-stopping smile is Charlotte's.

The same smile I fell in love with the moment we met in the elevator.

The same one I have been aching to see again ever since.

Jesus, is that Charlotte's baby? Our baby?

In a flash, everything seems out of focus, and my brain is in a thick fog, like driving in the early autumn morning. At this moment, it's working on overload, and it barely reminds me to breathe. It's all too much. *I could be a dad.* And judging by the way they're all looking at me, I'm starting to believe it's true.

I want to say something, anything, to break the silence, to ask questions. But my brain is frozen, too stunned to form words. All that comes is silence, and the shocked, questioning look on my face.

One by one, I look at them. First, to Jennifer, the one who brought me here. The one who never mentioned a baby.

Silence...

My eyes shift to the older gentleman. He's standing now, shifting his weight from one foot to the other. There's a puzzled, sorrowful look etched into his otherwise stone face, one that carries a hint of pity. And it hits me. He knows something... something I don't.

Silence...

At last, my attention shifts to the older woman. She hasn't moved from her seat, still cradling the baby gently as she rocks him.

She's attractive, an older version of Charlotte. The resemblance is undeniable. Unlike the man beside her, her expression is softer, more complicated. She looks anxious, yes, but there's something else there, too. A flicker of happiness or maybe hope. And I don't understand it. Not when Charlotte lies lifelessly in a coma just a few feet away. What in the world could possibly give her a reason to smile?

This whole situation, these people staring back at me, the baby's eyes that are just like mine, the quietness that is swallowing the room whole, is all starting to freak me the hell out.

"Jax," she says gently, finally breaking the silence. "Would you like to meet your son, Michael?" She rises slowly, her arms lifting the baby toward me.

And just like that, the world as I know it has changed. My body stiffens. And for a reason I can't quite explain, I turn to Charlotte, searching for reassurance, for answers she can't give. Her body remains motionless, silent, and still.

When I look back, the woman is smiling. A soft, trembling smile of relief. Like she's been waiting for this moment all along.

My hand reaches back, searching blindly for the wall behind me, anything to steady my legs that all of a sudden feel like strings of overcooked spaghetti. My head shakes slowly, disbelief crowding every thought. I close my eyes, trying to breathe, trying to process the impossible truth bomb unfolding in front of me.

All at once, it registers. And without skipping a beat, something inside me changes, awakens. A spark of clarity floods through me, and with it comes the overwhelming realization: The one thing I've been missing in life... is this. The chance to be a father... to be someone's dad.

Not a day has gone by that I haven't thought about that baby boy that Joanna and I lost. It was so long ago, yet it still feels like yesterday. Back then, fate robbed me of the chance to be a father. And now, somehow, I'm being told I *am* one.

I have a son.

When we lost our baby, pain was all I felt, heartache was all I knew. But I had to be strong for Joanna. I held her through the sorrow, all while swallowing mine. The heartbreak we felt was unimaginable, and I wouldn't wish it on my worst enemy.

In the months that followed, I played the part. To everyone else, I was solid as a rock, exactly the man Joanna needed. But what they didn't see were the cracks. They didn't see me breaking down, alone on the tractor, or in the shower when the water masked the tears. They didn't see the rage. The way I'd cuss, throw things, raise my fist to the heavens, begging for a reason.

Since that awful day, something's been missing. I never knew what, until now.

It's like a light inside me switched on. Finally, and now, more than anything in this world... I need Charlotte to wake up.

"Jax?" the woman says again, her voice is gentle. "Would you like to hold him?"

My eyes look at her. She's still smiling, even though I see her chin tremble a little. And then I look at him... *my* son.

My heart answers long before my mouth does.

"More than anything in this world." As quick as a bullet, I walk over to my new reality and meet my son. A smile across my face, as wide as the ocean. With arms open wide, I reach for him, taking him in and holding him close, with plans of never letting him go. I breathe in the scent of him, baby powder and dried milk, as I pull him even closer, storing this memory, locking it deep down into my heart.

I hold him tighter and make a promise to him. "Daddy is here now, and I am not going anywhere... I already love you so much, little buddy."

Tear-filled laughter erupts from me, bubbling up from somewhere deep inside. It all sounds crazy, unbelievable, even. The world, as I know it, has changed in an instant. And the unconditional love I feel for this beautiful little boy is all-consuming.

And I welcome it, quite literally, with open arms.

Memories of Charlotte flood my mind like deja vu. From the moment I met her in that elevator, I felt that pull. Even then, I knew we'd be connected somehow.

I lost her once. And I've regretted it every single day since. But I am not about to lose her a second time.

Cradling my son in my arms, I gently pat his back as I walk over to Charlotte and lean down, just enough so that our faces are only inches apart. The closeness sends a shiver through me, stirring something deep inside, awakening every sense. It overwhelms me. *Oh, how I have waited to be this close to you.*

Just over a whisper, I close my eyes and lean in, speaking only for her ears to hear. "Charlotte... It's me, Jax." I swallow hard, my voice heavy with emotion. "I'm standing here, holding our beautiful son, Michael." A breath catches in my throat. "I've missed you so much, and I'm sorry for every second of every day that you thought you had to do this alone." Michael wiggles in my arms, freeing his tiny hand from my grasp. He reaches for his mommy. And I let him. "I'm here now," I whisper softly. "And I'm not going anywhere, no matter how stubborn you are; we both need you," I reiterate. "Please, Charlotte. Don't leave me now. Not when I've finally found my way home to you." My voice breaks.

"Open your eyes," I beg. "Open our eyes!" I feel my heart pounding in my chest. "I've been lost this past year without you... I love you."

And with everything I have, I press a kiss on her soft, warm cheek, then step back, hoping and praying. Waiting.

It takes every bit of strength I have to pull myself away from her, but I know there is nothing more I can do. As I step back, Michael is still nestled in my arms, and I look up and realize we're no longer alone by the bed. Everyone else in the room has gathered around.

Tears stream down each of their faces, silent and steady. Every gaze is fixed on Charlotte. I get the feeling that they, too, believed my presence, our presence, might be enough to pull Charlotte from this horrific nightmare. As if somehow, love alone could bring her back. *I failed.*

So, we wait. All of us want her to wake up. One by one, we speak to her softly, each voice begging, coaxing, hoping. Asking her to open her eyes, to move a finger... any sign that she's still in there. That she's coming back to us.

"Alright, Charlotte! Enough is enough!" her mother snaps, tumbling with emotion. "It's time you woke up, sweetheart. You hear me?" she now demands.

"Charlotte honey," her father chimes in. "You need to wake up... just so I can beat you at Scrabble just one more time." A soft laugh escapes him, and the rest of us can't help but follow suit.

"Charlotte, if you don't wake up soon," Jennifer says, her tone serious but teasing. "I'm gonna start spilling all of the bad things we did together and kept from your parents. God knows… There are a *lot* of them." She pauses, eyes on Charlotte. "Like that one time when you stole a cigarette from your grandmother and smoked it while your parents were out. You had no idea how to hold it and dropped it, burning a hole right through the couch." Jennifer laughs. "And then you blamed your grandmother when your mom finally noticed."

Charlotte's mother slowly turns and gives Jennifer the full *stink eye*. We all burst out laughing.

"My poor mother," Charlotte's mom says, shaking her head. "I remember calling her that night and telling her that if she wanted to smoke at my house ever again, she'd have to do it outside." She lets out a huff, half-laughing. "She swore it wasn't her, and I never believed her." She points at Jennifer, narrowing her eyes. "And all this time, it was you two knuckleheads." The entire room bursts into laughter.

Everyone has tried, and still nothing, so now, all we can do is wait. And we wait some more.

* * *

Hours have passed, and nothing has changed. Hope begins to fade, dimming with each tick of the clock. Charlotte's mother, Edith, clings to her husband, her strength dwindling. She buries her face in his chest, sobbing quietly, a bible clenched in her hands, as his arms close around her. Tear-shaped droplets stain his once-pristine button-down shirt.

They are losing hope.

"I believed it would work," she chokes on her words. "I thought… I thought that Jax being here would be enough." Her voice cracks, rising with panic. Building with heartache. "Dear God… what if our baby never wakes up?"

Anger creeps into her words now, sharp and loud, and it scares little

Michael, his tiny body flinching at the sound, his wide eyes searching for answers, or maybe comfort.

He begins to cry, his small body trembling in my arms. I pull him closer, holding him tight, in hopes of calming him.

"I've got you, buddy," I whisper, gently rocking him. "I've got you."

Charlotte's father tries to calm Edith, placing a hand on her shoulder, but her anger grows. Before anyone can stop her, she spins toward the windowsill, swiping the bouquet of flowers with a sharp, sweeping motion.

The vase shatters against the floor, glass exploding into tiny shards, water and petals puddling on the floor. Her fist rises to the ceiling as she screams, yelling at the heavens above... a mother's pain, too big for her body to hold.

"How could you do this?" Edith screams, her voice filled with rage as she looks skyward. "Michael needs his mother!"

Her words echo off the hospital walls, shaking with pain and fury. "I need her! We all need her!"

Then, with little strength left in her, she collapses into her chair. She buries her face in her hands, defeated, broken, and begging for a miracle.

The doors burst open, and Charlotte's nurse comes rushing in, alarmed by the commotion. Part of her hair has slipped from its bun, and she quickly tucks it behind her ear as her eyes scan the room. They land on the pool of water on the floor, dotted with crushed petals and broken glass. Jennifer is already on one knee, quietly gathering the scattered flowers. She picks up the shards carefully, one by one, dropping them into the wastebasket beside her.

The room is silent now; tension is suspended in the thick air around us.

"What on earth is goi—" The nurse stops mid-sentence, her voice softening the moment she sees our faces, red and swollen. Her tone shifts, "Look, I know how difficult this is for all of you." The empathetic way she says it tells me exactly why she's a nurse. And right now, I'm grateful that she is Charlotte's. "I understand you're angry and scared, but this is still a hospital. We're already breaking the rules by allowing all of you in here at one time." She continues. "You could all use some rest... how about *one* of you stay throughout the night, and the rest of you go home... get some rest... then come back in the morning?" Charlotte's nurse pleads.

The room becomes quiet. No one speaks, no one dares to decide who should stay and who should go. And in the silence, a new fear rises in me, the fear that I might be the one asked to leave her... again.

After everything, I can't bear the idea of walking away again. Not now.

Not when she needs me most.

"I know you don't know me, well, at all, even, but I'd like to be the one who stays, if that's okay?" My voice is shaking with nerves. I shift Michael from one hip to the other, his tiny weight grounding me in this impossible plea. I know this is a long shot. To them, I'm a stranger. But I have to try.

"I have spent the past year trying to find my way back to Charlotte," I say, looking each of them in the eye. "An entire year missing her. Not seeing her perfect smile. And I can't lose another second... even if she doesn't know I'm here." I plead with the three of them. "I'm not asking for forever... Just tonight. Please."

Silence once again fills the room as I stare at them, waiting.

"It's not that crazy of an idea," Charlotte's dad says softly, directing his words to his wife more than anyone else. "Let Jax have his time with Charlotte." His voice is calm. "All of us have been here every day since the accident... around the clock for days," he adds, looking at Jennifer too. "We could all use the rest."

He gives a small nod toward the bed, toward his daughter, Charlotte. "And maybe she needs this, too."

Edith collapses into Leonard's arms, surrendering to his request, as exhaustion finally swallows her whole. The weight of sleepless nights spent in the hospital, the ache of uncertainty, the mental strain of watching their daughter remain unresponsive... It's all too much. It's destroying them all.

"I promise I won't leave her side. I will take good care of her," I say, and I mean every word.

They gather up their belongings in silence, assuring me that they'll be back first thing in the morning.

"If anything changes," I promise, "you'll be the first ones I call," I say, and we exchange phone numbers in case anything does.

I turn to Michael, holding him close for one last moment. "Daddy will see you in the morning," I whisper, pressing a kiss to his forehead. "I love you."

Jennifer takes him from my arms; her eyes filled with emotion. As they all leave the room, the door clicks behind them. I sit back down beside Charlotte. And I think: I am someone's *daddy*.

CHAPTER 35

The hospital room grows quieter with every passing minute, now that everyone has gone home for the night. Leaving only me, here alone, with Charlotte. I watch her as she lies still, in the same position she had when I first arrived, motionless.

Her nurse has already come and gone, moving through her nightly rituals. She checked Charlotte's temperature, blood pressure, and pulse ox, all within normal range, thank God. Then came the stretches, precise movements to keep the blood flowing, to prevent clots from forming, one of the many risks that come with lying still for so long.

It's all routine, but I watch every move like it's my job.

I settle in for the night, pulling the chair closer until I'm right beside her. I take her hand in mine and begin to talk, just like I would if she were awake. For a moment, it feels almost normal. Just like the countless hours we spent driving cross-country, talking each other's ears off. A year ago, we couldn't get enough of each other's voices.

"You really are stubborn, you know that?" I say with a smile. She looks like an angel as she sleeps, so peaceful and still, like she could wake at any moment. *Please just wake up.* "By the way, our little boy is perfect... I love that you named him after my dad... he'll be ecstatic when he hears." I laugh, imagining his reaction. "I guess I should tell him I have a child first." I laugh even harder, still comprehending the fact that I have a son.

To help fill the silence, I tell her stories of the past year. One story at a time. The good and the not-so-good. Everything that she missed.

"I wish you could see it," I say, leaning back against my chair, "Work has been insane. Business has doubled since last year," I say.

I boast about the truck I purchased a month ago. A brand spanking new black Chevy Silverado. "You know, because every self-respecting American should own a Chevy." I can almost hear her laughing inside, trying desperately to let it out. *I wonder if she can hear me?*

"I'd give anything to see you in the passenger seat again, eating all the pineapple-flavored gummy bears before I can get one." I squeeze her hand.

I go on to explain the entire story between Joanna and me, the pregnancy, the miscarriage, our marriage, and our divorce.

"I know it sounds crazy, but she helped me deal with my pathetic life after you drove away that day," I confessed to her. "I was a mess for a long time, and she helped me find my way back to reality. But as friends, like we're supposed to be."

No topic is off limits; anything I can think of, just to try and jolt her awake. It's almost three in the morning, and exhaustion is taking hold; my eyes flutter open and shut every few seconds. My yawns are relentless and so loud, I wouldn't be surprised if they're keeping the other patients awake. It's been such an emotionally exhausting day, from the anticipation of seeing Charlotte, to the shock of her accident, and then learning that I have a son. It's all so much, wreaking havoc on

273

my tired mind, as I try to wind down.

"I'm gonna take a little rest," I tell Charlotte, even if she doesn't hear me. It can't hurt. I'll stay right by her side, holding her hand and lying my head against her arm. I give in to the quiet and close my eyes, just for a minute.

C - *Jax, I can't believe you're here...*

J - *Of course... I came as soon as I heard. I'm so happy you're awake...*

C - *I've missed you so much...*

J - *I've missed you too...*

C - *I could hear every word you said to me while I was asleep...*

J - *I'm so sorry for all the pain I have caused you...*

C - *It's okay, honey... I see you have met Michael... Our son...*

J - *I did, and he couldn't be more perfect... I am already in love with him... He reminds me so much of you...*

C - *He has your beautiful eyes...*

J - *I love you, Charlotte. I have loved you from the moment I met you...*

I wake up and can't get over how real the dream seemed. It felt like her hand was actually in mine, squeezing it. It all felt so real: the conversation, her confession of love toward me, the touch of her hand. It's everything I have dreamt about for the past year. The two of us, as a couple, and spending a lifetime together, as a family with little Michael.

But it was all a dream.

I look over her body, unmoving, still, and asleep. I want so desperately to close my eyes once more and escape back to sleep, where I can hear her voice again. *I have lost her again.* I lay my head back down against her in quiet defeat, my eyes locked on hers, but hers remain closed.

"Just wake up," I whisper, and any hope I have left begins to fade. "Please."

The grip on my hand tightens. My eyes never leave her, and that's when it happens, the slightest twitch of her fingers in mine. If I hadn't been holding her hand, I might have missed it.

Just like before, her fingers move again, and then her eyelids begin to flicker. Opening and closing in rapid motion, fluttering like the delicate wings of a butterfly. With each tiny flutter, her focus sharpens. Groggy and disoriented, she tries to speak, but no words come.

"Relax." My heart begins to race, pounding so hard I can feel it in my throat. "Take your time... The words will come." I'm barely breathing. "I love you, Charlotte... I'm sorry." A tear of relief slips from the corner of my eye, cutting a clean line down my cheek. "I've got you."

Frustration settles in as Charlotte shakes her head in defeat. She tries once more, and this time, the words break through, finding their way, slowly and more clearly. She turns her head toward me, her cheek still resting softly on the hospital pillow, and in the faintest whisper, she says, "Take me home."

And just like that, she found her way back, just like I knew she could. Just like I needed her to do.

"I wouldn't take you anywhere else, now that I've got you back." I laugh through my tears, the sound broken and full of utter relief. "You, our little guy, and I have a lot of catching up to do," I tell her, then lean in and press a tender kiss to her dry, delicate, chapped lips.

I remember I'm not the only one waiting for her to wake up.

"We need to call your parents and Jennifer... they've all been so worried... And I'm sure Michael can't wait for a big momma-bear hug from you." I say, grateful beyond words. She smiles softly at the mention of Michael, and a single tear escapes her, tracing a fragile path down her cheek.

I grab my phone, search for her mother's number, only stored just hours ago, and push the "call" button, then I hold it to Charlotte's ear.

"Mom?"

CHAPTER 36

Charlotte

8 months later

The smell of sweet buttercream and vanilla fills the air, clinging to my clothes, and let's be honest here, everything else, now that little Michael is toddling around. I'm working on his first-birthday cupcakes, theme, farm animals, of course. My piping bag bursts at the seam, and a dollop of green icing lands on the floor. Quick as lightning, Michael already has some in his mouth. He's the picture of pure chaos, like our life these days, missing a sock, green face, all wrapped in a perfect little package. Ironically, he's standing a few feet from a mountain of gifts, all wrapped in rodeo-themed paper, not that he will be able to know how to open them. I laugh at his cute face, looking like a tiny green monster, and call for reinforcements.

"Jax... I need you." I call out, trying not to laugh as Michael lets out a squeal, clearly pleased with his floor snack.

I hear footsteps, and within seconds, Jax appears in the kitchen, shirt untucked, and a toy horse peeking out from under one arm. He stops in his tracks when he sees the mess, eyebrows raised.

"A little green dinosaur eating off the floor, really shouldn't shock me... not with this kid." Jax shakes his head but can't help but laugh at the sight of Michael, now licking the floor.

"Well... I mean... he is your son," I say, teasing him, just before another glob of icing hits the floor.

Jax scoops up Michael seconds before it lands on his head. "Yeah, I see the resemblance. He has my appetite for sugar and your talent for destruction." *Touche*

"Excuse me?" I shoot back. And we laugh, loud belly laughs that echo through the kitchen.

Michael joins in, his hands flailing with excitement, leaving a smudge of green on Jax's t-shirt.

"Well, this didn't last long," Jax says. He wipes at the stain, but it only makes it worse. "I'll take him up and get him ready... change my shirt and pack his bag." He says, scooping a finger full of icing into his mouth. "You know, mom stuff." He laughs and is smart enough to jump back a step at his remark. I try to swat him with my spatula, but he is too quick for me, and I miss.

"Love youuuu," he yells at me, laughing through his words. And I can't help but think just how lucky I am at this moment.

I pipe the last swirl of frosting onto a cupcake, pack them away, and head to the stairs to get ready, just in time to pass Jax and Michael coming back down. Mischievous grins on their faces.

"You two look like you're up to something."

Jax grins, "Who... Us... Never?" he laughs, shifting Michael on his hip. Jax leans in and kisses my cheek. "I'll load the truck and make sure the cupcakes survive the ride."

"Are you excited to see all the animals?" Jax asks as he hoists Michael up into the truck and into his car seat, then steps aside to let me finish buckling him in.

"Horsey, Horsey!" he screams back.

After securing him in, I ask, "Are we going to see horsies for your birfday?" The way I speak is in a childish way that only he understands.

He squeals with excitement, flailing his hands in the air and accidentally swatting me in the face as I lean in to kiss his cheek. I laugh, brush it off, then close the door. And of course, Jax is right there, by my side, holding the passenger side door open, like he has since the day we met. I blow him a kiss through the window just before he shuts it, then watch as he rounds the front of the truck, that familiar grin on his face.

Its massive engine roars to life as we pull away from the house, headed to meet our family and friends at the rodeo for Michael's birthday celebration. The idea, all Jax's, given that farm animals are Michael's most favorite obsessions these days, second only to floor frosting. *Like father, like son, I guess.*

I still have yet to go, so not only will it be Michael's first time, but it's also mine. We are both equally excited. We've only heard about it a million times this week, from Jax.

"Memorial Day weekend and opening night… It's gonna be a good one," Jax assures me with that confident grin of his, the same one that still makes my heart skip a beat. "Opening night is always the best. I can't wait to see your face as you watch the bull riders." He says to both Michael and me. Only I get the pleasure of Jax's touch, as he gently takes my hand in his and presses a kiss to the back of it.

"Well, what can I say? I am a sucker for cowboys." I say with a grin, watching Jax tip his hat and flash a smile.

"When are you gonna let me make an honest woman of ya?" he questions, and holds up my hand once more, rubbing my finger where an engagement ring would be.

"I told you, after Michael's birthday party is over, we can start talking about marriage. One thing at a time, Mr. Lange... Hold your horses." Pun intended.

"I'll give you something to hold onto." He winks.

"Dork!" I laugh, shaking my head. *God, I love him.*

Once we arrive, Jax starts rambling about what to expect; clearly, his nerves are kicking in. I think he's worried I won't enjoy the rodeo as much as he's hyped it up. But honestly, none of that matters. We could be lost in the woods for all I care, and I'd still be happy, as long as we're together. I have a beautiful family I never knew I needed, and, somehow, I found my soulmate all on my own. If anything, these past two years have taught me that every day is a gift, and I'll never take it for granted. I won't ever let him go again.

We weave our way through the crowd, passing the sweet scent of funnel cakes as Michael rides high on Jax's shoulders, giggling at the new surroundings. I've got a tray of cupcakes secured safely in my hands, and we're on a mission to find the rest of our crew, who've already claimed seats for the three of us. Of course, we're running late; some things never change. I couldn't leave without double and triple-checking the front door, making sure the stove was off, the curling iron unplugged, and who knows what else. It's a wonder we ever get anywhere on time.

Both sets of grandparents are here, along with Jennifer and Sean. I can't help but notice how close the two of them are sitting, their knees practically touching. The way she looks at him, like he hung the moon, makes me wonder if something more than a friendship is brewing between them. Sean reaches into the cooler at his feet, pulls out a beer, and hands it to her with a devilish grin.

Oh, you little hussy, I think, laughing to myself.

The idea of those two as a couple makes me smile, and I make a mental note to dig into it later.

Just behind them, on the bench, are Joanna and her new husband, Steven. Yep, you heard that right. She and Jax managed to stay close, even through the divorce. They both knew their marriage wasn't meant to last, and I couldn't be more grateful. She was the one who helped him through last year, and from what she told me, Jax was just as miserable and lost without me as I was without him.

We've become good friends, surprisingly enough, and she's awesome with Michael; he adores her. She and Steven fit right into our chaotic, perfect little family. And with a baby of their own due in a few months, spending time with Michael has turned into the perfect warm-up for them.

Joanna waves her hand high in the air like the massive American flag rippling above us, trying to catch our attention. "Guys...here!" she yells out, patting the empty spot beside her. I follow her cue and slide into the seat, settling Michael on my lap. Jax takes the spot on the end, his shoulder brushing mine as he sits. I look around at the people surrounding me, and just like that, we're all together, right where we were meant to be.

Michael marvels at the bull riders and has found a new love for barrel racing, too, and pretty much everything else the rodeo has to offer. But of all the things here, the creepy rodeo clowns keep his attention. Laughter explodes from him at each corny joke they tell. He giggles as they ride on their own pretend toy "horsies." The same ones that were made from the handle of a broomstick and a stuffed horse's head glued to the end, purchased from the tents at the rodeo entrance. They were the first thing Michael spotted when we walked through the gates. Jax already promised to buy him one on the way out. Along with a cowboy hat and child-size lasso to complete the look. *Just like his father.*

The clowns are an obvious favorite, but the funnel cake is a close second. The powdered sugar dusting both his shirt and mine is a dead giveaway. I don't mind the mess, though; they've always been my favorite. Looks like he inherited one thing from me, I guess. I may or may not have bought one for myself, too. I laugh as I watch him devour it with more joy than should be legal. Most of his traits are Jax, through and through, which I love, but this little shared love for funnel cake? That's all mine. It could be worse, I guess.

"Hon… he's getting powder all over you," Jax says as he points to my shirt.

"It's fine. Funnel cakes are my favorite, too; the mess is part of the fun." I brush off some of the remnants from my shorts. "This ain't my first rodeo, you know?" I say with a smirk. "Oh, wait… it *is.*" We both laugh at my corny joke, the kind that's become second nature to us.

Then he leans in, his lips brushing against my ear, and in the softest voice, for just my ears, he says, "I Love You, Charlotte."

Given this *is* my first rodeo, I didn't know what to expect. But I have to admit… I love it. It's different from what I'm used to, but something about it feels right. Like home. I could definitely get used to this.

It takes me back to when Jax first gave the idea, *our* first date at the rodeo, if I'd allow it. I remember how excited I felt at just the thought of it. But sitting here today, celebrating Michael's first birthday, surrounded by the people we love, is so much better than any first date ever could've been.

God, I love this man.

It's nearing the end of the show, but there is still one more surprise left. Jax insisted on making a call to the rodeo director, "to make our boy smile." And honestly, if there's one thing I've learned about Jax, it's that he'll do anything… everything… to make Michael happy. And if I had to guess, this won't be the last deal he makes in the name of fatherhood. Not by a long shot.

He's the best Dad I could have hoped for, I think, as I catch a glimpse of him wiping away powder from Michael's cheeks with a baby wipe, he pulled from the diaper bag. Cleaning him, good as new. He's talking to him softly, smiling the entire time, totally unaware that I'm watching him, and that he just made my heart swell two sizes.

"It's time." Jax cries out with excitement. He's practically bouncing in his boots, eyes wide, waiting. I think he's more excited than everyone. It's cute how nervous he is that he wants everything to be so perfect. For Michael, for me, for this moment we'll never forget.

The announcer's voice booms over the loudspeaker. "Ladies and gentlemen, let's all wish a very special cowboy a happy first birthday, to Michael!" He pauses. "Whoever's holding the birthday boy, stand on up so we can all see him."

Of course, that's me. I rise, placing Michael on my hip as his eyes grow wide. A second later, the entire arena bursts into song. Echoing beneath the sky.

Michael claps, and squeals, and buries his face in my chest, while I blink back tears. I glance at Jax, who's watching us with that same look he had the day he first told me he loved me.

It's perfect. And I can't help but think, how could anything ever top this? As the last note of the song fades into applause, I turn to make my way back to my seat... but in an instant, I'm stopped dead in my tracks. Jax is no longer beside me.

He's down on one knee, right there in the aisle of the stands, a small velvet box in his hand, his eyes locked with mine. I can feel my heart pounding out of my chest.

He takes a breath; his voice is strong and steady and not wavering. "Charlotte Evans, I never believed in fate until I met you. And now, I believe in everything. You and Michael helped me find my way home. Will you do me the honor of allowing me to be your husband? To be my forever date to the rodeo."

I pause, holding Michael a little tighter as my eyes fill with tears. For a moment, I'm speechless. My heart is racing, my cheeks are burning, and all I can do is stare at the man I love. To say I am shocked would be the understatement of the year. Never in a million years did I expect *this* tonight.

The crowd begins to chant, *"Say yes! Say yes!"* Thousands of eyes, all watching, including little Michael, are waiting for an answer.

"Yes... Mommy..." Michael begs me, his tiny blue eyes bore into me.

I look down at Jax, then back at our son, who's reaching for his daddy with white sticky fingers. I laugh through my tears and finally remember how to speak.

"Yes! Of course! A million times... Yes!" I say louder than I mean to, but it feels right.

* * *

Michael rides high on Jax's shoulders, holding his pony stick like a prized trophy, just as promised. The three of us walk through the crowded parking lot, love and laughter still hanging in the air. Tonight was more than just a birthday party; it's a core memory embedded deep in my heart forever.

As we reach the truck, I slide my arm around Jax's waist and rise on my toes, lips brushing his ear, "You better be ready," I whisper, my voice playful, "because I can't wait for you to *take me home.*"

A naughty grin blankets my face as my hand slides down and gives his backside a firm squeeze. Jax jumps slightly, almost giggling, and shoots a look at me that promises I've just started something he's very ready to finish.

Take Me Home

May we never forget the nearly 3,000 lives
lost on September 11, 2001.
To the innocent victims, the survivors, the
first responders, and the heroes who ran
toward danger when others fled – we honor
your courage.
To the military members who served in the
years that followed, the families who
endured unimaginable loss, the volunteers,
nurses, doctors, and all who carried the
weight of that tragedy – your strength will
never be forgotten. This story is written
with deep respect for every life touched by
that fateful day.

Charlotte's Favorite Buttercream Recipe

Ingredients:

- *1 cup of unsalted butter (salted is fine too)*
- *1 cup vegetable shortening*
- *2 lbs sifted powdered sugar*
- *1 teaspoon salt*
- *2 teaspoons of vanilla extract*
- *Milk (start with 2 tablespoons, then add more for consistency)*

Instructions:

1. *In a large bowl or mixer, cream together the shortening and softened butter until smooth and creamy.*
2. *Add the vanilla extract and mix once again.*
3. *Gradually add the powdered sugar, one cup at a time, beating on low to medium speed to avoid a sugar cloud. I like to add the salt during this process. Scrape the sides and bottom of the bowl as you go.*
4. *When all the sugar is mixed in, add the milk. Beat at medium speed until smooth and fluffy.*

Tips:

For piping sugar roses, add a bit more powdered sugar, and for a softer, more spreadable icing, add more milk.

Acknowledgments

I want to thank my husband and children. You've been my biggest fan through all my crazy adventures. Without your constant encouragement and support, I would never have started this book, let alone finished it. What began as a fun way for me to pass the time, while one of you was at basic training, ended up as a full-fledged novel that I didn't know I had in me. For nearly three years, you have stood by me proudly, even on the days when I may have failed to cook, clean, or possibly even shower. And trust me, there were more of those days than I care to admit. Thank you from the bottom of my heart for stepping in and filling in the gaps. When you weren't giving me moral support, you were rescuing me from every computer, laptop, and software disaster imaginable. This story began as handwritten notebooks, then lived on two of your personal computers, before I finally broke down, entered the twentieth century, and purchased my own laptop. It's been carried by patience, borrowed keyboards, and a lot of love. Huge thanks to my boys for that. While there may have been a few eye rolls, you patiently walked me through the entire process. I know it couldn't have been easy teaching this old girl new tricks, and I will never forget everything you've done for me. It's extremely humbling when you must ask a ten-year-old for help. Lol. And to my oldest daughter, I am forever sorry for traumatizing you. It cannot be easy reading a spicy scene written by your mother. Therapy is probably cheaper than talking about it.

For my mom and dad, who taught me that love is the most powerful force in the universe. Thank you.

Thank you to Kathie. Without you, I would never have brought this story to life. You were the one who pushed me to write it – even if it took a few margaritas before I agreed. You are a talented author, and an even more incredible editor and friend. I admire you more than you know, and I can only hope to be half the writer you are.

P.S. You really aren't annoying... Well, maybe a little. And I love you all the more for it.

To my book club – thank you for resisting the urge to kick me out, even after months of not reading a single book because I had to focus on writing mine. I am simply not capable of doing two things at once, and you all know it. Thank you for loving me anyway.

To Jeff and to Dick (may he rest in peace), thank you both for keeping me sane and getting me safely home during a time when the world stood still. I will be forever grateful. And Jeff, I look forward to – and truly cherish our yearly 9/11 anniversary calls.

To Elly, for rescuing me in the final days before publication and generously lending her graphic design expertise. Thank you.

And last, but not least, I want to give special thanks to everyone who read my story in its rawest form, who answered endless questions, and who gave me honest feedback. I know I was a relentless pain in your behinds. Lol. This book absolutely would not exist without your good, bad, and sometimes brutally honest input. You all know who you are, and I appreciate each one of you. (Kathie, Danielle, Sallie, Joanna/Dummy, Mary, Mia, Erin, Andrea, Heather, Denise, Cathleen, Marie, Julie, Val, Chloe, and Courtney) Please forgive me if I've somehow forgotten anyone. My menopause brain is in full effect these days. Lol. And of course, to Miss Bill, I never imagined I'd be grateful for, let alone smile at, your infamous red pen corrections.

About the Author

M. A. Morris spends her time with her husband, their children, and what she jokingly refers to as "a backyard farm with every animal known to man." a lifelong lover of love stories, writing a romance novel was both a bucket-list dream and a deeply personal project inspired by her children - especially the weeks her son spent at basic training, which reminded her how fast life changes and how important it is to follow your heart.

When she's not writing, she can be found living in glorious mom-chaos: cheering on the sidelines of field hockey, mat-side at wrestling matches, or juggling whatever sport is currently in season. A baker by trade, she believes sugar, butter, and a good sense of humor can fix almost anything.

She loves reading, a perfectly made mojito, date nights with her husband, and creating lasting memories on family vacations - especially to Disney. She's a puzzle junkie, a hummingbird enthusiast, and the kind of person who decorates her house to look like a Hallmark Christmas movie… even when it's still 80 degrees outside.

M. A. Morris writes heartfelt romance filled with hope, humor, resilience, and the belief that love always finds its way home.

You can connect with me on:
Amazon Author Central - M. A. Morris
Facebook - Pages by M.A. Morris
Instagram - @pagesby.m.a.morris (M. A. Morris Books)